YOU
PAY

ALSO BY TERESA DRISCOLL

I
WILL MAKE
YOU
PAY

TERESA DRISCOLL

THOMAS & MERCER

Published by Thomas & Mercer, Seattle

www.apub.com

Amazon, the Amazon logo, and Thomas & Mercer are trademarks of Amazon.com, Inc., or its affiliates.

ISBN-13: 9781542092234
ISBN-10: 154209223X

Cover design by Ghost Design

Printed in the United States of America

I
WILL MAKE
YOU
PAY

CHAPTER 1

ALICE

'I am going to use cheese wire on you.'

That's what he says. The first time the voice is in my ear. In my head. In my life.

It is a Wednesday – 3 p.m. – but I do not yet realise the significance of the day because the truth has not yet dawned on me that it all began earlier – that this is actually the *third* Wednesday.

At first it simply feels unreal. The voice on the phone is distorted through some kind of mechanism. I'm so thrown by this – the robotic echo – that I hang up immediately. Later I will regret this, wishing I'd listened more carefully, for very soon the police will be asking a lot of questions – *Did he use your name? Background noise? Rhythm of voice?* – and I will feel embarrassed that I do not have the answers.

Me – supposed to notice things for a living.

For now I sit, suddenly alone in this busy, noisy office, not at all sure how I'm supposed to react. I am shocked to feel not just afraid, but also that most British of responses – embarrassment. Yes. Inappropriately and maybe even ridiculously, I feel *embarrassed* to be this easily shaken. There is still this strange disconnect between me and the room. An over-awareness of the physical so that I can feel my pulse in my fingers, still gripping the phone, returned to its stand.

I look at the flesh on the back of my right hand and the echo of the robotic voice – *cheese wire* – makes me draw my hand back into my lap. I picture the staff in my local deli using the razor-sharp wire to slice through an enormous slab of cheese. I think of that same wire cutting into . . .

No. I straighten my back. I wonder why anyone would say such a horrible thing. Even think such a truly *horrible* thing . . .

I turn to my right to see Jack walking back into the newsroom. He moves quickly to his seat next to mine, a coffee cup in his hand. A light is flashing to signal a new call. He picks it up and I hold my breath but it is clearly not the same caller. Jack's expression moves merely from puzzlement to irritation. He rolls his eyes, switching the phone from his right to his left ear, to explain that *we do not cover divorce cases routinely, madam* . . .

He clears his throat, pausing to listen to his caller again for a moment before continuing.

Yes, I'm quite sure it is all very desperate for you, but I'm sorry; we just don't cover divorce. Not routinely . . . not unless—

I can hear the response; someone shouting. Jack holds the receiver away from his ear, the caller's swearing bleeding into the room, then he puts the receiver back to his head. *I wish you well with the case, madam, but I'm going to have to ring off now.*

As Jack takes a final slurp of his coffee before firing the cup into the bin, I turn to my left, where Adam, our crime correspondent, is hunched over his keyboard. He is on a deadline, typing furiously; a court report wanted right now for the online edition of the paper. I don't like to interrupt him or Jack or anyone, because I still don't know how to process this. How I'm *supposed* to feel.

We get weird calls all the time. Last week a woman came in complaining that a cloud was following her . . .

'Are you all right, Alice?'

'Yes. Course.'

No. The problem is I have never had *this* kind of call before. I turn my head back towards the question; towards Jack. I am still thinking of cheese wire. Razor-sharp. Cutting slowly and easily . . .

'Jeez, Alice. You don't *look* all right. Do you need water?'

Only now do I hear how laboured my breathing sounds.

'I'm fine.' I take in a deep breath through my nose and let it out through my mouth, trying to steady myself. 'Just picked up a dodgy phone call. Threw me for a minute.'

'What kind of dodgy?'

Finally I look Jack in the face. 'A nutter. Just got a call from a nutter. It's nothing.'

'Doesn't look like nothing. So, what did they say – this nutter?'

I pause, realising that I don't want to repeat the words because I don't want to give them life; I don't want to take them forward.

'What did they say, Alice?'

'It's nothing.'

'Please. Tell me . . .'

'A man. It was a man using some kind of voice changer. He said, *I am going to use cheese wire on you.*'

'Jeez.' Jack rakes his hand through his hair and stands up. 'Bloody hell. A *voice changer*? Right. I'm getting water and we're going straight in to see Ted.'

He darts to the water cooler and returns with a cup which he places into my hand, staring right into my face.

'Drink this. Sip it. Slowly . . .'

It is ice cold, and I look at the cup and think of the contrast – the cold water on my tongue and the warmth of the flesh of my fingers against the plastic.

Cheese wire . . .

Jack is watching me closely.

'I'm fine, Jack. Honestly. Just a wind-up. A fruitcake.'

'What line? Your line or a general line? I mean – was it random? Did they use your name?'

The first of the sensible questions that I will struggle to answer. I glance at the little row of lights by the phone. Middle light? Yes.

'Line 301. I use it for my column but it's listed as general too. I don't think he used my name.' I pause, trying to remember for sure. 'No. Look. Come to think of it – probably just an attention-seeker. I shouldn't have let it throw me.'

Jack shakes his head. 'Random swearing we ignore. Direct threats with voice changers we take to Ted. Come on. Protocol.'

I pick up the cup of water and follow him to the editor's cubicle in the corner of the office. Jack knocks on the open door.

'What now? I hope this is a new lead because I've just had the lawyer on and he's giving me an ulcer . . .'

'Sorry, Ted. Alice just picked up a phone call from a nutter. Threat from a guy using a voice changer. Thought we'd better report it.'

I repeat what he said and watch Ted suck in his face.

'Right. So did he ask for you? Did he use your name, Alice?'

'No, Ted.'

'Good. That's good.' Relief on his face. 'Probably some random loon who hates something we wrote. And did you answer using your name?'

I feel a frown as again I rewind. 'No. Just the name of the paper.'

'And he definitely didn't use *your* name?'

'No.'

Ted is nodding. 'Good. OK. Random fruitcake, then. I'll put this on the log, but good that it's not personal. Nasty though. The voice changer. Was it software then? Can you do that on a phone?'

'I don't know.' I wonder why I hadn't considered this myself. For some reason I had imagined some physical device. But maybe Ted is right. Voice change software? An app perhaps?

'You OK, Alice?' Ted says. 'You want to finish early? Get yourself some air?'

'No, no. Course not. I'm fine. Just thought we'd better mention it in case he calls again. Upsets someone else.'

'Sure. Like I say, I'll log it so it gets shared across the departments. If it happens again, we'll report it to Alan. In fact, I'll probably mention it to him anyway.'

Alan is the press officer for the local police. A drinking pal of Ted's. A good egg.

'Thanks.'

And then I go back to my desk, and already the distance between the call and this new place where Ted needs to get back to the lead story makes me feel better. They're right. It's random. Probably someone with a grudge against the paper – someone who didn't like a story. Court case maybe? Back to work . . .

'Sorry, Jack. I should have shrugged it off.'

'Don't be daft. Just don't answer 301 for the rest of the day. I'll pick it up. Just in case he gets off on it and tries again. Bastard probably gets a wank out of it.'

I grimace.

'Sorry, Alice. TMI.'

'No. You're right. I'm fine now, honestly. Think I'll fetch a decent coffee from next door. Fresh air. Want another?'

'Yeah. Cappuccino, please. Want me to come with you?'

'No. I'm good now.'

I lean left to nudge Adam, making a cup-tipping motion, but he shakes his head, still engrossed in his story. I grab my bag and head downstairs, grateful at last to be out on the street. There is a soft breeze, the buzz from the traffic. The roar of a motorcycle. The bleeping of a pedestrian crossing. Familiar sounds and a familiar bustle, which make me feel settled again.

It is only when I get to the café next door and see through the window the owner writing my name on a small cup – my usual order – even before I step inside, that I feel a shift again in my stomach.

'You psychic suddenly, Giovanni?'

'No. Guy just rang in your order. Said, *Alice will need a double espresso. She's on her way . . .*'

'What guy?'

'Dunno. One of them in your office playing prank. You nice girl, Alice. You want to tell them boys to grow up.' He is wagging his finger.

'I have no idea what you're talking about. What guy? What prank?' I am thinking of Jack but he's not one for messing about.

'The joker with one of them voice changer thingies. Creepy.' He snaps a lid on my drink and pushes it towards me. 'You tell them boys in that office of yours – they can ring in orders but *no pranks*. What if one of my girls picks up the phone? Eh? Not nice.'

CHAPTER 2

ALICE

Just a few hours later and I am home, waiting for Tom. This new and paranoid version of myself.

I have checked both doors and all of the windows. I have set the landline to caller display. I have turned off location services on my mobile, I have reset my passwords for Facebook and Twitter and have switched my Instagram account to private. I have made an appointment for a security company to check over my rented two-bed first thing tomorrow. I have ordered a 'police-approved personal alarm' which should arrive in the morning post. In short, I have done all the things the police have advised – along with googling pepper spray, which they most definitely did not.

Still I do not feel safe.

Though the police were thorough and kind, the bottom line as I sit here alone is sinking in.

Alan from the press office brought a woman detective sergeant from CID. She took statements from me and the coffee shop staff next door. At first all this official fussing felt good; as if it would lead to something positive. I'm not sure precisely what I expected – but a full stop of some kind? Pretty soon I realised, as Alan and the policewoman exchanged knowing little glances, that they were going through the motions as a favour to my editor.

'So what happens now?' I asked.

The awkward pause and their expressions said it all.

Turns out that unless I can suggest an obvious suspect – someone I've upset through a story or someone who's been hassling me – nothing much happens now. The report goes on file. And we just wait . . .

The important thing from here is to be vigilant and gather evidence, Alice. If he calls again or anything unusual happens, you must keep very precise records. Bring us right up to date. The best hope, of course, is that this was just some random nutter who guessed about the coffee shop.

What surprises me most of all is they don't seem especially worried he might be actively watching me. I am. That's what's worrying me most of all.

I mean – how did he know I'd be at the café? What my order would be? The police say these kinds of individuals often punt a bit. It wouldn't take rocket science to guess reporters use the café next door. The guy may have phoned previously with an excuse to check on my regular order, to spook me. Or just made a guess.

But he used my name when he phoned the café. Knew I was going to the café . . .

And yes, they said, this made it more of a worry and they were taking it very seriously. That was when they gave me this big to-do list of general precautions. The security visit and personal alarm, *blah blah blah*. They gave me leaflets.

But since arriving home I've been surfing websites about this – stalking and anonymous threatening calls – and it makes pretty depressing reading.

Seems these callers know very well that they have the upper hand. The police can't give you a bodyguard. Or a new car. Or a new address. And unless and until things 'escalate' (I don't even like to think what the hell that means), it seems they can't actually do very much at all.

Basically, I'm on my own with this.

I look around the room again and then stand up to pace. I draw the curtains, even though it won't get dark for another hour. I make another coffee and then realise, even smelling it, that I have drunk far too much coffee today and pour it down the sink.

Finally I am sitting at the kitchen table, staring at the bolt that is pushed across the top of the back door, when I hear the key in the front door.

I find that above all I am deeply disappointed in myself. So that by the time Tom walks into the house, I have burst into tears.

'Hey, hey. I came as quick as I could. So, what's happening with the police? What did they say?'

I let him hold me for a moment but then pull away, wiping my face with my sleeves. Once more I feel both ridiculous and embarrassed; I don't like anyone, not even Tom, seeing me like this.

Jack phoned him from the office, apparently, while I was with the police, and he's keen for more details now.

'Look, I still don't know if I'm simply overreacting, Tom. To be honest, I'm all over the place.'

I babble that it is probably just some saddo who's hoping for this *precise* reaction, which is why I wish I could buck up.

I sit down on the sofa, and Tom sits alongside me and takes my hand. At first he is reassuring. He seems to think it was probably random. Someone who hates the paper. But as I share more of the story, about the call to the café, he suddenly looks more alarmed.

'So you're saying they phoned the café as well? This guy knows your name? Could actually be *watching* you?'

'Possibly. Probably not. The police reckon it could be a lucky guess. Or the caller may have done some research just to spook me.'

'But he used your *name*?'

'Yes.'

There is a pause, and Tom's expression is changing. He stands and is at first still. He seems to be thinking and then starts pacing.

'So this guy targets you – you *specifically* – and the police just let you drive home in your car on your own? To just wait and see what happens?'

I tell him that the office offered to arrange a taxi but I didn't want to leave my car behind. And I felt reassured by the police. *A bit*, anyway. I explain that at this stage there isn't really anything they can do. It may just be random. He may never call again.

'No, no. I don't like that he knew you were at the café. What if some nutter *is* watching you? Followed you here? They shouldn't have let you just drive off, Alice. Not after two phone calls like that. A voice changer, for Christ's sake.'

I don't tell him that Jack offered to bring me home and wait with me.

'Can't the police give you some kind of protection? Surveillance or something? At least until we know if this is a grudge against the paper. Or a grudge against you personally.'

'No. Apparently not. Not on the basis of a couple of phone calls. They don't have the resources, Tom.'

'So you just drove straight home?' He glances at the door as if someone could be out there right now watching us.

'No. I drove around a bit actually. Took a couple of detours. Just in case.' I do not want to tell him that I actually drove several miles in ridiculous circles for the best part of an hour, taking random eleventh-hour turns this way and that, just in case someone *was* following me.

'Right. I'll cancel dinner. Obviously. We can order in.' He is back alongside me, holding his palm to my cheek, and I look into his face and feel the guilt I always feel when Tom looks at me this way.

It makes me think of that other face. From years back. Also Jack's face. *Stop it, Alice.* I glance across to the other side of the room and feel another punch of guilt before I turn back to Tom.

I need a moment and so I ask him to make me a coffee. My house is open-plan downstairs and I watch him move over to the kitchen area, staring at his back as he flicks on the kettle and reaches for the coffee canister on the shelf above the cooker. I realise that what I feel, along with all the confusion, is still this powerful disappointment in myself.

I am someone who has always admired resilience in people. I see it often in my job. Write about it regularly. The truth? I had hoped and believed that deep down I was tougher than this. I have interviewed people who have had their lives utterly devastated and yet have risen above it. A man who had his foot blown off in Afghanistan and went on to run a marathon. A woman who threw herself in front of three children when a drunk driver mounted a pavement. I watch Tom's back as he pours the boiling water into two mugs, and I think of so many stories. So much courage.

And the first time I am tested?

'No, Tom. We should go out as planned. I need to get a bloody grip. This is completely ridiculous. Precisely what he wants.'

'Dinner doesn't matter.' Tom carries the drinks back to the sitting room area and places them on the coffee table.

'It does matter, Tom.' The booking this evening – Tom's favourite restaurant – was supposed to celebrate things going so well for him at work. He's pushed incredibly hard the last couple of months, working long hours to win a big new corporate client. His firm is delighted.

I sip my drink, new emotions pushing to the fore. Anger now. 'That's precisely what this creep wants. To mess with my head.'

'I honestly don't mind about this evening, Alice. We can order in. Chinese. Thai. Whatever you fancy.'

'No. I mean it. I'll have a shower. Get changed. Stuff the saddos of this world – we're going *out*.'

For all my bravado, I find – on the way to the restaurant – that I keep turning to check the cars behind us. By the time we reach the parking area, I'm almost dizzy with the flip-flop of emotions. Afraid then angry. Worried then furious. Yes. Livid, actually, that someone on the end of a telephone for less than a minute could do this to me.

So that, once we've ordered, I come clean. 'Do you know what, Tom? I feel ashamed. Me – always banging on about the resilience of people, and look at me.' I hold out my hand to show him that it is actually trembling.

'Oh, Alice. Why always so hard on yourself? It's no wonder you're shaken. It was nasty, what he said. Anyone would be shaken.'

I do not answer. I try not to think of the deli; of the wire slicing slowly through the slab of cheese. I wonder what would make someone *say that* – such a horrible image. I tear at my bread roll and spread far too much butter on it.

'OK. So has the paper upset anyone recently – any trolling online? Complaints about any of your copy? Court cases? Anything like that?' He is using his lawyer tone, practical and steady now, leaning in so I can see my reflection in his glasses.

I shake my head. The police asked this too, but I can't think of anything or anyone; I haven't covered court or crime for ages.

'I've been on features mainly – busy on the Maple Field House campaign.'

'And no one has kicked off about that? The campaign?'

'A few local politicians are still embarrassed to have been shown up. Otherwise, quite the contrary. Everyone's delighted how it's turned out. I mean, I shouldn't be taking the credit. The residents have driven the campaign. I just wrote it all up.'

Tom lets out a sigh of exasperation and fidgets as if trying to think of some other motive.

The truth is I've been so busy on Maple Field House stories that I haven't done any meaty news for ages. I've been the lead reporter on the campaign for the best part of a year, and Ted's been delighted to have so much copy out of it.

Maple Field House is a dreary and dated U-shaped mall of shops with three storeys of flats. In its heyday, it was apparently quite smart; the shops busy and successful. But changes in customer habits and the poor building design have taken their toll.

Most of the shops are now empty – just a few converted to charity shops. The flats above them are extremely damp and dreary, with all manner of structural problems. They're owned by the local council, but the block hasn't been upgraded in years because the housing committee couldn't decide whether to reinvest in the flats or relocate the residents to a new low-rise development of houses and maisonettes.

Because of the indecision, conditions got worse and worse. The whole building has some kind of dry rot. The communal rubbish chutes kept getting blocked. Fed-up residents started a campaign for the whole place to be demolished. It was largely ignored until I started to run features on the damp affecting children's health – especially the kids with asthma.

Finally it all came to a head – the council got tired of the embarrassment caused by all the stories in our paper, the *South Devon Informer*. The housing committee agreed to demolition and the relocation of all the residents. Plans for a joint scheme were swiftly drawn up with a housing association.

Everyone is now in temporary accommodation, and the first families are moving into the early phase of the new development.

To be honest, it's made for easy copy for me. The constant roll of story updates keeps me busy; it's good to work on something worthwhile and it keeps my editor happy too.

'You know I've been off the court rota at work for ages,' I add. 'People are always upset with the paper, Tom – you know that – but

I've not personally covered anything controversial for ages. At least not that I can think of.'

I stare at my fish. Sea bass with perfect crispy skin. I separate the flakes with my fork but then find myself staring at the glinting metal.

I am going to use cheese wire on you . . .

'Not hungry?'

'I think I just had too much at lunchtime.' I put the fork down.

He finds a smile. 'Well, you're right. Probably just a nutter you won't hear from again.' Tom saws into his steak. 'Though if you'd like to stay at mine – or me at yours – until we're sure?'

He isn't looking at me and I don't know how to respond. The truth is I don't like the idea of sleeping on my own, but we normally stay over only on weekends or after dates like this. Tom's now in commercial law. His work takes him to London quite often and that rather suits me. I'm not ready to *live* with anyone. Not again . . .

'How about you stay over at mine tonight as planned and then see how we go?' I say. 'I'm sure I'll feel better tomorrow. Probably just a one-off. It'll all settle once I know it was a one-off.'

'OK. So long as you're not just being brave.' He pauses and tilts his head with a smile. 'Or stubborn.'

'*Moi?*'

We both laugh, and I realise it's the first moment I've relaxed since I took the wretched phone call. And that feels good; like some tiny triumph.

Tom smiles at me again and I want to fast-forward to the day when we can look back on this as a dinner party anecdote. *You remember that nutter who tried to spook you . . . ?*

Yes. I feel defiant suddenly. I pick up my fork again. I scoop a large flake of fish into my mouth and find that it is delicious.

Everything will be back to normal very soon.

CHAPTER 3

ALICE

The box arrives the following Wednesday. Courier. Ten a.m.

It is a bakery box with a sticker on the top from a local firm which recently won an award. I did a feature on the owner just last week, and she emailed to say how thrilled they all were with the coverage.

'Someone get the coffees in.' I raise my voice and stand to make a little show of the gift. 'It's from that award-winning bakery. Should be good.'

I am pleased to be feeling my old self today. For the first forty-eight hours after that stupid phone call, I was all over the place. Nervous in the car. Nervous in the office; afraid to answer the blessed phone. But as the days passed – Thursday, Friday, the weekend – the impact of the phone call faded. I felt more and more foolish for overreacting.

I went to the gym as normal on Saturday afternoon. Visited mum Sunday morning and had a cinema date with Tom in the evening. Then, on Monday, I stopped thinking about it so much, and yesterday I covered stories as normal. Answered the phone. Even went to the café next door.

I am thinking of all of this as I look at the box, pleased to have a treat to share with my colleagues. The only question going through my head is – will it be one large cake or individual cakes? Ipso facto, will I need to find a knife?

The top of the box has a kind of envelope closure – the paper slotted neatly into slits like the lens on a camera. I carefully pull out one flap, then a second.

By this time Jack is next to me – standing close to get a good view. A cake lover. Hollow legs. I open the final flaps.

The shock that it *isn't* a cake inside takes a moment to sink in. By now there are three of us peering into the box – Jack, the editor's secretary Samantha, and Nigel, one of the older photographers.

'Flowers?' It is Samantha's voice first, her tone all puzzlement. 'But they're completely ruined. Look at the stems. How odd.'

'Oh no . . .' Jack moves forward and begins to close the top of the lid to try to stop me seeing, but I move my hand to push him back.

'I want to see.'

'No, Alice. It's another wind-up. We need to phone the police. There may be fingerprints.'

Again I push his hand away.

Pink peonies. My mother's favourite.

'What's going on?' Ted has come out of his cubicle.

'Oh – so is this from the *cheese wire* guy?' It is Samantha's voice again, her hand up to her mouth.

I stare at the flowers. *How the hell does he know about peonies?* These are deep pink and shaped as if for a hand-tied bouquet, but the stems have been tightly wrapped with wire – a cheese wire with little wooden handles, the type used in professional delis – so that most of the stems have been deliberately severed and the flowers are all dying.

Worse, there is a large card inside . . .

'Christ. Right.' Ted lets out a huff of air. 'Leave the box there. I'll phone Alan again. Get someone down here from CID. See if they can't rustle up someone a bit more senior this time.'

'Seriously. We shouldn't touch it, Alice. It's evidence,' Jack is saying, but I can't help myself; I push his hand away again to pick up the card and start to read it.

'Dear Lord. My *mother*.' The message on the card is such a shock that my heart is immediately pounding and my whole body temperature seems to change. First hot. Then cold. Then back to hot. 'I need to check my mother is OK.' My hand is trembling and I have to sit as I reach for my phone to dial.

'Why? What is it, Alice? What does the card say?'

'Shh. Shh.' I wave my hand for quiet as I wait for the line to connect – *come on, come on* – I press the receiver closer to my ear as I read the rest of the card.

And that's when I realise for the first time, my heart still pounding with fear for my mother, that the day is significant.

Wednesday.

Also that the phone call last Wednesday wasn't the beginning of this.

CHAPTER 4

HIM - BEFORE

He sits on the end of his bed staring at the rockets and stars which zoom and flash across the duvet. He is five years old and his gran says he is growing up way too fast.

My little rocket man.

It is his gran's voice inside his head right this minute, which is odd because she is really next door in the kitchen. He gets this strange little punch in his stomach as he remembers the day they picked out the duvet cover in the special shop where everything is cheap. It was in a big, bright red plastic bin. Like a dustbin, only smarter. SALE. He remembers trying to spell out the letters, with his gran helping. So proud.

You're such a clever boy . . .

He gets this odd and confusing explosion of feelings inside. Like the noise and the flash when a rocket launches. Sort of muddled and loud and strange. He doesn't know if he is angry or not. Mad. Sad. Bad?

My brave little soldier.

It is the other thing his gran calls him. He stares up at the door as there is some kind of clattering from the kitchen. She always says that on Wednesday . . .

He gets chocolate flakes for breakfast on Wednesdays. And ice cream after his tea. She is making it now – fish fingers, chips and beans. His favourite.

And ice cream with chocolate sauce for my brave little soldier.

Only he isn't brave, is he?

That's the problem.

In school they are learning to read in groups and he is in the top group. Red Group. The best in the whole class. He has a book about a girl who is frightened of the dark and who meets a bear who is frightened of the dark too.

He wanted to tell the teacher this morning that he's frightened of the dark as well. But he's not allowed. It's a secret.

Wednesdays are *their secret*. Him and gran . . .

'You OK in there, lovely?'

He realises that he wants to kick something very, very hard and is a wicked boy. Mostly he loves his gran. Mostly he wants to throw his arms around her and hold on tight, tight, tight.

But on Wednesdays he doesn't understand grown-ups at all. He wants to kick and bite and scream at the whole world.

He can feel tears coming right this minute, and he thinks of last Wednesday in school when Patrick caught him crying in the library corner. And he had to push Patrick right off his stool.

He is six next birthday, and he wonders if he will feel braver when he is six.

CHAPTER 5

MATTHEW

Matthew Hill stares at his daughter lying on the ground in the middle of the biscuit aisle. He's on the verge of giving in. The shameful whisper – *don't tell Mummy* – right on the tip of his tongue. But there is suddenly a problem; Amelie's spectacular lungs have attracted an audience. Several shoppers are staring at him now, apparently waiting for his next move.

Matthew tries to calm his face for the crowd – his options all at once limited. No one warns you, he is thinking. Just six months back his daughter was a cherub in floral dresses.

'I hate you!' Amelie again stamps both feet in turn on the ground, her little fists clenched into tight, angry knots. Knuckles white. She flips her back up and down off the floor like some furious seal.

Matthew looks once more at the spectators; bribery sadly off the table. Too many *witnesses*.

'Daddy's going to leave now, Amelie. Are you going to stay and live in this supermarket or do you want to come home with me?'

'I want Pippy Pocket biscuits.'

Matthew glances at the display on the shelf as two middle-aged women widen their eyes, apparently eager to see if he will fold.

'And if you had been a good girl, you might have been allowed Pippy Pocket biscuits. But this is the fifth time you've lain on the floor, Amelie. So no Pippy Pocket anything today. We're going to pay and leave.'

The screaming, once it starts up again, is spectacular both in volume and pitch. Matthew instinctively raises both his arms and swings to face the little crowd. 'Look. Not guilty. Not touching her.'

'Terrible twos?' The voice from just behind him sounds older. Its owner then steps forward to stand right alongside him, and he turns to take in the white hair. Thick coat despite the mild day.

Matthew tries to find a small smile – any expression which might suggest he's coping.

The truth? If there were no audience, he would definitely go with the bribe. He would buy the sodding biscuits just to get the child up off the floor and out of the store. But he can already hear his wife Sally's voice in his ear.

You mustn't give into the tantrums, Matt. If you keep giving in, we're doomed.

The word resonates. *Doomed.* He stares at the child on the floor and wonders what happened to the angel baby placed into his arms. The sweet girl with blonde curls in a high chair who was always smiling. As a new couple peer around the end of the aisle to find the source of the screaming, Matthew reflects that the word *doomed* pretty much sums up his life right now.

'How about you walk off and pay and I keep an eye on her. She'll throw in the towel.' The overdressed gran has moved closer to whisper her proposed strategy.

Matthew looks at the woman more carefully. She doesn't look like a child-snatcher. The problem is, his years in the police force and now as a private detective make him suspicious of everyone. 'We're fine, thank you.'

'Up to you, but she looks settled in for the night to me.' The woman is watching Amelie, still kicking her feet on the floor. 'I had one like that. Especially stubborn, I mean. Expect she's bright? Yes?'

Matthew narrows his eyes. He glances at the till and realises that the reflection in the window beyond will save the day, allowing him to monitor his daughter and the granny child-snatcher quite safely.

'Thank you,' he whispers finally. 'I appreciate it.'

'Right then, Amelie. Daddy is going now. I hope you like living in the supermarket but I should warn you it gets very cold at night here. And they switch off the lights.'

He turns his back and pushes his trolley towards the tills, all the time watching the scene in the window reflection.

Amelie stops screaming almost immediately but stays on the floor. After a little while she lifts her head to check his progress. The gran stands guard. One more minute and Amelie gets up, looking utterly bemused. Then a tad worried. As Matthew places item after item on the rolling belt, humming a little tune, Amelie starts to walk slowly along the aisle. He glances again at the window reflection, that familiar beat of surprise at how much taller he is than everyone else in the queue, but he does not turn round.

Very soon he feels his daughter's body pressed against his left leg and can hear her quietly sobbing, her little shoulders heaving up and down with the full weight of defeat. He pats her hair but continues with his task. 'Want to help Daddy unload?' The trick, he has learned, is not to make eye contact just yet; to limit her humiliation which could so easily morph into another tantrum. He passes a cereal box, which she puts on the trolley belt. Then a loaf of bread in its paper bag.

They continue their double act until finally the sobbing ceases and the shoulders still.

'I sorry, Daddy.'

And now his heart explodes. He pats his daughter's hair again as a sign it is OK between them. He wonders if it will always be like this.

Love. War. Love. War. He wants suddenly to go back and buy all the Pippy Pocket biscuits on the shelf to show how much he forgives her and loves her. But he knows he must resist and so he strokes Amelie's hair some more and just keeps passing the lighter items of shopping.

He turns now to lift his hand as a thank you to the mystery gran, who is smiling at them. He remembers his own mum warning him on their last family visit that he must not wish time away, however hard it gets. She says these years will go too fast and he will look back one day and wish he was right back here. Tantrums and all.

The problem, he thinks, is that when you *are* here – right here with this unpredictable two-year-old who will not sleep, will not put her coat on, will not get into the car seat and will not get up off the floor – it is all so permanently exhausting. And so you can't help wishing for the next phase. For a bit. More. Calm.

As they finish loading the belt, his mobile sounds. He sees from the display that it is a call automatically forwarded from his office in Exeter. *Damn.* He is starting late this morning to allow Sal to visit the hairdresser's, but doesn't like to appear part-time to his clients; he also hates anyone realising that he still doesn't have a secretary or assistant.

'Hello – Matthew Hill, private investigator.'

The woman on the till raises her eyebrows and Matthew widens his eyes in return.

'Hello, Mr Hill. Right. Um. My name is Tom Stellar.' The voice sounds thirties. Nervous, which is par for the course. Most clients find it hard to make the leap. Make the call. 'I'm wondering if you might be able to help me. Well, my girlfriend actually.' There is a long pause.

'Go on.'

'She's being harassed. Some kind of stalker, we think. Nasty phone calls at first. I was hoping it would pass, to be honest, but instead it's getting worse. A delivery to her office. I'm really very worried. The police don't seem to be able to do very much and so I was wondering . . .' He's talking faster and faster.

23

'OK, Mr Stellar. I hear you, but I'm on a case right this minute and it's difficult for me to talk properly right now. I've logged this number, so how about I call you back very soon. Within the hour? Would that be OK with you?'

'Oh.' The man sounds deflated. 'It's just I'm so very worried. It's urgent.'

'I absolutely promise I'll get back to you shortly. Then you can tell me everything and we can decide how to move forward.'

'Right. OK. She's with the police at the moment but she's very upset, and I don't have much confidence in the police, frankly. Last time they seemed to just fob her off. Sent her home – on her tod, would you believe.'

Matthew sighs, still stroking his daughter's hair. He doesn't like to hear the police criticised. Deep down there's an old loyalty he cannot shake. Most officers do their best. It's a tough job; he of all people knows that from his past. But the truth is that stalker cases are the force's worst nightmare. So difficult to handle; to get right. And never enough resources to do what officers would like to do.

He realises this is the first time he has been asked, as a private investigator, to get involved in a stalker inquiry, and isn't at all sure what to say. Whether to even consider the case. Deep down he doubts he will be able to help very much. Not on his own.

'I'll call you back very soon, Mr Stellar. Try to get an update from your girlfriend meantime, and we can see where we are.'

CHAPTER 6

ALICE

I am in the editor's office now and look up at the window on to the newsroom, several faces looking in. They turn, embarrassed, as I catch their eyes.

'So you're saying you think this is the *fourth* thing?' The woman police officer is staring at the evidence bag on the desk between us, turning it over to read the card which was inside the cake box with the dying flowers. 'Each thing happening on a Wednesday?'

I nod. I want to speak but I am afraid that I'm going to cry and there is no way I want to do that in front of this woman or the other journalists still glancing in. It is good that Ted loaned us this space but I wish it had blinds. More privacy.

The only relief is that my mother is OK. I've spoken at length to the staff at her home. A carer is with her and they've reassured me about their security; they log all callers and won't allow any visitors to my mother without my say-so.

I look back across the desk at the police officer. She seems very nice, understanding completely why I freaked out over my mother. I'm embarrassed now that I don't remember her name. She's a DI, which suggests they're taking it more seriously – or Ted has leant more heavily on his mate Alan. From her initial questions, she's clearly competent; sharper than the officer they sent last week, I would say. She has a warm and open face but she is heavily pregnant, and for some shameful reason this really troubles me. You will struggle to find a more outspoken feminist than me, but right now I feel a complete fraud – all my thoughts betraying the sisterhood.

I can't explain it but I don't like the idea of sucking this nice, pregnant woman and her unborn child into this horrible thing that's going on. This man who talks of using cheese wire, who sends nasty decapitated flowers, who mentions my *mother*, and who I now believe has been into my home. I find myself glancing at her belly. It makes me think of my sister – how protective I felt of Leanne when she was pregnant. I am thinking of the new life starting there; the wonder that in a few short months it will be a real, little person. The innocent child. And then I think of this cruel and horrible man . . .

'I think he's been in my house.' I reach for the cup of water as I speak. I didn't even plan to say this yet. I'm still trying to work out in my head if this can really be true. I have to take out my phone for my diary, to check all the dates again.

'Right. No hurry, Alice. When you're ready, talk me through it from the beginning. One step at a time. Why do you think he's been in your house?'

I stare at my phone and scroll through to check the date I went to London and then the emails to my landlord. Yes. *Jeez.* It really fits.

'OK, so when I got that phone call to the office – the one using the voice changer last week, I thought it was the first thing. Was hoping it would be the only thing.'

'Yes. I've looked back at the statement my colleague took. There was no mention of any other incidents.'

'That's because I didn't realise the connection then. But this box turning up today with the message, mentioning my mum.' I stare again at the evidence bag containing the little card, still on the desk in front of the officer.

She turns it over again and reads it aloud.

'Your mother's favourites? Like the flower on your car? Oh – and did you miss the light bulb, Alice?'

'I'm sorry. I've forgotten your name, Officer. So rude of me but I'm a bit all over the place and I didn't really take it in properly earlier.' I can feel myself blushing. Did she say Mandy?

'DI Melanie Sanders.'

'Right. Thank you.'

'You're welcome to call me Melanie.'

'OK. Thank you.' I pause. 'Melanie.' I don't like to say that this doesn't feel right at all; to call her by her Christian name. As if she is my friend. My buddy. As if I can know yet whether I can trust her.

'So talk me through this card, Alice. The flower on the car. What's that about?'

I let out a little huff of air as I picture it. The peony on my windscreen. Why didn't I realise right from the beginning?

'When I read that on the card – about the flower – I suddenly realised it was him. The first thing, I mean. About a month back. The first Wednesday. I just checked the date in my diary. I was up in London at the headquarters of the housing association involved in a story I'm working on. Demolishing the Maple Field House complex and building new homes.'

'Yes, I read about that. Good outcome.'

'I've been doing the campaign stories; all the features. So I went up to London for an interview about the place of housing associations in a landscape where councils fund so little new social housing. I used the train from Plymouth and I left my car in the railway car park. When I got back – quite late because I wrote and filed my story from Paddington station – there was a single flower on my windscreen with a business card. I'm not going to lie – it did startle me a little bit because of the coincidence that it was a peony. It's my mother's favourite flower, you see.' There is a slight crack to my voice. I cough, hoping she didn't notice this. 'But the card seemed to be from a florist, and you often get flyers left on cars in car parks. I thought it was a gift. A gimmick – just some clever marketing. The choice of flower a coincidence.'

'What did the florist's card say? Have you still got it?'

'No. Unfortunately not. Mine was the last car in that section of the car park and I just assumed all the cars would have had them. I took the peony home and put it in water. But I threw the business card away.'

'Try to remember, Alice. What it said. The name on the card. Close your eyes if you like; that can help sometimes. Try to picture yourself sitting in your car with the card in your hand.'

I feel self-conscious but she widens her eyes in encouragement, so I do as she says and am surprised to remember something almost instantly. Yes. The card had a pink border. Lacy, like trellis work. But it was matte. Thin cardboard. Not very professional.

'It was one of those cheap business cards, like the ones you can order online or print off from a machine. It had a fussy pink border and the name was . . .' I screw my eyes closed more tightly and start to see the word. 'Oh hell.'

'What is it?'

I open my eyes, shocked to picture it so precisely. '*Wednesday Wisdom. Say it with flowers* . . . That's what it said. You know, like a Twitter hashtag. Wednesday Wisdom. I thought it was the name of the florist. But it wasn't, was it? Oh, dear Lord . . . it was the beginning of this.' I can hear my voice changing; can feel myself trembling.

DI Sanders is leaning forward.

'OK. So try to stay calm, Alice. Your mum is fine. We've checked with the home too. But we need to get to the bottom of why this person even mentioned your mother. We're going to help you. All of these things are horrid. Upsetting. But it actually helps that you're putting it together now, because all these pieces of information add to the picture.

More evidence for us; they are all things we can check out. The business card, I mean. But what about the choice of flower – the peony on the car and now the peonies in this posy. Why is that significant? And who else would know that it's your mother's favourite?'

I look away to the left, frowning as I take in the three tall stacks of newspapers on a side desk.

'It's not a secret. All the family know that they're my mum's favourite flower.' I find that I hate talking about her in this context; as if sucking her into this. I think of her with her oxygen. Her wheezing . . .

'I've probably mentioned it to quite a lot of people.' I realise I *have* told loads of people. Too many. 'Oh goodness, I may even have written about it in a column for the paper. Sometimes we take turns to write a personal column.'

'OK. So we'll need to take a look at those. Can you pull up copies of all your personal columns over the past . . . say, six months?'

'Sure.'

Next, DI Sanders – I can't see myself calling her Melanie again; not yet – wants to know about the light bulb, and why I think this man has been in my house. I know it's going to be difficult to explain. Only now am I remembering that I wrote about that in one of my blessed columns too.

I need to buy time to figure it out in my head, and so I say I feel a bit odd and ask if I can have a cup of tea with some sugar.

As we wait for someone to nip next door to the café for drinks, I realise that it all goes back to the rapist case. The first thing. The light bulb. I feel a bit sick even thinking about it.

Adam, our crime correspondent, covered the court proceedings, but we discussed it a lot in the office and it spooked the life out of me. There was this rapist on the very edge of our patch – about six, maybe eight months back – who had a particularly nasty MO. Four cases – all in South Devon and all similar. He would watch single women living alone to work out their shift patterns. Then he would break into their houses while they were travelling home from work in the winter after dark. He would remove the first light bulb in their house – from the hallway or sitting room – so that they would think the bulb had gone and would move, oblivious, into darkness. Then he would pounce. In a mask.

He was jailed – the rapist. But I got so wound up by this horrible, horrible case that I started carrying a torch in my handbag, sometimes even in my pocket, just in case. Got so spooked for a while that my heart pounded every time I arrived home after dark. And I wrote about all that in a personal column.

I can feel my eyes narrowing as I wonder how I could have been so stupid. To expose my feelings to everyone. In a local newspaper column. In print and online, too. Why the hell did I do that? Why do we writers share *so much*?

I think again about me and my stupid soapbox – my obsession with courage and cowardice. Always banging on about it. That's what the column was about really; trying to assess whether the fear we feel is defining. Or simply human. I remember using a quote from Nelson Mandela. Probably a bit pretentious of me. *Courage is not the absence of fear* . . . I wrote that previous generations had proved themselves through wars. But most of us these days have never had our temperament truly tested. Brave? Or coward? When the chips are down . . . which will we be?

Once tea has arrived and I have taken a few sips, I tell DI Sanders about the rapist and my column and how three weeks back – on a Wednesday *again* – I came home to find that the first bulb in my rented house had blown. It was in a light fitting high up in my entrance vestibule, which is an odd design, covering the full height of the two-storey property. So it was impossible to replace the bulb myself. The fitting is a very contemporary design – covered by smoked glass. I just assumed the bulb had blown and it was too high for me to do anything about it.

'Because of the rapist case, it spooked me. I mean, I knew the guy was in jail but it was such a horrible coincidence, and it really unnerved me not having a light at the entrance. So I emailed my landlord straight away, asking him to arrange for it to be replaced,' I tell the policewoman. 'That's how I realise now that it was a Wednesday. I just checked the email.

'The landlord hasn't sorted it yet and I've been really cross. I've sent a couple more emails. But now I've seen the message on that card . . .' I nod to the card in the evidence bag on the desk. *Did you miss the light bulb, Alice?* 'I'm worried that this man, whoever he is, read my column and somehow got in my house and took the bulb to upset me. Frighten me.'

DI Sanders' face changes completely, and she turns to the male detective sergeant beside her. His face changes too. 'OK. So we'll need to come back to the house to check this light fitting. Whether the bulb is still in place, I mean – just blown. Or actually missing. You say it's up very high?'

'Yeah. It needs a special ladder.'

'I'll get our CSIs on to all of this. The cake box. The card. Your home. I'm wondering . . .' Again she glances at her partner. 'Once we've done the checks for fingerprints and so on, is there somewhere else you could stay? Just for a bit? While you get the locks changed and so forth, and we finish all the tests we need to do? And if that light bulb *is* missing, we'll need to know who else has had a key up to this point.'

I feel this sinking deep in the pit of my stomach. I had a private security firm do a check on my home last week, not realising that someone may already have been inside. A part of me was hoping she would simply counter my theory. *No. It's unlikely he's been in your house.* I had wondered if I was being overly dramatic. Paranoid. The fact she is taking this theory seriously makes me feel so much worse.

'Um. Keys? My landlord, obviously. A neighbour keeps a spare for emergencies. And my partner Tom has a key.'

'We'll need to talk to your partner and neighbour. And the landlord about their security over the storage of keys.' Again she is looking at the sergeant, who is making notes in a book.

'Right, yes. Of course. Tom will be keen to help—'

'And now' – the policewoman's face is even graver – 'I want to talk about the reference to cheese wire, Alice.'

I feel extra fluid in my mouth suddenly. Have to swallow. Cough.

'It's a horrible thing to say. Deeply unpleasant. But it's also unusual, Alice. And I want to know if there is any reason – any person or any incident that you think could be connected? Someone who works in a deli? On a cheese counter? Does anyone come to mind?'

I shake my head, not wanting to think about it. The image of cheese wire – razor-sharp – slicing not just through cheese . . .

I am going to use cheese wire on you.

'I'm sorry. Could I have some water? There's a dispenser in the newsroom.' I glance at the partition glass, and the detective sergeant moves from the office to fetch a cup.

DI Sanders continues. 'So – have a think, Alice. Have you done any stories on any cheese companies? A delicatessen? Anything like that?'

Again I shake my head.

'And you don't use cheese wire at home, Alice?'

I find myself rubbing my hands suddenly. I really, really wish she would stop talking about this. I mean, I know she has a job to do. But . . .

'No, no. Goodness. I just use a knife. I mean – I've *seen* it used. Cheese wire. They use it at the local deli. And at my supermarket. But I've never seen anyone use it at home.'

'Right. We'll need to take the names of the supermarket and deli that you use, Alice. Just a long shot. Just ticking boxes.'

'Right.'

The sergeant reappears with a plastic cup of water, which I sip.

'Thank you. I appreciate what you're doing. Really I do. It's just . . .' I try to sound calm but find that it suddenly all feels too much. I try pinching my lips tightly together but it's no good.

'It's OK, Alice.'

Her kindness makes it worse.

'Sorry.' I put the cup down and start scrabbling in my pocket for a tissue. I glance up again at the window through to the main office. Two people turn away as if embarrassed, but I can't make out who.

'Don't apologise. It's a lot to take in. But we're here for you. We're going to check all of this out, and we will find this man. And stop this.'

She is looking me right in the eye and I see that she means this. Or rather that she wants to mean it.

But I am still struggling to believe she is any more in control of this new nightmare than I am.

CHAPTER 7

ALICE

Four days later – a Sunday – and I am staring at my sister, thinking how much she looks like our mother. I can almost predict what she is about to say. I ready myself for the little punch of indignation at the word I so hate.

Don't be so stubborn.

I close my eyes and hear the echo of my mother's voice; buzz-buzzing right up close as I pouted my way through all those petty childhood disputes – anything from a challenge to try a new food to a row over household chores. I remember even when I was really small feeling this fury building inside me whenever the label was applied. Not brave. Not heroic. Not all those things I wished I could be . . .

Stubborn.

Back then, and again right now, I want to rip the word right off me – to feel the sting of its removal, like a plaster worn too long.

I feel the same hurt and the same defensiveness as I dig in deeper and deeper, while my sister Leanne stares back at me with the familiar exasperation that bridges love and every sibling argument we have ever had.

'You're going to *have* to tell them.' Leanne tops up my coffee mug from the large cafetière on the table. I stare at her coffee jug and think that it sums up every difference in our lives. It is designer. Beautiful. A sleek stainless-steel, double-skinned wonder which keeps the coffee hot while simultaneously looking magnificent. My plastic cafetière is from the local supermarket. Cheap. Cheerful. Serves me cold coffee with an orange, plastic grin.

'It's not relevant, Leanne.'

'How can you be so sure – so *bloody stubborn* – about this, Alice?'

I wince. *Buzz, buzz.*

She shakes her head. 'I'm sorry.' She raises both arms as if surrendering. 'I didn't mean to sound cross. With everything you're going through – but I'm so worried and I think you're wrong about this. You need to tell the police absolutely everything.'

We've been going round and round in circles like this for maybe half an hour, and I need her to move on from this. It's bad enough being grilled by the police and not having the right answers.

For now we have decided not to move Mum from her home near me in Devon. In the initial panic, we thought this might be necessary. Urgent, even. Leanne was especially keen to have Mum in London but the police seem happy with the Devon home's security. And we don't want Mum upset, not unless she is truly in danger.

'So. Are you still OK to drive us to see Mum, Leanne? Is that OK?' I hold her stare as a warning that I need her, please, to stop grilling me on what I have and have not told the police. I am so tired of thinking of nothing else but this wretched and faceless man. This stranger who in such a short spell has turned my life upside down. Turfed me from my home. My job.

Leanne nods and I reach out to touch her hand as a thank you. My olive-branch fingers brushing hers ever so briefly. I wonder how love can nestle so close to hate some days. No, not hate. But irritation, certainly. We dance always between the two – me and Leanne. Love – and something *other*.

As we finish our coffees, I look around her huge kitchen. Black polished marble worktops gleam in contrast to the white cupboards with their stylish handles – twisty knots of stainless steel. The blue double-width Aga displays no evidence of cooking. Not a single fingerprint on its perfect surface. My sister's shiny life.

Am I jealous? No. It isn't jealousy . . .

'I'm so grateful for you driving down, Leanne.' I mean it. She has dropped everything to join me here – leaving my niece and nephew with their nanny and their dad Jonathan in London. This is their second home – a gorgeous thatched cliché in Dorset. Security gates. Security cameras. *Safe*.

'You can stay here as long as you need, or come up to London. Whatever you prefer. I'm just sorry I can't stay down here longer myself.' She pauses. 'Jonathan was wondering if you wanted someone else here? I mean, the cleaner pops in a couple of times a week but I don't really like the idea of you here alone once I go back to town. Until they find this guy. Sort it out.'

'Who do you mean – *someone else?*'

'Oh, I don't know.' She blushes. Clearly she's been discussing a range of options with Jonathan. 'Security guard? Bodyguard? We could put the cost on the company. You mustn't worry about the cost.'

'And now you're sounding like Tom. I'm not a bloody pop star. I don't want a bodyguard. I want my life back, Leanne.'

'I know that, honey. It's just, we're all so worried.'

'Yeah, I know. But four days. No word from him for four days. That's good, don't you think? Maybe he's given up.' I try to sound hopeful but am convincing no one.

It's Sunday, I remind myself. The day we visit mum. A good day. A safe day.

It's not Sundays this man seems to be interested in.

In the car, I try very hard not to glance behind us; this new and constant worry that someone may be following me. Leanne is playing classical music. I don't know the composer but it is soothing. Beautiful.

I turn to look out of the passenger window – the blur of trees and sunshine blinking through the gaps as we head south. The pulse of the flashes of light makes me narrow my eyes and I am wondering if I remembered to put my sunglasses in my bag.

It was a rush, packing up.

When the police team confirmed that the light bulb was missing from my house, everything seemed to step up a gear. My landlord said he hadn't sent anyone round; hadn't given anyone access to a key. It made no sense . . .

Tom was grilled. The neighbour with a spare key was grilled. My colleagues at the paper were questioned too. Every decent person I know seems suddenly to be a suspect while the real culprit is heaven knows where.

But then – a new complication. The police discovered that a junior member of staff at the estate agents has been secretly breaking protocol for over a year. She's been letting workmen take keys to rental homes without being accompanied, to save her time. Strictly against the rules. I've had a few repairs over the past year – central heating and so on. It basically means anyone could have copied a key to my house. There was a huge meltdown over it – disciplinary action and a flurry of activity to change locks for a string of properties.

The police keep me updated but don't seem to have any real leads yet. The cheese wire enclosed with the flowers is readily available on the net. A cheap import from China with hundreds of reviews online. I checked them myself. One couple said they bought a set with handles to cut their wedding cake, would you believe. I was shocked; I had absolutely no idea that you could buy it so easily. That anyone would *want* to.

There were no fingerprints at the house or on the cake box. The courier was paid cash with a false name for the delivery and there is no joy yet regarding the fake florist's business card left on my car. Seems my 'stalker' is clever. Going to a lot of trouble. DI Sanders seems certain they're reading my columns and using the information in them to wind me up. The question is why. Who the hell have I upset so badly?

Leanne and I have rather worn ourselves out with the dilemma over whether we need to move Mum to a different nursing home. It was Mum who chose Devon – to be near the sea – rather than London. She likes it. The police theory is that this man, whoever he is, doesn't know where she is. Was just twisting the knife by mentioning her in his message after reading my columns.

I really don't know what to think; I just want to be sure that my mother is safe.

Tom meantime is losing all patience with the police and has arranged for me to see some private detective tomorrow. A guy based in Exeter who comes highly recommended. Like Leanne, Tom wants the reassurance of extra security while I'm on my own. I think he would have preferred me to move in with him immediately but I'm still not keen. I mean – he has to work in London so often these days that it wouldn't really be a solution. He can't be responsible for me 24/7; I wouldn't want that. And I'm not ready to live with him. With anyone. Not again . . .

No. For now, this Dorset house is a better option. It's like Fort Knox. Downside of being in the money, I guess – worrying about burglars. Though heaven knows how I'm going to juggle the geography once I'm back at work. The office for the *South Devon Informer* is between Plymouth and Ivybridge, about twenty minutes from my rented house. But it's a long haul from Dorset.

'How long did you say you're taking off work?'

I turn to Leanne. It's as if she can read my mind – or maybe my expression. And I've been going on about it because it's the thing that is bugging me the most. My editor has insisted I take all the holiday I have spare. Lieu days – the lot. He says it's sensible all round. But I feel this is like giving in – like punishing me.

'If it were up to me, I'd be back at work tomorrow.'

'*Stubborn.*'

'No. Not stubborn. I just want to see the Maple Field House campaign stories through. They're planning the demolition right now. There's loads happening and I don't see why I should have my life so disrupted. Have him stop me doing what I love.'

'It's only temporary. Just go with it, Alice. Please. Keep your head down and keep yourself safe until the police find this guy. Like I said, you can always come and stay in London, if you don't mind the chaos.'

'You know I hate London.'

'Great journalist you make. A reporter who hates London.'

'And what does that mean? The world doesn't revolve around the capital, you know. There are really good stories everywhere. Just as important. More so, actually, because they get overlooked. Never make it into the nationals.'

Leanne gives me one of her glares.

'Sorry. Didn't mean to rant.' It's another thing my mother and sister tease me about. *On one of your soapboxes.*

We are nearing the nursing home now, and I get the familiar contradiction of love and dread all mixed up together. I love seeing my mother. Hate seeing her *here*.

And I thought it was cancer that smokers needed to be afraid of . . .

Inside we sign into the visitors' book and I'm pleased to see a member of staff posted on reception, monitoring the main door and checking guest passes. I'm reassured yet again about the security in place. The back door has a special lock which requires a PIN. All of this was explained when we first checked out the place for Mum two months back.

'Your mother is safe with us.' The woman with *Wendy* on her badge is smiling. 'We look after all our guests. Security is always a priority.'

I smile back, but am afraid to speak in case my voice cracks.

Leanne is holding the bunch of peonies and I look at them – a gorgeous soft pink – remembering our garden back in Hastings when we were little. Peonies in every colour you can imagine.

Mind the flowers with your tennis, you girls. You mind the peonies . . .

'Ready?' Leanne takes a deep breath for us both. She touches my arm and I just nod, trying not to think of that single flower on my car. The peonies tied with cheese wire in the cake box . . .

My mother is in her room, sitting in a deep red, high-backed chair, looking out on to the garden. There's a book on the small table next to her and a glass of water. She is dressed in a lovely pale aqua blouse and matching skirt, her hair up in a neat chignon. It is only as she turns and smiles that the evidence of her new reality slaps my face. The heaving of her chest with every breath. The little tubes into her nose. The oxygen paraphernalia alongside her chair.

'Hello, my darlings.' She is beaming but has to pause to take a few breaths. Just three words can be a strain these days. She smiles but I read the frustration in her eyes that she wants to say so much more but cannot.

And so we move across to kiss her cheek in turn, and she reaches out towards the flowers. Next we play the game where for the most part we talk and she listens – joining in when she feels that she can. Each of us pretending that this is normal. Two daughters filling the silence because their mother cannot talk and breathe at the same time anymore.

'Gorgeous, aren't they? Every colour I see, I think – that's my new favourite. Until I see the next colour Leanne finds.' My voice has this almost sing-song tone. Trying too hard. I pause to check myself.

'Me too. Though I have to say this baby pink is hard to beat.' Leanne moves forward so our mother can stroke the petals for a while. Then she points to the corner. A shelf with books and two empty vases. Leanne nods and moves across to busy herself with the arrangement near the little sink. She takes a pair of scissors from her handbag, and I think *how typical* of my sister. To remember to bring scissors.

We chatter, the two sisters, about our lives, editing out anything but the pleasant. I do not, of course, mention my stalker. Instead we say that Leanne and I fancied a little break together and so are at the Dorset house, catching up.

'Not falling out?' My mother's expression says more than her words. She has learned that she can manage just three at a time. Words. Her speech is like waltzing now. *One, two, three . . .*

'Not too much. I haven't broken anything yet. Smashed any mirrors.'

My mother is almost laughing but has to stop herself. The breathing even more of a struggle when she's excited. *Try to keep things fairly neutral*, the nurse said once. *I know it's hard, but too much excitement can bring on an episode.*

I wondered what she meant by *an episode*. We soon found out.

My mother has end-stage COPD. It means her lung disease is in its final chapter. The oxygen is merely buying us all some time. Soon – we don't quite know when – no amount of oxygen will be enough.

Meantime, an 'episode' can see temporary transfer to hospital. The nursing home can cope with day-to-day care but doesn't seem to want to be held responsible for anything too serious.

We are equipped to handle your mother's condition while she is stable, the senior nurse told us in a meeting. *But you know that we don't offer end-of-life care here. We'll need to talk again if . . . well – when things change.*

So, quietly, Leanne and I have been looking into the local hospice and arguing over whether London – near my sister – would be better. Working out secretly where my mother should die.

I try so hard to put that future, that inevitability out of my mind – to spend every visit in the present – but it is a trick I have yet to learn. The cruel paradox for me especially is my mother is still so very beautiful; she looks strangely, almost hauntingly well in other ways. Her skin is good. Her hair shines.

I think of her packet of cigarettes on the kitchen counter and want to go back in time and snatch them away from her.

Instead I chatter, and when Leanne has finished the flowers, I suggest we find a nice spot in the garden so that I can read to her.

'This book. Yes?' I pick up the faded copy of *Wuthering Heights* and check to find a postcard marking the chapter I reached when I visited last week.

Leanne fetches a wheelchair from the corridor and we transfer my mother easily between us, placing the oxygen in the little pouch hanging off the back of the chair. We weave our way out of the room and along the corridors, to fetch a nurse who uses her pass to let us out into the garden.

Good, I think. They are true to their word; being careful about security.

Outside we find a bench for me and Leanne, overlooking the fountain centrepiece of the garden. A spot where you can just catch sight of the sea in the distance. And so I pick up where I left off last week. It is the chapter where Heathcliff runs away.

We stay in the garden for maybe an hour – Leanne fetching tea and biscuits as an interlude. My mother's breathing is still laboured but seems a tad steadier outside. Maybe that is my imagination, or maybe it is because she knows that she will not have to talk. Or walk. Or do anything much. She just watches the fountain and listens to me reading.

'Nice breeze today.'

One, two, three . . .

'Yes, Mum. Just enjoy it. Close your eyes if you like. Just listen. You know me. I love the sound of my own voice.'

A smile. My mother has the loveliest smile . . .

Later, back at the Dorset house, I have the words of *Wuthering Heights* mixed with the tinkle of the fountain, all echoing in my head as a text comes in from Tom, urging me not to be late for the private investigator.

I turn the words over in my head. *Private investigator.*

I have already played the journalist. Checked him out online. Matthew Hill made a bit of a name for himself, helping to solve the case of a missing girl a while back. I can't help wondering what precisely Tom thinks he is going to be able to do to help me.

But this is not just about me now. I close my eyes to picture peonies. The single flower on my car and the severed flowers in the box. I need to ask this man – this Matthew Hill – if he can keep my mother safe too.

CHAPTER 8

HIM – BEFORE

'Are you OK?'

In his dream there is someone shaking him awake in his cave. He thinks it must be his gran. She went out much earlier. But when he opens his eyes, it's not the cave. The room is too bright. A searing light hurting his eyes.

'It's all right. You just fell asleep again.'

The voice is familiar and he looks up. Not a cave – but his classroom. Miss Henderley. She is sitting on the edge of one of the desks. Everyone else is gone.

He looks around the room, not understanding. Next he sees three faces at the window, laughing at him. Bruce and Luke and Helena. Miss Henderley turns and waves her arms to signal that they should move away.

'Don't take any notice of them.'

'Is it home time? Do I need to go to after-school club?' He sits up straight. His arm feels a bit weird where his head was leaning on it. Also there is an odd lump right in the middle of his stomach. As if he has eaten his food too fast. He can't work out if he is hungry. Or too full. Or has a tummy ache.

'It's OK. You're not in trouble. I just want to have a little chat before you go out to play.'

'I didn't fall asleep. I was pretending.'

'It's OK. Like I said, you're not in any kind of trouble. It's just I'm a bit worried about you. It's not the first time this has happened. Falling asleep in class, I mean. Is there something wrong? Something at home? Is there anything you're worried about? Want to talk to me about? I was wondering if we should maybe have a little chat with your gran when she picks you up.'

'No. Don't do that. I'm fine.'

'I had a look in the book and it's always Thursdays that you seem so tired. Do you do sport or something on a Wednesday evening. Swimming lessons? Football? Something like that? Or do you stay up watching something on television on a Wednesday night?'

'No. Nothing like that. I'm fine. Can I go out to play now?'

'So – is it maths? Are you worried about that? I know we do a lot of maths on Thursdays but you're honestly doing really well with your work. Your reading and your maths are both very good. There's really nothing for you to worry about. I want you to know that.'

'I'm not worried.' This is a lie. He's worried about a million things.

He looks down to see sauce on his school sweatshirt. He remembers now that they had shepherd's pie for lunch. So it is the afternoon. Afternoon break. Nearly home time. Yes. After-school club. Then home.

He is all at once remembering other things too. The banging on the door last night. Dark. Late.

You in there? Someone in there? I know you're in there . . .

He remembers suddenly needing the toilet when the banging started. Sitting in his bed and being worried that he might make a mess. Thinking about it makes the feeling come back.

'I need the toilet, please.'

'Off you go, then. I'll see you later. After-school club.' Miss Henderley pauses. 'I'll look out for your gran. Tell her how well you're doing with your work.'

The rest of the afternoon seems to go on for ages. The after-school club also drags. He normally likes it but not today, because he is worried about what Miss Henderley is going to say to his gran. She stayed on in the classroom after the final bell, marking books, and said she would *see him later* which made the weird feeling in his stomach worse.

After-school club is held in the main hall. Tables and chairs are set up with boxes of toys and puzzles and games. When Louise, who is in charge of the club, tells them to start packing up, he tries to be super-quick so he can be first out and get away fast before Miss Henderley appears. But it's no good.

When he gets to the door, she is already standing there – out in the corridor – before Louise gets the register.

They all have to be ticked off, one by one, from Louise's list, as parents arrive to collect them. It's the rule. Through the glass of the double doors to the corridor, he can see Miss Henderley talking to his gran.

When Louise calls his name and his gran comes to the door, she says they just need to nip to his classroom for a little chat with his teacher.

Oh no.

In the classroom, they both ask him the same question – Miss Henderley and his gran. About why he is tired on Thursdays. And is there anything worrying him?

He again says, 'No, I'm not worried about anything' – and keeps looking at his gran.

His gran has lots of different faces. She has a face when she is pretending that she isn't tired. A face when she pretends she isn't cross.

46

Right now she is pretending about something but he doesn't know what.

When they get outside and are walking home, she holds his hand and then ruffles his hair and says that she's sorry. And she tells him not to worry. For some reason this makes him want to cry.

'I didn't say anything to my teacher.'

'I know, lovely boy. I'm not cross. It's not your fault.'

When they get home, she makes him hot chocolate in his favourite mug – the one with the big, green dragon.

'I have a new idea,' his gran says. 'For next Wednesday. We can try something different. You can come with me but we'll have to keep it our extra-special new secret. Like hide-and-seek. I'll need to find you somewhere to hide. Can you do that for me? Be very, very quiet. And hide. Like a game.'

This is the best news. The best news in his whole life.

'So I can come with you. For the new secret?' He is not sure he understands how this will work but it sounds much, much better than the old secret.

'Yes. A new secret. You still mustn't tell anyone, especially not at school. You can come with me but you will need to *hide*. So shall we try that?'

'Yes please.' He throws his arms around her neck and kisses her cheek.

CHAPTER 9

MATTHEW

Matthew has his feet up on his desk, leaning back in his chair. He has an odd feeling that is making him frown. He narrows his eyes, trying to place it . . .

Ah yes – *rested*; he had quite forgotten. This is what a good night's sleep feels like. He smiles as he remembers the shock first thing this morning.

He had been woken by Sal shaking him, her eyes darting from side to side in alarm. She then gripped his forearm, with her other hand in the air, signalling that he should listen. He had assumed a strange noise. Some evidence of an intruder?

He listened, already glancing for a weapon. A plan. But no – *nothing* . . .

Another look sideways confirmed something even odder than the silence. The alarm clock said 8 a.m. This could not be right. For the last five, maybe six months, Amelie had set her own clock.

To 4.45 a.m.

They had tried everything. They had read books and scoured websites. They had followed the guy on Insta with umpteen daughters, millions of fans and buckets of advice. Nothing worked.

Maybe she doesn't need much sleep, Sal's mother had mused over their last Sunday lunch together. *Like Margaret Thatcher. She didn't need much sleep . . .*

The comparison made Matthew go cold.

They tried putting Amelie to bed later. Earlier. Dropped a nap. Added a nap. Cut out dairy. Increased dairy. Nothing worked . . .

Until today; until this blessed morning when their clever, brilliant and totally wonderful daughter slept through, not just until eight o'clock . . . but eight thirty.

Matthew taps a pen on the desk. He hums. He smiles.

It's over, he says to himself, just as the phone rings.

He takes a deep breath, fearing it may be his new client couple cancelling their appointment. Sadly, this happens a lot – people losing their bottle. He checks his watch. His agency is doing OK these days – off the back of some high-profile success – but for all that, it's been a quiet month. He could do with some new bookings.

'They're back.' The voice on the line is familiar. 'I thought they had gone, Mr Hill. Do you remember? A good while back now. The last time I spoke to you we both thought that they had gone for good. Turns out we were wrong. They're back and there are more of them. You *have* to help me.'

'Still tiny?' Matthew asks, his heart sinking. His caller is a 'frequent flyer' named Ian Ellis who bombarded him with calls soon after he set up the agency. Ian believes miniature people want to kidnap him. *Like Lilliput.* He has been ringing on and off for years.

'Yes. Thumb-size still. Different clothes though, now. I think it might be something to do with Brexit. They look European. And they're armed. I've told them I voted remain but it's made no difference. They won't let me cross the hall to the bathroom. And I very much need the toilet. I do not wish to be indelicate here but we are in danger of an accident, Mr Hill.'

Matthew bites into his lip. Ian became horribly persistent at one point, ringing several times each day. Matthew tried to be kind and he tried to get Ian help. He was clearly one of the people on the fringes of society who had sadly stretched the patience of his GP, the local hospital and the emergency services. As a nod to his former police colleagues, Matthew often in the past tried to 'talk him down' to limit Ian's 999 calls.

There would be spells with a lot of calls. Then long spells with none. And then eventually the calls stopped completely and Matthew had rather forgotten about Ian – hoping his problems had resolved.

'Right – well, this is a surprise after all this time, Ian. So could anything have triggered this? It's just I thought we'd agreed they'd gone for good the last time we spoke. Anything happened lately that might have brought them back?'

There is a pause. Matthew can hear Ian sucking in a long breath. He expects the usual blabbering describing the activities and the clothes of the 'little people' to ramp up a gear, but instead there is another sound. Matthew strains to make it out and pushes the receiver closer to his ear. To his horror, it sounds like distant crying.

'Are you all right there, Ian?' Matthew is used to feeling irritated by Ian. Sad. Frustrated. Angry that society has no resources to deal with people like him. A whole range of emotions, in fact. Now, for the first time, he feels truly shaken. Also very guilty.

'Nothing has happened, Mr Hill. Nothing has triggered this. Why did you have to ask that? You people always fishing for your blessed *triggers*. You have *absolutely no right* to ask me that.' And then – another first. Ian is the one to end the call.

Matthew sits up straighter. He finds that he is uneasy – both to hear from Ian again and also how this particular call has made him feel. And then the intercom announces the arrival of the 'stalker' case couple. He presses the button to invite them upstairs, still thinking about Ian as he warns over the speaker about the steep flight of stairs that he always worries will be the death of someone.

By the time he is standing – door held wide, ready for his clients – Matthew has decided to break a promise to himself. Yes. If Ian rings again, he is going to arrange to visit him.

'Sorry we're a bit late. Parking trouble.' Tom, who rang him in the supermarket and later booked this appointment, is stretching out his hand. Firm handshake but nervous face. This is not unusual. He has his hand protectively on his girlfriend's back and Matthew glances between them as he signals for them to sit down, offering coffee.

'I have a decent machine in the kitchen next door. Bear with me while I get things going and then we can chat properly.' Matthew likes to watch his clients from a secret vantage point, through the crack in the door, to try to assess what he is dealing with. He and Sally now live in a cottage near the sea but he has kept this flat adjoining the office and finds it terribly useful.

He watches as Tom takes his girlfriend's hand and gives it a squeeze. Tom is athletic-looking – dark hair cut short. A close-fitted T-shirt beneath a very nice blue jacket. Flat stomach. Matthew would guess mid-thirties? His girlfriend looks a tad younger; late twenties, fair and slim – even borderline frail – in a floral dress with a denim jacket. Tom is smiling his encouragement but she is very pale and clearly not comfortable at all. Matthew wonders if this is the result of the stalking, or reluctance to attend the appointment.

As he brings the tray through with their three cups and a jug of foaming milk, Matthew decides to plunge right in.

'Right. So Tom gave me quite a lot of detail over the phone, Alice. An awful time for you. I'm truly sorry to hear what you're going through. But before we talk about options going forward, I need to know how you feel about coming here. Involving me, I mean.'

'We both feel that the police aren't doing enough. That they don't seem to have the resources.' Tom is leaning forward. Agitated. 'It's quite a shock to us both. How little they seem able to do.'

'Is that right, Alice?' Matthew widens his eyes. He sympathises with Tom's concern. If it were Sally, he'd be exactly the same, but he needs to hear from Alice.

Finally she glances at her boyfriend, finding a small smile for him, before turning back to Matthew. 'I'm not going to lie. This was Tom's idea, not mine. He's very worried about me. Hoping that you can add to what the police are doing.'

'Or aren't doing,' Tom interjects, the sarcasm in his voice barely disguised.

'And where are you at with the police? Who's handling it?' Matthew keeps his gaze on Alice.

'They've put DI Melanie Sanders on the case now. I'm told she's very good. Is that right? I understand you worked together a bit.'

Matthew narrows his eyes. So Alice has been reading up on him – checking him out. He takes in a slow breath, remembering that she is a journalist, after all.

'Yes. I do know her and she is. Very good, I mean. We trained together. And we sort of worked on a missing persons case quite recently. You're in good hands.'

'But they won't provide surveillance.' Tom is leaning forward again. 'Doesn't that surprise you? I thought it would be the first base – that there would be some kind of protection offered. I mean, this guy is actually threatening her. May have been in her house. May even be *watching her.*'

Matthew taps into his computer to call up the notes he took from his second chat with Tom on the phone, when he called him back after getting home from the supermarket. 'So has there been nothing from Forensics? From the light fitting, the house or the cake box?'

'Apparently not,' Alice says. 'He must wear gloves. Be quite clever. Or at least experienced at this. The police seem to think it's someone who reads my columns in the paper. May have some personal grudge.'

'And you really can't think of anyone. Ex-boyfriend? Someone from a court case you've covered? Anything like that?'

'I honestly can't think of anyone.' Alice's face changes and Matthew watches her closely. He notices that she lets go of Tom's hand. Interesting.

He glances between them. Tom looks so worried, his foot flicking up and down. Matthew again takes in the expensive jacket. An alpha guy. Yes. Privileged-looking. Probably used to being in control of his life. He will dislike this feeling of helplessness. Matthew's already checked Tom's LinkedIn account and profile with his law firm. A high-flyer. Private school, then a first in Law from LSE. Matthew's not naturally drawn to the public-school type and so bristles. He tries to process this response and checks himself; it's unfair to judge Tom because of his background. It's understandable that Tom would hate this. Matthew couldn't bear it if Sally were ever targeted . . .

'So I was wondering if you could agree to surveillance,' Tom says. 'To look out for Alice on Wednesdays. This guy – he seems to target her on a Wednesday . . .'

'He's not a bodyguard and I'm not a celebrity, Tom. We can't expect Mr Hill to trail around after me. I can't go through my whole life expecting protection.'

'I don't do personal security per se,' Matthew says.

'Yes, I know that. I saw that on your website.' Tom's voice is more agitated. His face anxious. 'But I was wondering if we could book you for a day a week to work on this case. And if we made it Wednesdays, you could keep an eye on Alice and hopefully nail some evidence to catch this guy at the same time. Put an end to this.' Tom's eyes are really wide. Pleading.

Matthew twists his mouth to the side. He takes in Tom's desperation and finds that he likes him after all. He can't deny that a regular booking would be welcome. But it's not the kind of agreement he'd normally make. A bit too much like security. He's worried about setting a precedent.

'What do you think, Alice?' Matthew keeps his tone neutral.

'I don't honestly know. I mean – I *am* afraid. I hate admitting that. But I do dread what's coming next from this guy. I would feel better if someone was at least working actively on this. I have no idea why Wednesday is significant. Or whether it's just a coincidence so far.'

'It looks more like a pattern than a coincidence to me,' Matthew says, glancing again at his notes.

'Yes, I agree.' Alice is looking at him more directly now and he sees real fear in her eyes. For some reason he finds himself thinking again of his wife. And his daughter too.

'I tell you what. How about I agree to work on this case this coming Wednesday. Keep an eye on things from first light through to when you feel safe. Say, when Tom is able to join you in the evening? Did you say you're staying in Dorset?' Again he glances at his notes on the screen.

'Yes. My sister's place. It has very good security; I feel reasonably safe there. But I have an interview set up for Wednesday and I really don't want to cancel it. If you could come with me, or watch out for me, I would feel much happier.'

'I thought you were taking a couple of weeks off work?' Matthew is still cross-checking the information Tom gave him on the phone.

'Yes. I'm not going into the office at the moment. While we wait for this to quieten down. But I set this interview up a while back. It's with a local actress who's not often available. It's a bit of a coup so I don't want to give it to someone else. Professional pride.'

'OK. I'll email you to sort arrangements. Then we'll see where we are after Wednesday and regroup. Yes?' Matthew takes a deep breath for the tricky bit. 'And you know the fees . . .'

'Just invoice me directly. Money's not a problem.' Tom is now sitting up very straight.

'Tom. Please. I'm quite happy to deal with this—'

'No argument. My idea, so my expense. You invoice me directly, Mr Hill. Whatever hours you feel this needs. However long it takes. Yes?'

Matthew nods as Tom again takes Alice's hand.

'You don't think he truly means any of it, do you?' Tom's voice is suddenly quieter. 'I'm assuming he just wants to scare Alice. That's what he gets off on? Yes?'

Matthew thinks very carefully before he speaks.

'DI Melanie Sanders is one of the best police officers I know. She'll do everything she can to stop this. But I'm not going to lie to you. Police resources can be stretched, and stalker cases can be very difficult. And very stressful, of course, for the victims. All I can promise is that I'll do everything I can to boost what the police are already doing.'

Matthew does not add what he knows from his research. That the real answer to Tom's question depends on what kind of stalker Alice has.

The good news is that most stalkers are not killers.

The bad news is that a lot of killers are stalkers first . . .

CHAPTER 10

ALICE

Tuesday. I keep looking at the shorthand – *Tue* – lit up on my phone. I've honestly not given much thought before to the shape of the week, but now suddenly it is all I think about. The day. Where we are in the week. Sleeping less and less, the closer we get to Wednesday.

In the past, I never worried about the day per se; all I worried about was whether I was working or not. For me as a journalist, there's no clear midweek-versus-weekend routine as we work on a rota to cover weekends. Some weeks I may get Tuesday off for a Sunday on duty. Another week it may be Monday off for working a Saturday. Never the same, one week to the next, and so I have always simply marked my days off in green on the calendar on my kitchen wall, and smiled over my morning coffee as the green squares get closer.

It is other things that in the past have shaped my week. Pilates on a Thursday night. French conversation classes on a Tuesday.

And now? I am sitting alone in my sister's Dorset kitchen, asking myself what today really feels like now. *Tuesday*. The new answer is very simple – too close to Wednesday.

I can't relax because I'm wondering: What the hell next? What might he do tomorrow? Am I safe? Is my mother safe? Will having

Matthew Hill watch my back truly solve this? Keep us all safe? In fact, have I even got this right – is this man going to target me in some way *every* Wednesday, or has the day been a coincidence so far?

My editor is still insisting I use up all my spare holiday. I tell myself this is him being kind and sensible but wonder, deep down, if Ted simply wants the problem moved out of the office. He won't allow me to write about the stalking or harassment or whatever we choose to call it. He says we should treat it like bomb hoaxes were in the old days. *Do not give these things the oxygen of publicity. That is what they want, Alice. We say nothing in the paper. No columns. Nothing.*

Ted still talks about 'the paper' as if the physical version is the most important thing – which, of course, it no longer is. The readership of our weekly paper is dying. Literally.

Our South Devon 'paper', like every other, runs each story and photograph online first in a fruitless attempt to devise a new advertising and revenue strategy.

The reality is we are in financial freefall. Our few remaining readers are aged. As I say . . . literally dying off. Advertisers have given up on the physical paper but we have yet to find a way to make adverts work for us online. So much competition. It means we will probably all be out of a job very soon. The wise ones have already moved into 'communications' – PR and marketing, or the mystery that is search engine optimisation.

All I have ever wanted to do is write, and I'm not sure I have it in me to switch to *sales*.

I check my watch. Only 10 a.m. It's too far from Dorset to make my French class later, and I see a muddle of boredom and anxiety stretching ahead of me. I cannot imagine counting down the hours, just sitting here in Fort Knox, and so I head upstairs to my room to find my sports bag. Thank heavens I thought to pack my swimming kit.

At first it feels contrary to even contemplate leaving the house on my own. The security blanket of the camera system and the alarms. Leanne would be furious. She had to return to London and her family, and wants me to stay indoors until all this 'blows over'. I wonder if I should just watch another film?

I turn the options over in my head. I glance around the kitchen and take in the large television in the corner. I think of all the blessed films I've watched already.

I am rather sick of films. And I'm sick of feeling so cooped up. Defeated. Controlled. I hold my car keys in my hand for several minutes before finally deciding. Next there is the surreal, rich-kid novelty of the gates that open automatically for my car. My sister's smart life.

Even as I pull up the first hill, I am wondering when there will be an end to these push-pull questions now controlling my life. Is it madness to leave this safe haven? Possibly. Probably. Should I turn around and stay home? Possibly. Probably.

I turn up the radio a little too loud and drive a little too fast. By the time I reach the main road, I fancy that a red sports car is tailing me. Five minutes and my heart is starting to beat faster and faster. Then the car suddenly turns off at the traffic lights and I feel foolish.

My own gym back in Devon is much too far, so the only option is the public swimming pool. I can't remember when I last used a public pool but I seem to recall my sister saying her children had top-up swimming lessons here and it's good. It's unlike Leanne to use anywhere without private membership, so that means it really must be OK.

The satnav makes it an easy find. Plenty of parking. And I am starting to feel that it is a good idea to be somewhere busy – somewhere with lots of people around me. No one can target me in a crowd, surely? I change quickly, surprised to find a smart row of single cubicles as well as the communal space. No shortage of lockers. Lots of room. The water is warmer that I expect and very soon I am relaxing into the rhythm that always transports me.

Stroke, stroke and breathe . . . Stroke, stroke and breathe.

I complete one length very fast, using the 'serious lane' which is separated from the rest of the pool by bright orange rope with small blue buoys. On the second length I slow a little and let my mind wander.

For some reason I am picturing Jack, trying to appease the divorce woman when I took that first phone call in the office. *I am going to use cheese wire on you.* I remember how steady Jack was. Worried eyes but measured and sensible – just concerned enough to make me feel less stupid, but not so much to make me feel worse.

Not for the first time I wish with all my being that I had not crossed the line with Jack. Made that stupid spectacle of myself. What was it – seven, maybe eight months back? Just before I met Tom.

Lord knows what I was thinking. The poor man had barely lost his wife – the hell of ovarian cancer. Less than a year as a widower and there I was, practically asking him out. Put him right on the spot. *Just Italian if you fancy it, Jack. You know – save us cooking one night. What do you think?*

Maybe he just said yes to be polite. Who knows. We got along so well in the office and I felt so sad for him. Losing his wife like that. But yes, I'm going to be honest here. *Stroke, stroke and breathe . . .* I really fancied him too, so I was probably being a bit selfish as well. Shameful of me.

Whatever. It was a complete disaster. We had gin and olives. I found that I was incredibly nervous, being with him away from the office. I hadn't thought it through at all and so I talked too much. Asked too many questions. Drank too much too quickly. By the time the main course arrived, Jack was pale and I was getting tipsy. Then, horror of horrors, I could feel myself starting to properly flirt. Somehow I knew it was the alcohol and I knew, deep down, that it was a terrible idea, but I just couldn't stop myself. At one point, I reached across the table and touched his hand. Poor Jack. He looked puzzled and then embarrassed. I drank more wine. I reached for his hand a second time and he pulled it back as if burned. I was much drunker than I realised; he was suddenly mortified – mumbling about mixed messages and a terrible misunderstanding.

I'm so sorry, Alice. But I shouldn't have said yes. I can't do this. This feels . . . I don't know. All wrong. I think it's best I go.

He didn't even finish his meal. Paid the bill. Ordered me a cab and then disappeared.

For a good while afterwards, it was excruciating in the office. Me blushing. Him blushing. So that when Tom suddenly appeared on the scene a few weeks later, I started dating him with almost ridiculous enthusiasm.

An out . . .

I finally bought Jack a coffee and openly apologised.

I'm sorry, Jack. That Italian restaurant thing the other week? I honestly didn't mean for you to think it was like a date or anything. God, no. I didn't mean that . . . I have a boyfriend, actually. Tom. Lawyer. You must meet him. We're having drinks soon. I'll introduce you.

That's great, Alice. I'm sorry I was a bit odd at the restaurant . . .

Don't be. Entirely my fault. I had way too much wine. Anyway – I wanted to say sorry so that things can be OK between us again. Mates, I mean. And you must meet Tom. You'll like him.

I duck under the little rope of blue buoys and swim to the side of the pool. I take off my tinted goggles and hold on to the side as my eyes adjust to the brightly lit room. I scan the crowd, taking in the faces of all these strangers. There is a man with two small children in armbands and I wonder why he isn't at work and why the children aren't in school.

On a raised chair, a lifeguard is scanning the pool too. He looks bored stiff and I fancy he may almost enjoy the odd drama, to at least feel useful. No. That's cruel.

I wonder how Matthew Hill truly feels about his work. Trailing after me on Wednesday. Does he hope that nothing happens? Or secretly hope to be useful?

Like a journalist when we make our routine 'check calls' to the police and the fire brigade – morning, noon and night. We hope that no one is hurt; we wish no ill.

And yet? We secretly want a story all the same.

CHAPTER 11

MATTHEW

Matthew Hill glances at the door as a woman with a buggy negotiates the small step into the café. He wonders if he should help – or at least hold the door? He tenses for a moment and watches carefully, but no. A man nearer the entrance holds the door and she's fine. Better than fine, actually, as the child – dummy in mouth – is still asleep.

It's Tuesday and he's booked to watch Alice tomorrow. He's feeling unusually anxious about this case and badly needs a steer of some kind. He checks his watch, turns back to the pyramids of sugar sachets and checks the table for stability. The napkin under the right-hand table leg has done the trick. He has four pyramids on the second layer already and is starting to think he may actually achieve a third tier today. Great that this coffee shop has not switched to those skinny, straw-shaped sachets. He gently picks up two new paper squares, shakes off the stray sugar granules and leans forward . . .

'So, you don't change, Mr Fidget Fingers.' Melanie Sanders' voice right alongside the table has a smile in its tone. She must have followed the mother in without him noticing. He turns too abruptly – his pyramids collapsing.

'Mel!' He immediately regrets the shock in his tone but the sight of her is difficult to take in.

'Yes – I know. I'm huge. A whale. And I still have a month to go at work. Don't even pretend not to be appalled.'

'I'm not appalled. But seriously – are you sure it's not twins?' He kisses her on the cheek, eyes wide at her enormous bump.

'If I had a pound for every person . . .'

'Sorry. But really? No twins in the family?'

'I had an extra scan to check. Just a very large baby. It may even be a mistake. Maybe I'm carrying an elephant.'

He smiles and stands to signal the counter. 'Coffee? Cake?'

'Both please. Carrot cake if they have it. Stuff eating for two. I'm eating for Britain. Maybe that's why the baby's so big.'

Once back at the table with her drink and cake, Matthew decides to wait for Mel to take this forward. They have worked together unofficially before – and very successfully – but it is still a risk for her to meet him. Swap info on a live case. He knows this. She knows this.

Melanie dips her finger into the froth of her cappuccino and sucks the milk and chocolate powder off it before sighing. 'OK. So tell me again – how come you're working on the Alice Henderson stalker case?'

'Boyfriend Tom hired me. I suspect you know that he doesn't think the police are doing enough.'

'Oh yes. He's made his dissatisfaction *very* clear. And what do you make of him – this Tom? We've checked him out, of course. No record. No obvious flags – and cast-iron alibis. But should he stay on my list? I found him pretty straight myself, if a little irritating.'

'Yeah. Me too. Bit spoiled. Bit of a silver spoon there, I suspect. I get the feeling he's keener on her than vice versa but he seems genuinely concerned and she seems happy to have his support. I've tried to explain to both of them about police resources.'

'Yes. Well – we both know that we can't do as much as we'd like. They only put me on this because the chief knows the paper's editor and I'm supposed to be winding down to maternity leave. They seem to think this is one I can run mostly from my desk.'

'What's your instinct so far then, Mel?'

'Well, as I say, your Tom's in the clear. We've done the full checks and found absolutely nothing. A high-flyer by all accounts. Popular. Squeaky clean. And he was in court each time Alice has had hassle.'

'So where are you looking? Anything on the cheese wire angle? Alice told me you pressed her on that. Certainly an odd threat.'

'We've checked staff at her deli and supermarket. Nothing there. To be honest, I'm thinking we're looking for an ex-boyfriend or someone she's upset with one of her stories. But the latter is a needle in a haystack. Unbelievable the amount of stuff each reporter writes. I had no idea they were so prolific. She writes quite personal columns sometimes which may have stirred some nutter's nest. So what's your brief then, Matt?'

'To keep an eye on her every Wednesday and see if the day really is significant.'

'Security gig, you mean?' She raises both eyebrows. 'A bit Kevin Costner, isn't it? Didn't think that was your style.'

He blushes and finishes the last of his drink. 'I wouldn't normally have taken it, Mel, but she seems nice – this Alice. And these kinds of cases are so frustrating all round. We both know there's not much we can really do without surveillance. I've said I won't play bodyguard per se, but I'm happy to do twenty-four-hour surveillance once a week.'

Melanie lets out a long sigh. 'OK. Well, strictly between us, I'm very happy you're working on this too, because we both know I'm highly unlikely to get the manpower to do much unless things escalate. Forensics have found nothing so far, so our guy clearly knows what he's doing. I'm a bit worried about the mother, actually. Whether she's genuinely some kind of target too and we're missing something. Or whether this guy just referenced her to wind Alice up some more. We're checking the finances. Who would gain if the mother comes to harm.'

'So what's the security at the mother's nursing home like?'

'Not bad at all. They've got cameras and good door security. I'm sending uniformed round once a day to keep the pressure on them. But their protocols seem good.' She pauses. 'Might be worth you popping by to double-check; make sure they don't just let you sweet-talk your way in. If you have time.'

'Good idea. I'll do that.' Matthew then lets out a long huff of air and stares into Mel's eyes.

'Are you thinking about the Rachel Allen case, Mel?'

She nods.

'Yeah. Me too.'

When they were in police training college together, there was a stalker case in Devon that they studied as part of their training. Matthew and Mel spent time with the team involved. A waitress in her early twenties was being stalked by a bartender who had developed a crush on her. Lots of phone calls and texts. Flowers, chocolates and teddy bears delivered to her flat. There were no threats as such and the bartender had no record of violence. Matthew and Mel had to report back to their colleagues on how it was all going. One of the police recruits was reprimanded in class for cracking a joke – *I wish someone would send me flowers and chocolates.*

The feeling on the investigating team was that the guy was probably harmless and the crush would blow over. Matthew remembers the signal from the old-timers that they were probably wasting their time . . .

Until Rachel Allen was found strangled in her shower. Matthew has never forgotten the photographs.

The bartender had climbed in through a window of her flat and lost it when she screamed for help. He strangled her with the belt of her dressing gown. In his interview he said that he knew that they were destined to be together. *But Rachel kept fighting it . . .*

'OK, Matt.' Melanie's face has darkened and Matthew wonders if she is remembering those dreadful photographs too. 'Ideal world we find this guy while I can still waddle. We keep Alice *safe* and get enough evidence for a prosecution. That will also get me brownie points with the boss so I can go off on maternity leave to eat a lot more carrot cake. Which means that anything you can do to help me, I'll be grateful.'

'I'll stay in touch, Mel. Anything I get, I'll share. Let's see how this Wednesday goes and talk again.'

'Good. Thank you. And dare I ask how your Sally managed to have such a neat little bump? I seem to remember she was barely showing at this stage.' Mel is staring, crestfallen, at the huge expanse stretching her shirt to the limit of the fabric and forcing her to sit back from the table.

'Absolutely no idea. But if it's any consolation, the neat little bump that was Amelie has suddenly turned into the devil child. Strictly between us, I have an exorcism booked for Monday.'

CHAPTER 12

HIM - BEFORE

His gran talks a lot about 'work' but he doesn't understand any of it. He can see that teaching is a job. And driving a bus and being an astronaut or a superhero. But he can't see how making cups of tea and sandwiches can be a job.

That's what his gran says she does on Wednesday nights. She does it in the daytime too on Monday, Tuesday and Friday, but Wednesday is different. She says it's called a night shift. *My job is to make sure everyone is comfortable. Sometimes people can't sleep so I make cups of tea and sandwiches. Help take people to the bathroom. That sort of thing.*

He asked his gran why she couldn't stay home and make *him* cups of tea and sandwiches and call that her job but she said, *Life doesn't work like that.*

I do things for you because you're my little soldier and I love you. I don't get paid for doing things for you, darling. I do it because I love you. A job is when you're paid for things. So I can pay our bills – for the flat and the food and your football club.

He had said lots of times that he would pay her to stay home on Wednesday nights. They could go to the thingy in the wall which gives out money. He could pay her lots more than the stupid job. But she said it didn't work like that. And there wasn't enough money in the thingy in the wall.

He loves his gran ever so much but he gets fed up when adults say the same things over and over again.

Life doesn't work like that . . .

He feels in his pocket to find a sweet that George gave him in school at break-time. Good. He is sitting on his bed in his room with his little rucksack, ready for their new secret. Gran says he has to promise to be quieter than a mouse. And brave. They are going to play a sort of game – like hide-and-seek but he will have to hide and snuggle up for a sleep for quite a few hours. So he has two juice cartons in his little rucksack and a packet of biscuits and a torch. And the sweet which George made him promise to save so they wouldn't get in trouble in class. He looks at the rucksack and worries that his gran has told him to pack a torch. He hates the dark but she has told him not to worry – that the torch is *just in case.*

'You ready, my little soldier?' His gran's voice through the doorway sounds a little bit weird. And when he walks through to their little kitchen and sitting room, her eyes have that funny look when the words and the feelings don't quite match. Like a lie, but not a wicked lie like a robber or a murderer. Just a lie to avoid trouble, like when he told the teacher everything was fine at home. He looks at his gran and decides not to say anything more just now about the dark and the torch. He will ask about that when they get there.

They walk down the stairs holding hands. He hates the stairs because they smell of toilets and you have to mind your feet. And then afterwards they walk right along the high street for miles and miles to the bus stop. This makes the funny feeling in his tummy come back. When his gran goes to work on Wednesday nights, she always says that she isn't too far away. He used to sleep at a lady called Jan's flat on Wednesday nights, but Jan has moved away so he can't stay over anymore. His gran can't find anyone else, and that's why they have to keep their secret. She says there will be terrible trouble if he tells anyone she can't find a new babysitter, and people will come to take him away.

For weeks and weeks his gran has said he must just be brave; and that when she was a little girl on the family farm, she often had to stay on her own when her dad was out lambing at night. It was perfectly safe, and so he is to go to sleep like a good boy in his bedroom and he mustn't answer the door or ever, ever tell anyone their secret – and she will be back before he knows it. Before he wakes up. But he sees now that it isn't true about her working nearby. It's miles and miles away . . .

He has been trying to figure out if he could run and run and find it in the dark but he can't remember the turnings already. Too many.

The bus is a double-decker and his gran lets them sit upstairs. It's cold and it also smells a bit like the stairs and the toilets in school, but his gran puts her arm around his shoulders and they play I Spy. And he wins.

When they get off there is a lot more walking, and then they get to the place his gran works. It's called the Daisy Lawn Nursing Home but he can't see any daisies or even any grass. It looks a little bit like a school but with no playground. He wonders if the people who live here don't get to play.

They go in through a door around the back so no one will see. His gran has a special card to scan to get in, which she wears on a ribbon round her neck. She puts her finger up to her mouth to say that they must be quiet like mice and she leads him along a corridor to a small room.

The room does not have a window but has lots of shelves with all sorts of things. Blankets and pillows and boxes and stuff.

His gran takes down some pillows and blankets and spreads them out in the corner to make a sort of bed for him. She says this is where he will sleep for the new secret but he is to be ever so quiet and ever so good.

He doesn't like the little room. Not at all; it is even smaller than his bedroom and he hates that it has no window.

'Can't I come and help you with the tea and the sandwiches? I'll be very good.'

'No, darling. You're not really supposed to be here when I'm working but I need you to get more sleep so you're not so tired in school. It has to be our secret, so you need to go to sleep now and I'll come and check on you whenever I can.'

'What if I need the toilet?'

'Do you need the toilet now?'

'No. I don't think so.' He keeps very still and tries to think for a moment – to feel properly, deep inside, if he needs a wee. He shakes his head. 'I'm OK.'

'OK. Good. I'll come back soon and ask you again. How does that sound?'

'Can you leave the light on?'

'Yes – of course. And if there's any problem, you have your torch.'

'What problem?'

'Never mind. Try to go to sleep now so you won't be tired in school. I have to go and do my work. Be a good boy for your gran. Yes?'

Once she is gone, he looks around the room and can hear his heart in his left ear. He used to worry that his heart had moved up into his head and that it would explode but his gran says this happens when it's too quiet and he's not to worry. It's normal. He looks at the towels on the shelves and he counts the towels and then he tries to count sheep.

It doesn't work. He is sort of tired but also not tired. He takes the sweet from his pocket and pops it in his mouth. It is pink but is not the strawberry flavour he was expecting and it tastes a bit like cough medicine. At first it is just a bit odd but then it gets hotter and hotter in his mouth until he feels that his mouth is on fire and he is going to choke.

He sits up, coughing and spluttering and realises it is a joke sweet. Some of the other boys were talking about this very thing last week. George has played a prank on him. He is furious and spits out the sweet on to the blanket but it is too late. His mouth is burning. Hot like a volcano.

He tries to be quiet but it's no good. As he coughs and wheezes, the door of the room swings open. He is terrified that his gran is going to be ever so cross but it is worse.

It is not his gran. It is a very fat man with a bright red face, wearing some kind of uniform. The man steps to the right, so he can see him properly around all the shelving.

'So what the hell is going on in here?'

CHAPTER 13

ALICE

I check the window to see Matthew Hill's car still parked outside. *Wednesday.* I wave and he flashes the lights in reply. He texted at 6 a.m. when he first arrived, and I offered coffee but his message said he has a flask and will wait on the drive unless I need him.

I let go of the curtain and sit back on the bed in Leanne's guest room. I feel utterly exhausted. Couldn't sleep. I remember the glow of the digital clock by the bed: 3 a.m., 4 a.m., 5 a.m., blinking in green digits on black. I check my watch – 8 a.m. now. Plenty of time for a shower to try to wake myself up a bit, then a final check of my notes before I set off for the interview.

Under the stream of hot water, I try so hard not to think of the day. Of that man. I think instead about the actress Melinda Belstroy and wonder what she will be like in the flesh. You can never tell. I've called it wrong so many times – looking forward to meeting a celebrity, only to find them dull. And on other occasions being surprised to sit laughing and enjoying the company of someone whose politics make me shudder.

Melinda Belstroy is fronting a new campaign for a bipolar charity, seeking support and tolerance in the workplace. She has only just admitted to having the condition and I've been lucky to secure this interview in person. The people in Melinda's league normally only meet the national press. We're lucky in the provinces to secure a quick phone call with someone like her. But Melinda apparently saw a feature I did on mental-health awareness in schools. She retweeted it and we've chatted on Twitter quite a bit since. So I got lucky when I bid for this chat. There was no way I was going to hand this interview over to someone else, just because the editor wants me to take a break. In my ideal world I'll be pitching again soon for some shifts on the nationals, and this will be good for my cuttings.

Dry and finally dressed, I check my iPad for my research notes and questions. Last night I watched that documentary again by Stephen Fry. The one where he questioned whether he would press the button which would allow him to be free of bipolar disorder. I will ask Melinda at the end of the interview. Yes. A bit of a cliché perhaps – but it will round things off nicely.

Downstairs, I check the wall unit which operates the alarms and cameras as Leanne taught me, to make sure that everything is fine before I leave.

Outside, Matthew winds down his window and says that he will drive me but I shake my head. He remonstrates but I'm really determined. I've agreed that he can follow me all day but I don't want to have to explain to Melinda what's going on. I want Matthew to be discreet. I promise him that I will keep his car in sight and he finally gives in.

The traffic isn't too bad. I feel nervous – this is the fifth Wednesday after all. The light bulb, the flower on my car, the phone call and then the cake box. Will he do something today?

I bite my bottom lip and glance in the rear-view mirror to see Matthew directly behind. He's ex-police and has a good reputation. He must do a lot of surveillance. *This will be OK, Alice.*

I am meeting Melinda at her agent's holiday home near Salcombe, and as the satnav steers me to the private drive, I can hardly believe it.

The house has three storeys with huge balconies to make the most of the glorious view over a small bay. Like Leanne's home, there are private gates, which open after I confirm my name into the little speaker. I say that Matthew in the car behind is also with the paper and will be sitting in on the interview, if that's OK. They don't seem to mind, which is a relief.

Melinda is dressed down in jeans and white shirt and no make-up. I think she looks better this way, and as we sweep through to an enormous library overlooking the bay, I try to play it cool – as if this is the kind of house I visit all the time.

She has her PR with her and so I know that our time will be limited. We chat easily and, to my relief, she allows a recording on my iPad. She is more open and relaxed than I expected and the interview goes well. Stories from her childhood when she first realised she was 'different'. Denial in adolescence when she thought she was just highly strung. And then diagnosis in her twenties, and drugs and therapy which she kept entirely secret, fearing it would destroy her career – until now. She's thirty-eight and tells me she cares less about what people think these days and wants to encourage others to be more open too.

Ten more minutes and I can see the PR shifting in her seat and so I ask the final question. Would she press the button? Be free of bipolar disorder if she could? I remind her that some people in the Stephen Fry documentary said their condition fuelled their creative lives and was a part of them. They had learned to accept it.

I watch her closely as she turns to look out to sea through the window. I am surprised to see her eyes tearing up. I feel guilty. And yet excited too, and I check that the recording is still running. I am already imagining how I will write this into my feature. Maybe it will give me an intro . . .

'I'll need to think about that, Alice. Can I email you later?' Melinda turns away from the window to glance at her PR, who looks worried, and so I step in and say that will be fine and hand over my card.

Outside, Matthew – who sat quietly drinking coffee throughout the interview – suggests we grab a sandwich and have a chat before we return to Leanne's house to map out the rest of the day. There is a café just along the coastal road and so I agree to follow him. After about ten minutes, he pulls in and I park directly behind.

I step out of my car first, turning to check behind as I hear a motorcycle approaching. And that's when it happens.

The rider has a bottle in his hand and freezing liquid is sprayed right into my face and down the front of my chest. Next I see Matthew bolting from his car as the motorcyclist accelerates away. And I hear screaming . . .

Mine.

CHAPTER 14

HIM - BEFORE

'So who the hell are you?'

Huddled in the pillows and blankets in the tiny, windowless room, he does not answer with his name. He remembers it is all supposed to be a secret. Suddenly he very urgently needs the toilet and wants to shout out for his gran.

'You tell me who you are right this minute or I have to call the police and the social services. Do you understand?'

He remembers that his gran said those words. The *social services* would come if he ever told anyone at school about Wednesday nights. She said they might take him away and so he shakes his head and says nothing, buttoning his lips tight, tight together.

He is terribly afraid that the police will come too, and he decides that he will fight and bite to stop them. But suddenly there is a new face at the door and relief floods through him. His gran.

The fat man still looks furious. His gran is also bright red in the face but she moves into the tiny room to kneel down and take him into her arms for comfort. Then she turns to the fat man.

'Please, Stan. Let me explain. It was just this one time. An emergency.'

'So he's with you? You brought him here?'

'He's my grandson, Stan. I normally have a babysitter for Wednesday night but she's unwell. I'm already on a warning and I can't afford to lose the job; you know that. I couldn't find anyone at short notice.'

Sitting on his little makeshift bed, he holds on to his gran and wonders why she is telling these fibs. There is no babysitter anymore. The lady on the floor below who used to have him to stay over on Wednesday nights moved months back. Why doesn't she tell Stan the truth? And what does she mean, she is on a *warning*? In school, it's bad to get a warning. Timothy is always getting warnings before he has to go to the headmistress.

'This is not allowed, Martha. You know that. We don't have the insurance. What if something happened to the boy. Unsupervised? We'd be in all kinds of trouble. An investigation. All hell would break loose.'

'But just this once. Just this one emergency. Please, Stan. Don't say anything. He's a good kid.'

'At nights I'm in overall charge, Martha. I can't let this go. More than my own job's worth. You should have phoned in and explained.'

'I'm already on thin ice, Stan. They want me to do two nights a week on the rota like everyone else and they're making an allowance just for now. If they find out . . .'

'Right. So this is what happens.' Stan has closed the door behind him and has at last lowered his voice. He pauses, looking at the ground as if he is thinking very hard.

'OK. Just this one time, I will say that you were suddenly taken ill, Martha. Vomiting bug. That I sent you home because I was worried about the residents catching it. I will cover you . . . but this one time. You are to take the boy home and this is never to happen again. Do you understand me? One final chance, yes?'

'You're a marvel, Stan. Thank you so much. I promise you this will never happen again.' His gran has stood up and starts gathering up the pillows and folding the blankets. 'Come on. We're going home.'

He stands and picks up his rucksack, staring at Stan and then at his gran. He tugs at her arm to pull her down to his level so he can whisper in her ear that he needs the toilet. She whispers back that he will need to hold it and do it in the garden when they leave so that no one else will see them.

And so he concentrates very hard to try to hold it in, all the while staring at Stan.

CHAPTER 15

ALICE

I can see the sky now so I must be on the ground. I am still screaming but Matthew is holding my arms and telling me not to touch my face.

'Water. That jug of water.' He is shouting at the people seated at an outside table near us. 'And an ambulance. Phone for an ambulance . . .'

I am gasping and bracing myself for the pain as Matthew is handed the jug and pours water slowly across my face. The water is ice cold and this is also a shock, almost as much as the spray into my face as the bike passed. I can feel my eyes darting from left to right, waiting for what is coming next. The pain and the burning? I am thinking of my looks. My eyesight. My face in the mirror. How bad this will be; how quickly acid works . . .

'Close your eyes, Alice. Keep them closed.' It's Matthew's voice again as he pours more water, first on to my left eye and then my right. But I cannot help myself. I'm holding on to his upper arms with my hands, frightened to let go, and my arms rise up as he moves the jug. Despite what he says, I open my eyes again briefly because I'm afraid of not being able to see. Relief. I still see sky. I hear Matthew demanding a lot more cold water. 'More jugs. Quick as you can, please.'

He continues to pour icy water over me and it is working. I close my eyes again and I can't feel the burning. The cold water is stopping the burning. I wonder how much damage it can stop; how long before I will feel the worst of it.

'It's all right, Alice. It's going to be all right. We're here. It's going to be OK.' Matthew has this low and steady voice and I'm thinking how incredible it is that he can do this. Not panic. His police training?

I open my eyes once more to find that he is staring at me very intently and I want to cry because I imagine he can see what is happening to my face. The skin changing? And then he stops pouring the water on me and frowns.

'No. Don't stop.' My voice is a whimper. I'm terrified of what comes next. Without the water, it will burn and I am very afraid of the pain . . .

'No. It really is OK, Alice. It's not acid. It can't be acid. You're OK. There's no burning. Your skin is completely fine.'

His shoulders sort of slump as he says this. I let go of him and I am suddenly very, very still – eyes darting once more from left to right as I try to process what he is saying.

Not acid.

Matthew then looks at me very intently before touching my face – briefly and then for longer.

'It's water, Alice. All of it. Water. It must have been water sprayed at you. Not acid.' His voice cracks as he says this, and the next thing I know Matthew is sitting on the ground alongside me, raking his hand through his hair, letting out little huffs of breath himself. *Huff. Huff.*

I look up at the sky and put my right hand up to my right cheek, touching ever so gingerly with the tip of my finger. No burning. He's right. Still no burning . . .

I smooth my finger right across my cheek next, to check the flesh properly. Nothing.

No burning. Not acid.

And then I'm crying with the relief and I close my eyes as I hear Matthew calling out to cancel the ambulance. Again his voice is steady and completely in control. The relief is seeping through me but I feel cold all over and am suddenly shaking.

'She's OK. It was water. She's going to be fine but she's in shock. She'll need a hot drink and a blanket, please, but we don't need an ambulance. Can you ask in the café? Tea with sugar and somewhere quiet for her to sit?' A long pause. 'But she's going to be OK.'

Ten minutes later and I am inside the back office of the café, wrapped in some kind of tartan rug, clutching a mug of sweet tea and still trembling. I can hear lots of voices beyond the door and imagine everyone gossiping about what has happened.

The café staff had wondered if an ambulance was still a good idea, given the shock, but both Matthew and I felt that was not what we wanted. Personally, I just want to get away now; I want to get back home. Or rather, to Leanne's home.

But Matthew reminds me that we have to deal with the police first. Local uniformed officers have responded to the 999 report but Matthew is now on the phone to DI Melanie Sanders. He is giving her all the details, explaining that he took a photo of the bike on his phone but that the number plate was covered. She's sending her own CSI officers to see if they can get any evidence. Maybe the bottle was discarded nearby? They are already putting a call out to check all CCTV and traffic cameras.

And then Matthew's face changes completely as he listens intently. He presses his phone closer to his ear then glances across at me. 'You sure, Mel?'

His expression becomes graver and graver and I get this sinking feeling, deep inside me.

'She's still in shock, Mel. But yes, of course. I'll ask her. And when we're done here, I'll bring her straight in to talk to you. Yes, of course. Absolutely. But she's had an awful time – a horrible shock, remember.'

Finally he rings off and moves to the seat opposite me.

'How are you doing now, Alice?' His voice is still concerned but there is some strange new edge that I don't understand.

'Better. A bit better. Just shaken. I feel warmer now. Have you spoken to Tom?'

'Yes. He's frantic. Also furious with me but never mind about that. We'll update Tom as soon as we can. Right now we need to speak some more to the police. Help them mop up any evidence.'

'Yes, of course.' I am looking into his face, trying to read what the new problem is.

'There's something else. Something Melanie Sanders shared with me. As a favour to me, really. Something I don't understand at all.' He looks upset, a frown deepening.

'What? What did she say?' Suddenly I can see my sister, looking across at me in the kitchen. The echo of her voice . . . *You have to tell them everything.*

Matthew takes in a long, slow breath – his eyes unblinking. 'I don't know what to say. I mean, I know you're still shaken. But she said she's just found out that your name isn't really Alice. And I'm to take you into the police station, firstly to investigate this attack. But also to explain yourself.' He pauses. 'We all need to understand who the hell you really are.'

CHAPTER 16

ALICE

I suppose I always guessed it would catch up with me.

Sitting in Matthew's car as we drive to face Melanie Sanders, I put my phone on silent. There is a string of voice messages from Tom but I can't face speaking to him yet; instead I've texted to say where we're going and that I'll update him as soon as I can.

I turn to look at Matthew's profile. His expression is stony. I try to imagine Tom's face when he finds out the truth, and the ball of dread in my stomach grows. I turn to the left to watch the blur of fields and hedges and trees, sweeping a patchwork green arrow to the chaos ahead of me.

Yes. I always knew I would one day be found out; I knew that today would come. I had just hoped it wouldn't happen while I was dealing with all this too.

I shut my eyes to picture him – *Alex* – and feel the familiar punch of fury at myself. He stares back at me from my memories – so handsome and confident and funny and smart. I can hear him playing the piano at the home we shared, shouting over the music for me to please make more coffee. And the worst thing? I can actually remember how in the moment, at the beginning of it all, I believed utterly in him. In us. I genuinely had no idea what lay ahead. I felt lucky. I cringe at that now but it's the truth. I actually felt *lucky.*

I met Alex at a fundraising concert in the Highlands. It was my very first month as a reporter, on a tiny weekly paper, and I had been sent to cover the concert with a photographer called Hugh. The snapper was old school – competent but well into the cynical zone; he wanted to get his pictures done as quickly as possible to head off for a curry with some friends.

But I've always loved music. I was pleased to be assigned the job and didn't mind staying the course, especially when the organiser was introduced to me. Alex Sunningham was impossibly good-looking and I had to struggle to contain an involuntary blush. I could tell immediately from his expression that he was thoroughly enjoying my response as he shook my hand. I imagined he was very used to women trying to contain a swoon and I hated myself for losing the upper hand.

While Hugh posed Alex at the piano along with various other performers, I took out my notebook and pretended to be jotting in shorthand, while occasionally glancing across at the ensemble. There were two violinists and a cellist. They played along with Alex in little snippets so that Hugh could get all his pictures. The sound was wonderful, and I started to think this might be a very enjoyable evening indeed.

Once Hugh had left, Alex took to the microphone to apologise to the arriving guests about the impasse for photographs, explaining that the publicity was crucial to achieve maximum fundraising. 'Please bear with me.' He said the concert proper would start in approximately ten minutes and then, to my surprise, he made a beeline for me.

'So what do you do now if there's a streaker or a fire?'

'I'm sorry?'

'Do you still run the posed pictures if something exciting happens?' He was clearly teasing.

'I'm sorry. The photographers never have much time. I'm sure you're used to that – and between us, Hugh's not exactly into culture. But I always have the camera on my phone.' I paused, lifting my phone by way of illustration. 'In case something *exciting* happens.'

'Well, we shall try not to disappoint you . . . Jennifer.' He lowered both the tone and volume of his voice as he said my name. And he held my gaze longer than was appropriate. I scurried away to my seat. Embarrassed. Confused. Interested.

The concert was extraordinary. Alex was both a brilliant pianist and a warm host, introducing the cellist and violinists as friends from music college who were doing him a favour to raise money for cancer research. Apparently the cellist's younger brother was currently under-going chemotherapy for a rare bone cancer, and I felt this pang as Alex explained about new research and the importance of doing everything possible to help a friend.

Later there were performances by Alex's pupils, and I realised from his banter on the microphone that he taught piano, both at a local school and privately. Some of the pianists were rather good; others were just starting out.

It was a charming evening, and as it drew to a close I felt the flut-ter of excitement in my stomach rise, confident that Alex would find me again.

'So are you going to tell me more before we meet Melanie? Do you not think you owe me that, Alice? Or Jennifer? Or whoever you really are?' Matthew's voice alongside me draws me back to the present. His tone is disappointed rather than angry. 'I mean, I do know you've been through a lot this morning. But this is going to get very serious now. And I have no idea what to think, quite frankly. I don't know how I'm supposed to help you . . . or even if I *should* at this point.'

I open my eyes and turn to Matthew. 'My real name is Jennifer Wallace. I was once engaged to a musician called Alex Sunningham. I thought he loved me and that our relationship was real. But it turns out he was using me as a cover for something else. There was a media frenzy about it. That's why I changed my name.'

'Oh Jeez.' Matthew does not take his eyes off the road. 'So what are we talking about exactly?'

'Look. I really don't want to go over it all right now, except to say I did nothing wrong myself. But it was still humiliating and dreadful and I will never shake off the guilt for failing to see through him, Matthew. But he's in jail now. It wasn't my evidence that put him there. I don't believe he bears me any ill will; in fact, I doubt he gives me a second thought. And he can't possibly have anything to do with what's going on now because, as I say, he's inside.'

I hear the echo of my argument with my sister in her kitchen.

I know he's still in jail, Alice, but you still have to tell the police. Won't they be furious if you keep this from them? They're bound to find out.

I think of how long it took poor Leanne to get used to calling me by my second name. Alice. I think of my mother, bless her, and those few close friends who also helped my reinvention.

'Right,' Matthew says. 'Well, one way or another, we need to talk again, Alice. Do I still call you Alice?'

I don't know how to answer because I don't even know what I think myself now. We are turning the final corner to the police station and Matthew has already warned me that he cannot risk being seen taking me right up to the entrance. It could prove tricky for Melanie Sanders. But he has promised her that he'll deliver me safely for questioning and so will wait for me to go in.

'You don't trust me to go in, do you, Matthew?' I watch him closely but he doesn't reply.

He pulls the car up within line of sight of the entrance and lets out another long sigh, raking his fingers through his hair – which I realise, watching him, is what he always does when he is struggling to compose himself. 'Like I said, I don't even know what to call you, let alone what to think or do right now. Don't think I don't feel for what you've been through today. But this is a pickle. Mel Sanders is a former colleague and a good friend, which means I'm seriously compromised here.'

'I'm sorry, Matthew.'

'Yes. So am I.'

CHAPTER 17

MATTHEW

Once Alice – or rather Jennifer – is inside the police station and liaising with the front desk, Matthew moves his car around the corner and parks up again.

He is genuinely stunned. He bashes the steering with the heel of his hand in frustration and anger and relief and confusion. Only now does he even begin to let out all the pent-up emotion from what happened earlier. When the motorcyclist swung past, he felt as if acid were being flung into his own face. The absolute horror of those first few seconds. As he was pouring water over Alice's face, all he could think was that she would be scarred for life, possibly blind too, and he had let . . . this . . . happen. He should have persuaded her to ride in his car; he should not have let her overrule him.

Idiot, Matthew. You complete and utter idiot.

The relief at finally discovering it was *not* acid was both wonderful and yet equally overwhelming and confusing. The seesaw of conflicting feelings was incredibly hard to control but all he could think of was the need to stay outwardly calm for Alice's sake. And then – just as he was managing the whole rollercoaster of emotions? This new twist.

It had honestly never occurred to him that Alice wasn't being straight. He realises, thinking back to that first proper meeting in his office, that he'd assumed her reticence to involve him was the result of being overwhelmed. Afraid. Confused. Now he feels that this fake-identity twist may have been a part of it. Was she worried that hiring a private investigator would increase the chances of all this being found out sooner?

Hell. What kind of a private investigator did it make him that he hadn't sussed this? And then he reminds himself that the police have only just caught up with the identity switch, so Alice must have been very clever about it; she must also have had the support of her closest family and friends to pull this off.

He calls up her profile on Facebook, which he checked thoroughly when he first took the case. All the pictures show Alice with her neat hair and her same, rather sweet look. Smiley. Delicate features. Hardly any make-up. Attractive but all very girl-next-door. No pouting or fake eyebrows or shots obviously enhanced by apps. The profile goes back several years and there is nothing obviously amiss, although he notices now that there are not as many friends as you might expect. But even that is not so very suspicious, as lots of people ditch their university profile and set up a new one – to step away from photographs, antics and friends they do not want to take forward in their life.

Next Matthew googles the coverage of the Alex Sunningham case. Several tabloid news stories appear instantly.

He'd wondered if Alex was secretly gay or committing fraud behind Alice's back, but it's far worse. He was jailed for sex with two underage music pupils. Matthew scans the copy, skipping from one online page to another for more details. It is now vaguely ringing bells but he doesn't remember it making the TV news. Did he see it in the papers or online at the time? He can't be sure.

The earliest stories say that Alex, engaged to journalist Jennifer Wallace at the time, had suddenly disappeared with a fifteen-year-old pupil. Alex and Jennifer had lived in the Highlands and the teenager took piano lessons at their home. The two runaways were initially believed to still be in Scotland somewhere, and there was a local police appeal. They were eventually discovered on the Isle of Skye when the girl fell ill and a local GP recognised her from the coverage. At first the pupil, who wasn't named, was loyal and devastated that their 'romance' had been discovered. Her initial story to police was that she loved Alex very deeply and they were going to marry at Gretna Green as soon she was sixteen.

But a sordid web quickly unravelled. A second pupil came forward to say that she'd had a relationship with Alex the previous year but he had dumped her, and so she'd made an excuse to her parents to give up her piano lessons. She was too afraid and embarrassed to tell anyone the truth.

Both girls were appalled to find out about the other and finally cooperated with the police, giving evidence which put Alex in jail.

Matthew calls up as many photos as he can find. The creep Alex is a looker. 'Smarmy bastard,' Matthew whispers out loud. He finds himself thinking of his beautiful little Amelie; he imagines her all grown-up and beautiful and feels this punch of fear.

Most of the papers carried photographs of Alex only, but one has an exclusive interview with the girl he disappeared with – she waiving her right to anonymity to warn others how easy it is to be duped. She is heavily made up in the photoshoot for the feature, and Matthew tuts. The picture makes him very uneasy.

Only two stories ran small pictures of the fiancée Jenny Wallace. The copy makes it clear she knew nothing of what was going on. She gave no comment on the record and her court evidence seemed to be insignificant compared to the two girls'.

In the photograph Alice looks very different. On closer examination she is recognisable, but as Jennifer she has long, dark hair. Now she has a chin-length, blonde bob with a fringe and is much slighter.

Just as Matthew is twisting his lips to the side, wondering what the hell to make of all this, his phone rings and Tom's name flashes up. He winces.

'Hello, Tom.'

'So what's happening? Where is she? And what the hell happened, Matthew? I mean, I'm paying you to keep her safe.'

Matthew takes in a long, slow breath. 'I can understand why you're so upset. Trust me, I blame myself too. It's shaken me. But Alice insisted. She didn't want to travel with me . . .'

'So have they tracked the bike? I'm on the way to the police station now but Alice won't answer her phone. She's not even answering texts. So have they caught the guy yet? Is it over? Have they found him?'

'I don't know, but I don't think so.' Matthew pauses. 'Tom. There are new complications which Alice will need to speak to you about.'

'Complications? What do you mean, *complications*?'

'Look, I don't have all the information myself yet, Tom. So you'll need to speak to her. I'm sorry but I'm in traffic right now. We need to decide about the rest of the day. If you want me to continue the cover, I mean, once Alice has finished with the police.'

There is another pause. Matthew fully expects to be fired.

'I'll take over supporting Alice for the rest of today. I think that's best.' Tom's voice is curt now.

'Fine. I understand. She's had a tough time. I'll catch up with you both when she's finished with the police. Hopefully we can find out whether there's any decent CCTV or other evidence.'

'Right. Good. OK then.'

There is nothing more to be said and so Matthew ends the call and immediately dials home, badly needing to anchor himself.

'Hi there. How's life as Kevin Costner?' Sal's voice is upbeat as she answers, and he can hear opera playing in the background. Her favourite. He pictures her in her sloppy red sweatshirt and jeans in their kitchen with a view of the sea, and would give anything this moment to be right there with her. For none of today to have happened.

'Gone a bit off piste, to be honest, but never mind about me – how are my two girls?'

'What does *off piste* mean? You OK?'

'Yes. I'm fine. So, what are you up to?'

'Oh. I'm doing housework, so feeling pretty fed up, actually. Your princess is currently taking a nap, which gives me a break from demands for Pippy Pocket biscuits. I have no idea what's got into her this week. Pippy Pocket this. Pippy Pocket that. I tell you, if Pippy poo-faced Pocket showed up right now, I'd sock her in the face.'

Matthew feels a smile for the first time today, remembering their daughter on the supermarket floor. The screaming and the little back flips.

'You do know we have the Barbie phase to come, Sal.'

'Don't remind me.'

'OK, so give her a hug from Daddy when she wakes up and I'll see you both soon.'

'You knocking off early? What's happened? I thought you were covering right through until this evening?'

'Her boyfriend's finished work early so he's taking over bodyguard duties.'

'Right.'

'So I'll see you fairly soon. Love you.'

'You too.'

Matthew throws the phone on to the passenger seat and stares at it for a moment as if longing to hold on to the connection just a little bit longer. He will tell Sally everything later but doesn't want her worrying meantime. Finally, he refastens his seat belt. With the click of the metal there is a flash from earlier. The roar of the motorbike. Alice screaming. He squeezes both hands into tight fists then fires the ignition, mentally planning a route home via the supermarket.

For Pippy Pocket biscuits.

CHAPTER 18

HIM – BEFORE

They are nearly home. There are no lights on as they walk up the path and he is glad that in the dark his shame is hidden.

'Stop worrying about it,' his gran says, squeezing his hand as if she can read his thoughts. 'It's just an accident. Not your fault. We'll soon get you sorted out.'

Back at the care home after Stan found them, he had tried ever so hard to hold it in. To save it for the bushes out in the garden – but he just couldn't. Stan watched them leave, and that somehow made it all worse. As they walked out the back door, he could feel the warmth trickling down the inside of his trousers. He looked down, praying there would not be too much, but there was soon a large wet patch and it seemed to come even faster.

'You can go in the bushes over there,' his gran had whispered, nodding her head towards the shadows. But then she twisted her face into a puzzled expression and turned to him. He could smell it too, and wanted to cry.

'Oh, right.' She was looking directly at the damp patch on his trousers. 'Never mind. It was my fault. Not yours. I'm so sorry, poppet.'

Now, as they creep up the stairs to their flat, the automatic lights come on and he hates that the wet patch can be seen again. He longs to be inside so he can hurry to the bathroom and strip off his trousers – but to his horror, as they walk along the corridor on the third floor, there is a noise from just inside the flat next door to theirs. His gran puts her finger up to her lips as she searches in her bag for her key, but suddenly the neighbour's door opens and Brian is standing there in his dressing gown.

'Everything all right there, Martha? I thought I heard something . . .' He is looking at his watch, frowning.

'Family emergency,' his gran says suddenly. 'All sorted now but I had to take the boy with me, obviously.'

'Anything I can help you with?' Brian's expression is still a little strange. 'Nothing too serious, I hope? At this hour . . .'

'No, thank you. All sorted. We're fine now. Just need to get to bed.' His gran sounds a bit flustered but she smiles at their neighbour. 'Really sorry to disturb you, Brian.'

His gran then unlocks their door and hurries him inside, whispering that he should pop his wet clothes into the laundry basket. She will run him a quick bath and fetch some clean pyjamas.

In the bathroom he strips naked and puts all his clothes into the big basket in the corner. When he was very little, he used to think it was a snake charmer's basket and his gran would let him take it into the sitting room and play his little whistle to charm imaginary snakes. Sometimes, when she was busy in the kitchen area, he would climb into the basket and put the lid on top to surprise her. Secretly he suspected that she knew he was in there, but she always pretended to be surprised.

Now he worries that the smell of his clothes will ruin the basket. He is very tired and he wishes that they had a shower like on the telly. He thinks that would be much quicker but he does not say this out loud because he is thinking suddenly about Brian. How he is fat like Stan and how he doesn't like either of them.

'I'm sorry,' he says as his gran moves into the room to join him. She is sitting on the edge of the bath, running the taps and adding a little bit of bubble bath. It is pink and he worried that it is for girls, but it smells quite nice so he doesn't say anything. Anyway – he likes bubbles.

'You need to be quick, my lovely. School tomorrow. But let's get you smelling nice and we can forget all about this.'

'I'm sorry, Gran, about making a noise. My friend gave me a trick sweet and it made me cough. I didn't mean to—'

She reaches out to brush his hair and leans forward to kiss his forehead but he pulls back. Even with his clothes stripped off, he feels a bit sticky.

'What are we going to do next Wednesday, Gran?' He is worried about it already and needs to know. He watches his gran test the temperature of the water before nodding to say that he should step in the other end. The water is warm and the bubbles feel lovely. He is so relieved for the smell to change.

He wonders if he should tell his gran what happened last Wednesday night when she was working. The knock-knocking on the door in the middle of the night. *You in there? I know you're in there . . .*

But his gran doesn't answer his question about next Wednesday. She just keeps checking the temperature of the water before turning off the taps. He watches her face very closely and is horrified. There is a sort of glistening to her eyes and he feels terribly afraid that she is actually going to cry.

He loves his gran and knows that this is his fault.

All his fault.

CHAPTER 19

ALICE

'So, your real name is Jennifer Wallace. And when precisely did you plan to tell us that?'

I half shrug, lips clamped tight. I stare at DI Melanie Sanders and want to ask if they have caught him. Never mind Alex Sunningham – the man I try every waking day to forget. Have they caught the man on the motorbike? The man who made me think just two hours ago that he had managed to melt my flesh. To disfigure my face . . .

'Do you have any idea how much time you've wasted, Jennifer – concealing this from us? Playing *games*.'

Jenny. I want to say that people only ever called me Jennifer in anger. Jenny was my real name . . .

DI Sanders still looks furious. She has a file in front of her on the desk and I find myself daydreaming. I let my mind wander because I don't want to be here. In this scene. At this desk. I stare at all the papers on the stained, wooden surface, and wonder when the police will go paper-free. Or if it's like a newsroom – just some ridiculous pipe dream. We all like to print things off.

Some of the sheets in front of her seem to feature cuttings from Alex's trial. Others seem to be from his prison records, but it's difficult for me to read them upside down. She clocks me narrowing my eyes, trying to read, and tilts the file up at an angle so I cannot see.

'I'm not playing games,' I say finally, surprised at how quiet my voice sounds. Inside I am angry and I had expected my voice to be stronger. I am not the criminal here. I have done nothing wrong. Alex Sunningham and this stalker are the criminals here.

I want to be angrier and I want my voice to be stronger but what happened earlier, outside the café, has completely knocked the wind out of me. I keep thinking about Matthew standing over me, pouring water slowly over my skin. I close my eyes, reliving those seconds of fear that I might go blind.

There is an odd sound of sucking in air, and when I finally open my eyes, DI Sanders is staring at me, her expression changed slightly.

'It was terrible – what happened to you earlier, Jennifer. We're still checking all CCTV. Nothing solid yet but we'll find him. Don't think I'm not sympathetic, but the reason I'm wound up here' – she pauses as if to control herself – 'is that we would have had a head start in this inquiry if you'd come clean with us.'

'This has nothing to do with Alex Sunningham,' I say.

'Oh, right. You're sure about that, are you? With your long experience of police investigations?'

'He's in jail. And unless he's escaped . . .' I raise my eyebrows, aware that my tone is inappropriate; borderline sarcastic. 'I had no reason to tell you.'

Melanie Sanders shakes her head and looks up at the ceiling as if in disbelief. Then she stares at me, unblinking, and takes a piece of paper from her file and turns it around to place it in front of me.

It is a photocopy of some kind of parole document. Sensitive details – email addresses and names and notes have been blacked out – but I am able to get the main gist of the message.

No. This can't be right.

'But why wasn't I told about this?'

'Well, you're not technically one of his victims, are you? And even if you were and someone wanted to let you know as a pure courtesy, we wouldn't know where to find you. With you changing your name and disappearing off the face of the earth.' She is tapping the document with her index finger. 'He's been out of jail on licence for nearly two months, Jennifer. All agreed by the parole board. Alex Sunningham was a good boy inside. Sentence shortened for exemplary behaviour.'

I can feel the blood draining from my face. Again there is a change of temperature. Cold. Then hot. Just like that first moment I saw the card in the cake box in the office.

Alex was sentenced to five years. I had never imagined he could be let out this soon. I had three years in my head as the absolute minimum he would serve; it's barely been two and a half years . . .

'But there's been nothing in the papers saying he's out.' I am staring again at the photocopied page. 'You're seriously saying a teacher can seduce two underage girls and he's out in a couple of years? And that's not in the news?'

'It's not unusual – a sentence shortened for good behaviour. He's on licence. Parole conditions. You know how it works.' A pause, during which DI Sanders' expression changes. 'Though it's a bit delicate at the moment. There's going to be a press announcement soon.'

'Why? What press announcement? You don't seriously think he could be connected to any of this? These things happening to me?' I can feel my chin pulling back into my neck. 'Look. My evidence didn't put Alex away. He has no reason to target me.'

'Do you seriously not realise that he should be topping our list of possible suspects, Jennifer? You – an intelligent journalist. You *are* aware of what this man is capable of? Lying? Deceit? No moral compass? We specifically asked you if there were any ex-boyfriends we should look at. Anyone who might have a motive; who might be tricky.'

I put my hands up to my head, a million thoughts suddenly swirling around my brain. I hadn't mentioned Alex because I thought he was still in jail. And I wanted to pretend I had never known him; that I wasn't this naive, stupid, gullible mug who was taken in by him.

And now, hands still clutching my head, I am back in court suddenly, trying to remember the way he looked at me. Was there blame? Did he look like a man who might one day *blame* me? Turn on me?

'No, no. I just don't see it. He blamed the girl's family. The one he ran off with. They were the ones who drove the prosecution and persuaded their daughter to give evidence. I genuinely had no idea what was going on. I looked a complete idiot, if you must know. And you're right. He has no moral compass but I don't see him as violent. Someone who would ever do the things *this* guy is doing.'

'Prison can change people, Jennifer. They can make contacts and they can get steered in a darker direction. He's had a long time to stew about this. We have to find him. And you have to start being one hundred per cent straight with me about everything.'

'Find him?' I feel my head pulling backwards again as I take this in. What does she mean – *find him*? I'd imagined they would have him in custody. If the police seriously suspect him, wouldn't they want to immediately check alibis against my nightmare Wednesdays – inquiries which I strongly suspect will simply discount him.

Suddenly the door to the interview room opens and a woman in civilian clothes steps in to whisper a message to DI Sanders, who nods. The other woman then leaves the room.

'Your boyfriend Tom is here, Jennifer.'

'I would prefer it if you called me Alice still. It's my second name. My birth name. I'm Alice now.'

'Well, we'll see. I'm told Tom is throwing his legal weight around. He's making a fuss at reception, demanding to see you. He's been told that he will have to wait. I take it he knows all about this Alex? About your past? Your name change?'

I move my left hand up to my ear, pulling at the lobe. I can feel my head sort of twitching. All the tension building inside me.

I don't want to think about Tom yet; about how the hell I'm going to explain myself to him. I am trying to deal with the echo of Melanie Sanders' voice, which makes no sense.

'Why did you say *find him*? Surely the probation service knows where Alex is?'

CHAPTER 20

ALICE - BEFORE

After the concert finished – that night I met Alex – tea and coffee and cakes were served by a team of volunteers, supporting the charity. I glanced around, disappointed to find no option of wine. And then a tad guilty at the longing for a nice glass of Shiraz.

I interviewed a few of the performers and a representative of the charity, all the while pretending that I was not aware of Alex watching me. He had that distinctive gaze of a man who is confident of his own attractiveness, and from across the room he was clearly willing me to look back at him. For as long as possible, I resisted. I planned instead to head home for that glass of wine.

And then finally, as people began to drift away, he was suddenly beside me, leaning in to whisper, 'Do you like dolphins, Jennifer?'

'Jenny. Everyone calls me Jenny. And of course I like dolphins. Isn't it illegal not to like dolphins?'

'So, are you free now?' He paused. 'Or not?'

I was entirely thrown by this. Up this close he smelled wonderful – expensive aftershave. Though I had been expecting an approach, I thought any invitation would be casual – for a drink one night in the future. I was not expecting this immediacy. I didn't like that he was so sure of my interest, and tried to hold on to my resolve to play it cool; I tried to think of the delicious sound of pouring my glass of Shiraz at home.

'Warm clothes. Flask of coffee. Dolphins.' He tilted his head. 'Interested?'

It was about 9.30 p.m. and exceptionally cold outside. I guessed now precisely what he meant; there was a famous dolphin-watching spot just a few miles away. I'd been there several times when I first took the job but had no luck. I wondered how he expected to spot anything in the dark. I imagined the wind and the cold versus my rich red glass of Shiraz.

In my head I said: *No. Definitely not.* But I made the mistake of turning to look at him so that 'Yes' spilled out of my mouth. Later, huddled in two huge blankets stored in the boot of his car, we sat on a bench, and after half an hour miraculously saw three dolphins in the moonlight. You couldn't make it up.

I was lost.

We didn't sleep together that first night but we did the second. And the third. And the fourth. Two weeks later I moved into his cottage, which was set high on a hill with a magnificent view of the sea. It was reckless, entirely out of character for me and also just a little bit magnificent.

As the light faded each evening, I would stand at the bedroom window, looking out for dolphins in the distance, and he would slip his arms around my waist and rest his chin on my shoulder. A quiet and entirely unexpected contentment.

'But you hardly know him,' Leanne protested on the phone when I broke the news that we were already living together. I sent her a picture on Messenger plus a clip of him playing his Steinway grand piano in his music room. *Jeez*, she replied. *Does he have a twin?*

And so I fell under the spell of Alexander Sunningham with not a clue what lay ahead for me. We cooked together, laughed together and took long walks in thick coats and ridiculous woollen hats.

I was on a trainee contract at the local paper on a modest salary and very soon felt the financial as well as the emotional benefits of sharing a home. Alex was a freelance piano teacher – tutoring pupils of all ages. One day a week, he went into the local primary school to teach on site and to accompany the pupils learning violin, saxophone and other orchestral instruments. He was also regularly booked to accompany pupils for their various exams. The rest of the time, he taught on his Steinway at home.

He worked haphazard hours to tie in with his pupils, and I became used to arriving home from my shift to find a parent drinking coffee in our sitting room, while their child bashed away on the keys with Alex alongside in the music room next door.

I had never lived with anyone before and was shocked how easily I adjusted to it, mostly because we let each other lead our own professional lives. The house, a beautiful red-brick terrace, had been left to Alex by his grandmother – along with the grand piano – so we were better off than most in the same stage of their relationship and careers.

It meant we took trips. London. Edinburgh. Barcelona. Rome. And then eight months into our relationship, Alex took me on a surprise trip to Sorrento and proposed. And I surprised myself by saying yes.

Are you sure this isn't all a bit too fast? My sister Leanne, though she liked Alex by now, was still a tad wary. My mother, who was in good health back then, ahead of her lung disease diagnosis, was for her part surprisingly relaxed about our haste. She, after all, had been pregnant when she married my father and that had worked out just fine, she said.

We planned to marry the following spring and, as I kept telling anyone who would listen, I didn't feel rushed; I felt lucky. I was enjoying my new career and I had a fiancé who turned heads everywhere he went and who actually wrote songs for me. What was not to love about my life?

Next came a small shift in routine which at first I hardly noticed. Alex asked if it would be OK for me to act, in effect, as the 'chaperone' for younger pupils whose parents were unable to stay for the lesson. This would be for occasional evening and weekend tuition. I remember him saying that it was wholly understandable for parents to want child-protection issues to be watertight, and he was also keen to guard his reputation.

I remember asking him whether this would involve me staying in the music room for the duration of each lesson. Would I need to actually sit in there with a book or something? Alex said – and I had to share this very carefully with the police later – that it would be fine for me to be in the adjoining sitting room, which was the routine chosen by the parents who did stay for lessons. The door to the music room would be left open so this protected everyone.

So that's what happened. Occasionally a pupil would be dropped off alone and I would read or watch a film on my iPad, with a clear view into the music room. I trusted Alex completely and felt this was purely for his protection, not the child's. I was actually worried that someone might make a false accusation if we weren't careful, especially as some of the girl pupils clearly had crushes on him.

It was probably two, maybe three months into this routine that something happened just once to unsettle me. It was the only thing I shared with police that I felt, with hindsight, I should have acted upon.

One cold October morning, just ahead of Alex's birthday, I walked into our sitting room after a shopping trip to find him pacing on his mobile, raking his fingers through his hair, clearly handling a difficult phone call. *You are not to do that. Now, come on, we've talked about this. You have everything going for you. You have a bright future. You have so many people who care about you . . .*

Alex glanced up at me and signalled with his expression that he was in a fix. I tilted my head to ask if I could help. He shook his head and continued, in a gentle voice to reassure the caller.

I moved into the kitchen, all the while listening to his end of the conversation. It alarmed me, as it sounded from Alex's side as if his caller was desperate; maybe even suicidal. Alex was patient and kind and reassuring, urging the caller to speak to someone; to get professional help. To remember that there was *everything to live for.* Over and over he kept saying that everything was going to be all right. That the caller had to look forward, not back.

The conversation lasted a long time and I found myself pacing the kitchen, feeling more and more unsettled. It was not only the worry that some young pupil was on the line with some kind of mental health crisis – clearly *crossing* the line – but that Alex was using a tone which was a bit odd. Sort of overly gentle. Borderline intimate.

When the call finally finished, he came into the kitchen looking drained.

'What the hell was all that, Alex?'

'One of my teenage pupils having a crisis. A complete meltdown. I suspected she might be self-harming because of marks on her arms. They show when she plays. But I had no idea quite how bad things were at home. I made the mistake of asking about it. The conversation got out of hand.'

I was stunned. Why the hell hadn't he mentioned her to me before?

'What pupil?'

'You don't know her. She's fifteen. Comes Tuesday mornings.'

'What. On her own?'

'Yes. On her own.'

'But I thought we had this chaperone rule. Parents or me.'

'For the younger pupils – yes. And when the parents are worried. But she's fifteen, Jenny. Practically grown-up. She doesn't need a chaperone. To be frank, what she really needs is a friend. Her parents sound a complete nightmare.'

I couldn't believe what I was hearing.

'Have you gone *mad*, Alex? It's you that needs the chaperone if she's fifteen. And unstable. Self-harming. We need to phone her parents right this minute. Or the Samaritans or something. We can't just let this go.'

'It's all in hand now. She's talking to her mum. Anyway, she's not truly unstable. She's just very unhappy.'

'So is that why you sounded so intimate on the phone?'

'I was not being intimate. I was being kind, Jenny.' His tone was now changing; he looked at me as if I had no heart. 'What would you rather I did? Tell her to piss off and kill herself?'

I began pacing. My mind was in overdrive. I felt deeply unsettled, and yet Alex was now making *me* feel guilty.

'So she's suicidal? Threatening to hurt herself? Well, I'm right; we need to call her parents. Social services. Her doctor, even. There are protocols for this, surely?'

'Of course. Yes. That's absolutely what I planned at first. But as I said, her mum's with her now. She saw her on the phone, crying. So she's in adult care. She's promised to speak properly to her mum. To get support.'

'But what if she doesn't? What if she made that up about talking to her mum? What if she hurts herself, Alex, and you're the last person she spoke to?'

'I'm pretty sure it was just a teenage girl being a bit melodramatic. I think she's fine. As I said, her mum is with her now. I was just worried when she was on her own. To be honest, you're the one being melodramatic now.'

'Me? *Melodramatic?* Jeez, Alex . . .'

We then had a full-blown barney. Our biggest and most unpleasant argument, in which he accused me of being heartless while I accused him of being naive and irresponsible. In the end, he agreed to phone the girl's mother right back to make sure she was in the loop. I listened in to the call and at last felt just a little easier.

Later I would have to share the full details of this episode and our row over it with the police. Unbeknown to me, the girl on the phone was the first fifteen-year-old that Alex had seduced and then dumped. Her mother, in reality, knew nothing of the girl's trauma. She was at work the whole time and received no phone call from Alex. He must have pretended to ring her.

But in my panic and rage at the time, I genuinely saw none of that. I saw Alex being supremely stupid. I worried that the girl might have a crush and that there was a real danger that Alex could come unstuck. That he would be in trouble for providing a shoulder for the girl and that she might wrongly accuse him of something. Or hurt herself.

I told him in no uncertain terms that he was not to teach her anymore.

He agreed immediately and promised to be more careful. Later, I would feel mortified by my own gullibility. But the whole episode was one tiny blip in this context where Alex seemed one hundred per cent solid, sensible, loyal and in love with me. I had no reason to suspect him of playing away, and never in my wildest dreams did I imagine he would do so with someone underage.

Looking back and sharing the details of that row with the police, I felt ridiculous. But it was the only fluttering of a red flag in all of our time together. And somehow Alex managed to manipulate our argument so that, in the end, *I* felt like the one in the wrong for being heartless.

The truth – though it sounds bonkers now – is that at the time I was worried about *his* reputation. I was furious because I was afraid the girl might become a problem, and that Alex was being too kind and naive for his own good.

CHAPTER 21

HIM - BEFORE

It is the Wednesday after the scene with Stan at the Daisy Lawn Nursing Home. The school day seems to go on and on and on – but the thing is, he doesn't mind this. He doesn't want the day to end.

He keeps staring out of the window at the clouds. In maths, during the afternoon, he finds that he is daydreaming for so long that his teacher becomes cross. He can hear her voice saying his name and he turns back to the room. Miss Henderley is asking him to answer a question but the problem is he did not *hear* the question. He's still sitting up on a cloud wishing that his mum wasn't dead – wishing that he had a normal mum and dad like Jim and Helena.

'I don't know,' he says. Everyone in the room is looking at him and the other pupils are laughing, saying that if he doesn't know then nobody will know. He normally gets all the sums right first.

'That's enough,' Miss Henderley says. 'Try to pay attention, all of you. You need to listen.'

When the final bell goes for end of school, his stomach feels bad and he dawdles in the cloakroom, putting on his coat ever so slowly. He thinks again of the clouds and wishes that he could fly. He doesn't want to go home. He doesn't want to have tea. He doesn't want the

Wednesday treat of fish fingers and beans and ice cream. He doesn't want to get into his pyjamas *nice and early.* He wants to fly around the world. Zoom, zoom. Like the rockets on his duvet cover.

He is one of the last to leave the cloakroom and he sees his gran across the playground in her blue mac and her pink scarf. On the days when she is on day shift and he stays in the after-school club, he likes the first sight of his gran. It makes him happy. But not on a Wednesday when she picks him up right after school and they have to *hurry, hurry.* It's raining and so he puts up his hood. He likes it when the hood stops all the noise around him. He often uses it as an excuse. *I can't hear you.*

His gran takes his hand and asks if he had a good day.

'I'm sorry, I can't hear you.'

She squeezes his hand and gives up with the questions, leading him through the gate and down the path past the line of oak trees. He knows they're oaks because they studied the different kinds of leaves in art last week. They had to collect leaves and dip them in paint and make pictures. He splashed them hard on the paper. Splash, splash, splash – squirting paint on Suzie, who was sitting next to him. The teacher told him not to use so much paint but he pretended not to hear then too.

It doesn't take very long to walk home from school and he wishes it were a lot further, like the journey to the home where Gran works.

She says she's trying very, very hard to find another job without night work but she's really too old and not very good at many things. He says he thinks she's brilliant at lots of things. She should be a dinner lady at his school but his gran says, 'Life doesn't work like that.' They already have enough dinner ladies at his school.

He sits at the table in the kitchen later, staring at his fish fingers and beans.

'Can't you stay home? Please stay home.'

Her eyes get all weird again as if she might cry, and she sits down on the chair right next to him. 'I know it's hard, sweetheart, but I wouldn't do this unless I absolutely had to. I've told you lots of times. I can't afford the rent here and all the bills unless I do my job. And Stan will report me if I don't do the night shift.'

She pushes his hair back from his forehead. 'Remember what I told you about when I was little on the farm and my dad had to go out lambing and leave me. I didn't like it either. I didn't have a mummy either, remember. She left us when I was very small. Just a baby. But it was always OK when my dad went out lambing. And we lived in the middle of nowhere. You're safe here. So long as you follow the rules. It's just sleeping.'

He digs his knife into his fish finger and cuts it up into two pieces. Then four. Then eight.

He thinks of his maths lessons and his teacher. She's nice.

'We could ask Miss Henderley to look after me on Wednesday nights. She'd do it.' He has suggested this lots of times before and doesn't understand why it's not a good idea. Miss Henderley looks after loads of them all day long. How hard could it be to look after one boy one night?

His gran suddenly looks very worried. 'We've talked about this, lovely, and it's way too dangerous to tell people, especially at school. Because they may tell social services I'm not managing. And they might take you away from me again. You don't want that, do you?'

He shakes his head. It's true; he doesn't want that again.

'So you'll be brave? Yes? Just until I can find another job? Now, eat up. Ice cream for pudding. Your favourite.'

Two hours later and she is back in her blue mac and her pink scarf. He's in his pyjamas even though it's quite early. Six o'clock.

She goes over the rules. No touching the cooker or any electrical things. No answering the door or the telephone. No matches or candles or anything to do with fire. He can watch telly until the small hand is on the eight, and then he must switch off the television and go to bed. Lights out in the sitting room and kitchen area but he can keep the little lamp on in his room.

'Can we get walkie-talkies?' He's looking right into her face.

'I can't afford things like that, love. And I don't think walkie-talkies would work.'

'In the army they work.'

'We're not in the army. You'll be fine. If you stick to the rules, you'll be fine. The only time you're allowed to leave the flat is if there's a fire. Then you get out and run. But there won't be a fire if you're a good boy and follow the rules, so you don't need to worry about that. You're safe in here with the door locked.'

She looks at her watch. 'Look, I'm sorry but I have to go. You're a good boy. Gran's little soldier. Remember, I'm not . . .' She stops.

She normally says that she's *not far away* but he knows now that isn't true. He remembers the bus ride and all the walking. He can feel tears in his eyes and she takes a deep breath. She kisses him on the forehead, squeezes him tight and then she is gone.

He watches telly but it's not good. Boring programmes. He drinks his juice and eats the biscuits his gran always leaves out for him. He can hear some kind of music in the flat below them and he likes that. It's later, when all the noises stop, that he doesn't like it.

It's a bit cold and so he puts on his dressing gown and climbs into his bed with his books. He can read some of the words but not all of them. It's why he's working so hard in school – so that he can read on Wednesdays when he's on his own. Sometimes, when he reads a book, he sort of drifts off right into the pages and completely forgets where he is. That would be good now.

He looks around his room and hopes there are no spiders. One Wednesday, there was a huge spider in the corner and so he had to go and take his duvet into the sitting room and lie on the sofa. He shut the door and put lots of cushions along the bottom so that the spider couldn't get out of his bedroom. When his gran got home, she said, *What the hell has been going on here?*

He stays in bed and curls up and tries to go to sleep but it gets quieter and quieter. He doesn't like this bit – when it gets so very quiet. And he doesn't like the dark. He never turns off the little lamp and he keeps his torch with him in case there is a power cut.

Often he cries, especially if anyone in school has been telling scary stories. He always runs off to play if someone starts all that. Ghosts and stuff.

His gran says there are no such things as ghosts but he's not so sure. He tries to stop thinking about it. He needs a wee but he doesn't want to go across the sitting room now that he has turned the light off.

He waits and waits and tries really hard but it's no good. He remembers what happened last week after Stan found him in the laundry cupboard.

He turns on his torch. He gets out of bed and he creeps across the room, shining his torch out into the sitting room. It is as he is crossing the room that the knocking on the front door starts up again. Just like a couple of weeks back.

'Hello? I know you're in there.' The voice isn't very loud – just enough volume to be heard through the door.

He keeps very still. This has happened only once before. He kept quiet that time and the knocking and the voice eventually went away.

He should have told his gran but he was worried she would be cross that he was out of bed.

There is knocking again. *One, two, three.* It is not very loud knocking. Again, it's just loud enough to be sure that it can be heard. Knock, knock, knock. *One, two, three . . .*

'I can see the light under the door. I know you're in there. Let me in or I'm going to phone the police.'

He keeps ever so still. *The police?* He thinks of his gran and how super-cross she will be if the police turn up. He tries to hold his breath but his heart is beating really, really loud. He thinks he should perhaps turn the torch off but he is too afraid of the dark.

And then someone is lifting up the letterbox in their door and he can just see a nose and someone trying to see right in. 'I saw your gran go. I know you're on your own. And if you don't answer the door right this minute, I'm phoning the police.'

And now he recognises the voice. It's Brian.

It's fat Brian from next door.

CHAPTER 22

MATTHEW

'What's up? What is it you haven't told me?'

Matthew doesn't answer his wife immediately. Instead he stares at her and then stares at his plate. Steak and chips. She has cooked the steak perfectly, resting it well so that it is juicy and delicious. But for some reason he's put off from cutting into the meat and so the steak is going cold.

'Why is it I can never get anything past you, Sally?' He looks again at the meat, wondering where his appetite has gone; he normally loves steak. But then he sees the red at the centre of the first slice of steak and realises . . . It is perfectly medium rare but the flash of rawness is making him think of something else. He is not normally squeamish but his mind keeps going back to that cruel fake attack. Flesh. Acid. The terrible moments when he was waiting for Alice's flesh to change colour.

'Witchcraft. On the quiet I'm a fully fledged white witch. Now, why not eat your steak while I check on our Pippy Pocket princess, and then you can tell me everything. Deal?'

He nods. He and Sally have been married a few years now. He loves her very much but wonders if he will ever truly understand how the female mind works. Sometimes he sits at breakfast and imagines

Amelie all grown-up. The two of them speaking in an entirely different language. About who said what and when. About fashion and gossip.

And *cushions*.

He smiles at Sally and feels guilty that he does not always listen when she's talking. He met her on a case – a difficult and quite emotional case involving two of her childhood friends. Sometimes he goes cold, thinking – what if Sal's friend Beth had picked another private investigator to help them? What would his life be?

Fewer cushions, he thinks mischievously – picturing the puzzle of their bed, which has a mountain of silk obstacles.

'Why are you grinning suddenly?'

'Doesn't matter. I love you, Sally.'

'You too. Eat your steak.'

Sally leaves the kitchen-cum-dining room and heads upstairs. He can just hear their daughter's voice protesting that she is not tired. Matthew smiles again. When does a child ever admit otherwise? There is some singing – Sally and Amelie together – and then a warning to *go to sleep*.

Finally Sally returns and he makes an effort with the steak.

'Good. You need the iron, Matt; you're looking a bit peaky. I was reading in a magazine the other day that iron deficiency is way more common than people realise. So – fire away. I'm listening.' She reaches for the wine bottle but he puts his hand over his glass and shakes his head. He's thinking once more of Alice and so is still unsettled. He may go out again; he hasn't quite decided.

'I sort of messed up today. Alice wouldn't travel in my car. I should have insisted but I didn't. There was a fake acid attack and it was horrible.'

'What the hell is a *fake acid attack*?'

He explains about the motorcyclist and the iced water in the bottle. How they assumed the worst.

'I guess it's a sign of the times. The biker knew we'd think it was acid. A truly horrible thing to do to her.'

'How absolutely dreadful. And strange too . . . to go to all that trouble for a fake attack? I mean – he could have been caught. Surely there will be CCTV?'

'Not so far. And I think this was a warning. Sort of, *see what I can do to you if I choose*. It's control-freakery. Classic stalker behaviour. This is about terrorising Alice.'

Sally looks shaken, and he tells her the rest of the news about Alice's double identity.

'So you're off the case? Well – good, I say, if she can't even tell you the truth about herself. It's getting way, way too complicated.'

Matthew smiles at his wife's loyalty. She wants to protect him and he likes that she's angry on his behalf, but the truth is he is over the anger now. He's read more about the Alex Sunningham case and feels sorry for Alice – or Jennifer, or whatever she wants to be called.

'You *are* off the case?' Sally leans in, trying to read his expression.

'Well, her boyfriend sacked me so – yes.'

'Good. We should do some more advertising. Try to get you some better work. It's good that the money's just come in from that corporate training you did. We're fine for a few months. And I don't like you taking on stuff outside your comfort zone. I always knew this was a bad idea. Borderline bodyguard work. That's not you. And in any case, if the police can't keep her safe, how are you expected to? On your own?' She has stood up now and is clattering about with plates and other dishes as Matthew's phone buzzes with a text. It's from Melanie.

Can you make our café in an hour?

He puts the phone in his pocket and stares at his wife's back as she loads the dishwasher. She will worry if he tells her he's meeting Melanie. DI Sanders still wants him back in the force, but Sally's not at all sure this would be healthy for him. She worries it will stir up old ghosts. Matthew left the force because he blamed himself over a child's death. He still sometimes has dreams about it. Sally will get very twitchy if he mentions Melanie.

'Just need to pop out. Nothing to worry about. Might be a new case. I won't be long.'

She turns. 'So long as it isn't the man who thinks little people are trying to kidnap him?'

'Might be.' He winks and then moves across to kiss her, parking the thought that – come to mention it – he might actually call in on Ian and his little people. If not tonight then some time very soon.

At their regular café, there's just an hour until closing. In the evening they serve burger and chips to boost takings, and Matthew is shocked to find he's almost tempted, despite the steak. He is lucky to have a skinny gene and a good metabolism but he needs to be careful as he gets older.

No. Very bad idea.

Melanie is just a few minutes behind him and looks even larger than the last time he saw her.

'Are you sure you have the energy for all this, Mel? Wouldn't it just be easier to go on mat leave early? Those triplets could be born any moment.'

She tilts her head and pokes out her tongue.

The waitress arrives to take their order – just coffee for him, though Melanie plumps for carrot cake again with her Earl Grey tea.

'So – a pickle. Alice turning out to be Jennifer.' He lifts a sugar sachet out of the little bowl on the table but checks himself and puts it back. No time for fidgeting.

'Understatement.' She pauses and then leans in. 'My boss is going ballistic. So. Usual rules here. We are not meeting and we are not talking.'

He raises his hands in surrender. 'Absolutely understood, and you know I won't breathe a word.'

'OK. So I've read Alice the riot act but, truth be told, I feel a bit sorry for her. Now I know the whole story. And given what happened this morning.'

He's relieved to hear this. Melanie is not someone to fall out with. Nerves of steel beneath the soft and very pregnant exterior. He bets she gave Alice a tough time.

'I have yet to tell Alice the whole story, Matt. She's determined we should keep calling her Alice, by the way. It's her second name and she claims her sister and mother have got used to using it. Anyway. I'm tipping you off because it's going to be all over the papers within twenty-four hours and I want to know what you think. Alex Sunningham has disappeared.'

'You're not serious?'

'Afraid so. Failed to report to his probation officer more than once. And now he's disappeared from his hostel. We were going to keep all this low-key for a bit but it looks like it's going to blow up very quickly. And not just because we want to question him about Alice. She needs to know – has a right to know, now that he's our principal suspect. I was rather hoping we would have found him by now . . .'

Matthew raises his left eyebrow. Melanie sighs and they both lean back as the waitress delivers their order. Once she's gone, Melanie sips her tea, then continues.

'The minor – the fifteen-year-old that he ran off with – has just disappeared from home as well.'

'You are *kidding* me.'

'I wish.'

'But I thought she spilled the beans to the nationals to warn others about grooming. I thought she now hated the guy. So what are you thinking? That he's got to her? Revenge?'

'At this stage, we don't know what to think. She's eighteen now. She's been doing A levels and has a place at university. Back on track. Her parents are in bits. It's completely out of character for her to disappear without contacting them. No one knows what to think. Whether this could be a coincidence. An aggressive move by Alex. Or something else . . .'

Matthew lets out a long sigh and sips at his own drink. The stories about Alex Sunningham are swimming through his thoughts.

'And you want to know what I think. Regarding the teenager and also Alice . . . Whether this is revenge?'

'Yes, I do. Jeez – Matt. I so wish you were working on this officially with me. But as you're sort of on the case anyway, I'm hoping you'll help. I trust your instinct. You know that. So what are you thinking? What should I be thinking here? Obviously, the terms of Alex's licence forbid him from having any contact with this girl. I'll be liaising with the other team investigating this girl's disappearance and Alex skipping parole. But do we assume he's violent now? What do you think? My head's all over the place, to be honest.'

'A few years inside could have turned this Alex into a different character. We both know he's a creep but he could have turned violent too. Plenty of time to get very bitter. Distort things in his head. I guess he could be capable of the stalking. And targeting the teenager for revenge. We daren't assume otherwise.'

'I agree. We have to find him very, very quickly. The plans are for a press conference if the girl doesn't turn up by the morning.'

'Which means the Alex Sunningham case will be hot news all over again.'

'Yes. And Alice – or Jennifer, rather – will need to decide how she's going to handle that. I'm happy for you to break this to her, Matt, but I want to know how she reacts. Agreed?'

Matthew finishes his drink and then gets out his phone. 'OK. But she's my client so it's tricky.' He pauses, remembering that this is in fact no longer the case; that he's technically been sacked. But the truth? He looks up and stares at Mel. He's not ready to let this case go. Not after the fake acid attack. And because he keeps seeing those dreadful pictures of the case from their training days too. Rachel Allen strangled in her shower. So young. Such a waste . . .

He strongly suspects it's why Mel is so agitated now. Frustrated, and worried about getting it wrong.

'I'm not sure quite where I am with Alice so I'll be straight with her that I'm liaising with you. Oh – and just one more thing, Melanie. Favour for favour.' He turns back to his phone and scrolls through the pictures folder. 'I'd like to know who owns this car. Black Golf.' He shows her a picture and she takes out her own phone to copy it as he zooms in on the number plate.

'Why?'

'Might be nothing. But I saw it twice in the hours I was keeping an eye on Alice. Might have been following us. I couldn't be absolutely sure. Got distracted when the bike showed up.'

'OK. I'll check it out and let you know. Meantime I want to let Alice sweat a bit overnight over misleading us. As a favour, I'll text you first thing if the girl doesn't show up so you can warn her just before the media get it. But the deal is I need to know how she reacts. I'll be honest, I think you've got a better chance of reading her than I do over this right now. I badly need to know whether you feel we can trust her going forward. Yes? And then I'll need to interview her again officially. She might have ideas where he's run to. She needs to cooperate with us, Matt. No more silly games. We need her to help us find him . . . for her own sake.'

CHAPTER 23

ALICE

We slept in the same bed but in that awkward way as if after a row, leaning outwards and being careful not to touch.

It's Thursday. I am still in shock from the attack yesterday. I am mortified they know about Alex now, and the police and Matthew and Tom are so angry with me. But I am also so relieved that I look the same in the mirror. I keep touching my face, sort of amazed still that I wasn't hurt; relieved too that I have a little time to regroup before anything else happens. Before *next Wednesday.*

'Coffee?' Tom's voice draws me back to the room. To his mood, which is difficult to read. He is wearing pyjama bottoms for the first time and I wonder where he found them – I did not even know that he owned any.

'Yes please.' I watch him scurry from the room and then glance around, taking in the order and the very masculine style which is so different from my own home. His flat in Exeter is on the second floor of a waterside block, with a large balcony and view of the River Exe. It's convenient for both the city centre and the station, which works well now that Tom spends so much time working in London. He used to work in criminal law but is now in corporate law. More lucrative and nearly all city-based.

Sometimes he talks about renting a place in London but, like me, he loves the country and the coast, and he is fond of this flat. It has good security so can be safely locked up when he's away. It has video entry and cameras so is also perfect for me just now – almost as reassuring in terms of security as Leanne's place in Dorset.

On the opposite wall to the bed there's a huge wardrobe which Tom had fitted a few months back at vast expense to house his work suits and coats. Proper wood – none of your veneer nonsense. There are two matching bedside tables but none of the clutter of my own bedroom back at my rented house. I glance to Tom's side of the bed where there is a framed photograph of his parents. Tom looks most like his father. His parents had him late in life and have retired early. His father was a surgeon, his mother a GP. No wonder all this is so outside his comfort zone. Tom doesn't realise what a charmed life he's lived.

At last he reappears with two mugs and I take one, trying to find a small smile.

'So – do I call you Alice or Jenny?' His tone is strained.

'Alice. I've decided I'm going to stick with Alice. It's my second name. My real second name, I mean, and I like it as my byline as a journalist. I've got used to it now.'

'Right.' He sips his drink, staring at the steam rising from the liquid, careful not to meet my gaze.

'Look – you're allowed to be angry, Tom. It's a lot to take in. I do know that. Why don't you just let it out. Be honest. If you need to be angry with me, be angry.'

He keeps very still for a moment and I can see hurt in his eyes, which is once again like a slap. That is what was most difficult after he picked me up from the police station and brought us back here yesterday. Hurt rather than anger.

'I'm not exactly angry. I'm just a bit shell-shocked still. I mean – a *paedo*, Alice. You were seriously living with a paedo . . .'

'There was no way I could know, Tom. Trust me, I beat myself up about it every single day, wondering if there was anything I could or should have done to protect those girls. But I had absolutely no idea. None.'

'Right. Yes. Of course. I shouldn't have said that. It must have been absolutely terrible for you . . .' Finally, he looks at me. 'Is that why you find it hard?'

'Sorry?'

'With me, Alice. I mean – I try not to push it. Give you space and let things move at their own pace. But the truth is I never really know where I am with you . . .'

I open my mouth to answer but my phone rings on the bedside cabinet and I check the screen. 'It's Matthew. I'd better take this.'

'I'm surprised he has the nerve. Some help he turned out to be.'

I turn away towards the window and press the phone tight to my ear. I don't blame Matthew for the fake attack, even if Tom does. It was my own fault for insisting on driving separately. I'm expecting him to want an update on the quizzing by Melanie Sanders so it's a shock to find he sounds almost breathless.

'Right. I'm not going to dress this up, Alice. Better you hear it straight. Alex Sunningham has broken his parole conditions and gone AWOL. The teenager he ran off with in Scotland has also disappeared. She's still not been in touch with her parents this morning and so there's going to be a media appeal to find Alex. Chances are the tabloids will be all over it like a rash. Maybe TV too. We felt you should be warned. And the police are going to want to interview you again today.'

I press the phone tighter, tighter to my ear until I can feel the imprint of the screen. For a moment, I can't speak.

'What is it?' Tom is now alongside me.

I lower the phone to my chest for a moment, squeezing my eyes tight in a bid to regroup, and then I move the phone slowly back up to my ear.

'I don't know what to say, Matthew. I don't know what to think. What are the police thinking? Do they really think she's gone off with him, this girl? Or that he's abducted her, or *what?*'

'They don't know. She's an adult now but that's not the point. The terms of his licence forbid any contact with her and he's now a key suspect in your case too, so they need to find him urgently.' There's a pause. 'Look – I want to be honest with you. Melanie Sanders asked me to report your reaction to her but I can't split my loyalties here. She's a very good police officer, Alice, and you need her on side, as do I. No more keeping things from her. You need to be one hundred per cent straight with her and with me. So, do you have any idea, any inkling at all, where this Alex might hole up? Does anywhere come to mind? Friends? Relatives? Special places? Anything we can share with the police teams looking for him?'

I try to think. I glance from left to right but can't quite process this. I've tried so hard for so long *not* to think about the wretched man. To have to suddenly conjure him up and imagine him free. Out there. Missing. It's too much to take in.

'Look – I have absolutely no idea where he might be, Matthew. That's the truth, I swear. I never want to hear about that man again, quite frankly. But I get what you're saying. From here on I'll be straight with you. And the police. I promise. And thank you for telling me, Matthew.' I pause. A new thought. 'So do you know when this will be made public?' Oh no. *My mother.* I look at the clock and start to get out of bed. My mother always watches the TV news. *Jeez.* I take in that Tom is still watching me, his frown deepening.

'I don't know. I'll let you know if I hear any more. Now, are you feeling safe, Alice? You're not on your own? I mean, I know it's not Wednesday and that I'm off the case but—'

'I'm with Tom. He's still angry with me and with you too.' I turn to look directly at Tom as I say this. 'And I don't blame him. But personally I'd like you to continue to help us, Matthew. Are you prepared to do that? To help me still? We'll pay you – I mean, *I'll* pay you if need be.'

There's a long pause.

'OK. Unfair question. You don't have to answer that now. I'll ring you after I've seen my mother.'

Tom is now glaring at me as I end the call. 'You're kidding me? You seriously still want Matthew Hill on this? After what happened?'

'I do. *Please*, Tom. I know you're pretending not to be furious, bottling it up, but I need you to bear with me. Please. Will you come to see my mother with me? It's going to be all over the news. Alex Sunningham has done a bunk. I'll explain on the way but I need to warn my mother. She'll worry herself sick otherwise.'

An hour later we park up outside Mum's nursing home. Tom is now in a different mood, more worried than cross. Reluctantly he's agreed to keep Matthew on the case after all. I watch Tom from the passenger seat; the news that Alex Sunningham has gone AWOL seems to have knocked him completely sideways. He says he feels helpless, which is the only reason he's agreed to re-engage Matthew. Like DI Sanders, Tom thinks Alex is bound to be behind the stalking, although I still find this difficult to believe.

'Do you want me to come in with you?' Tom looks anxious and is glancing around the car park, checking if anyone has been following us.

'No. The security is good. It's fine. I feel safe here.'

'And have you told your mother about the stalking?'

'No, no – of course not. She's just not well enough. But she obviously knows everything about what happened with Alex and why I switched my name. I need to hurry. Do you mind waiting here?'

'No. Of course not.'

I check my watch. *Damn* – one minute past the hour, which means news time. I hurry inside but am slowed down by the reception security. I'm logged into the visitor book, given a pass and then accompanied to my mother's room by a nurse.

But the timing could not be worse. As I walk into the room, my mother has the TV remote in her hand and is switching between news channels, her eyes wide and staring. One bulletin is dealing with an arson story. Another has moved on to the weather. But my mother then flicks back to a satellite news channel and there he is. Alex Sunningham. His picture full-screen. The voiceover outlines the police appeal to trace him and then there's a film recapping the background story with an older picture of him at his grand piano, beaming.

My mother turns to me as I stand in the doorway. She's suddenly struggling even harder than usual for breath, her chest heaving and her eyes still wide with worry.

'It's him again. On the telly . . .' And then she's truly gasping for breath, her right hand up to her chest. Too many words. She's pushed it too far.

I clutch at the nurse's arm. 'Help her. Please. It's a big shock for her. This story on the news.'

The nurse moves swiftly to adjust the switch on the oxygen supply, coaxing my mother to breathe more slowly. *Steady breaths.*

'Don't try to speak, Mum.' I lean in so that our foreheads are just touching. 'It's OK. I know about all this on the news. It's all right. That's why I'm here. Please don't be upset. Try to catch your breath. You don't need to worry about this. I'm OK. Everything's going to be OK.'

CHAPTER 24

MATTHEW

It's mid-morning now and, even as he rings the bell, Matthew wonders if he's making the most terrible of mistakes. He checks his phone, skimming for the headlines. The press conference regarding Alex Sunningham has made several key bulletins but there's no update from the police. No leads and no apparent sightings. Matthew had originally planned to make this quick call on 'Ian and the little people' last night, but everything ran too late. He didn't have time then and he doesn't really have the time now but he can't put the sound of Ian's quiet sobbing on the phone out of his mind.

When the door is finally answered, Matthew is entirely surprised. The man is older than his voice, slim and immaculately dressed. Shirt and tie, a clean if slightly shabby cardigan, and trousers with a sharp crease down the middle.

'Ian Ellis?'

'Who wants to know?'

'I'm Matthew Hill. We've been talking on the phone about the little people.'

'Oh, right. Oh goodness – so you're finally taking the case?'

'Not exactly. Look, I haven't really got much time to be honest, Ian, but I thought I'd check in on you briefly. You sounded a bit upset the last time we spoke.'

Ian blushes and looks at the ground as if considering something. Then he jerks his head back upright to challenge Matthew with a very direct stare. 'Right – come in, come in. They're upstairs. We'll need to be quiet.' Ian puts his finger up to his lips and leads the way up a steep staircase, creeping ever so gently. On the landing he stands opposite an open door that leads into what appears to be a large bedroom. He nods towards the floor at the entrance to the room.

Matthew leans forward as Ian again signals with his eyes towards the carpet at the bedroom's entrance. 'I'm sorry, but I'm not seeing anything, Ian.'

Ian lets out a puff of air as if deflated. 'Ah, yes – they do that.'

'What?'

'Make themselves invisible when it suits them. Just between us, I think they've configured themselves just now so that I'm the only one who can see them. Part of their plot.'

'To kidnap you?'

'Well, yes.' Ian frowns. 'Obviously.'

Matthew pauses. He can just see into the room now. It appears to be a woman's bedroom. There are pink slippers on the floor and a soft, fluffy dressing gown is draped across the bed. There is a smart, green dress hanging on the wardrobe as if ready for an outing. In the corner he can just make out a dressing table with perfume bottles and little china bowls and trinkets.

'I tell you what, Ian. How about we have a quick cup of tea. Go over what we've got.'

'Excellent idea. I knew you'd be interested once you realised what I'm up against.'

Downstairs in the kitchen, Ian sets about making tea with the enthusiasm and chatter of someone unused to company. Matthew had guessed loneliness would be a part of the picture here and is worried he will make things worse, not better – offering some kind of false hope. Ian's quite a bit older than he expected. On the phone he sounded late fifties, maybe sixties, but in the flesh he is clearly well into his seventies.

'The truth here, Ian, is I'm still feeling I'm not the right man for your investigation, but I wondered – if I had a bit more detail – if I might see some way forward.'

'Suggest another investigator, you mean?' Ian puts a selection of biscuits on a plate – Hobnobs, digestives and two chocolate-covered wafers – and leads the way into the sitting room. Again it's in immaculate order. Matthew imagines Ian having nothing much more to do than clean; he feels his heart sink further.

'So, do you mind me asking if you live here alone at the moment, Ian?'

Ian holds out the plate and Matthew shakes his head.

'It's just I noticed that the bedroom upstairs – the one the little people seem to be interested in – it appeared to be a woman's bedroom. Partner? Daughter? Other relative?'

Ian dunks his biscuit in his tea and examines it as if waiting for the precise softness before moving it swiftly to his mouth.

'You're observant. I expected that. But you're not going to start going on about triggers again, are you, Mr Hill?'

'No, no. I was just trying to gather the information I need here, Ian. To try to suggest how someone might help you.'

'I have just one child – a daughter who lives abroad. Canada. Jessica.' Ian puts down his tea and biscuits and moves across to select a photograph from a dresser. From the frame a large, jolly woman in her late forties or early fifties beams alongside a huge black dog. 'I haven't seen her in a few years, sadly, as neither of us has very much money. And, well, travel is spectacularly expensive. Also I worry what might happen. If the little people followed me, I mean. An in-flight emergency. I couldn't have that on my conscience.'

'Quite.' Matthew puts his hand up to his mouth to conceal a smile. He's surprised to be rather liking this strange little man.

'Anyway. Phoning is very expensive too so we just swap cards, me and Jessie. You know. Birthdays and Christmas. She has an email address and says I can write to her using that but I can't be doing with any of that. Apparently you need a module.'

'Modem?'

'Whatever. Mobile phones give you cancer. I'm not holding one of those up to my ear.'

'And does Jessica know about the little people? The plots?'

'No, of course not. I can't be worrying her on the other side of the world, can I. I mean – what kind of father would that make me? What can she do?'

'And is that Jessica's old room, then? Upstairs.'

'Oh no – no, no.' Ian suddenly looks crestfallen. 'That's Barbara's room.'

'Barbara?'

'My wife.'

At that very moment, Matthew's phone buzzes. Melanie Sanders.

'Look, I'm very sorry about this, Ian, but I need to take this call. Will you excuse me?'

'You know that mobiles fry your brain, don't you, Mr Hill? There's a conspiracy to cover it up. The government knows all about it but they want the taxes. That phone will give you cancer of the brain . . .'

'I'll have to take the risk, Ian.' Matthew moves out into the hall and lowers his voice to answer.

'Hello, Mel. So is this good news regarding Alex?'

'No. Sorry. No update there. I just wanted to let you know that I'm heading into Alice's newspaper right this minute to speak to one of her colleagues.'

'Because?'

'Because that black Golf you thought might be following you and Alice belongs to one of the other reporters. Jack Trenter. I'm thinking just a quiet word at this stage. Alex is our main focus, obviously. But do you know anything about him – this Jack character? Has Alice mentioned him?'

'No. Not at all. Let me know what you make of him, will you? As I say, I wasn't one hundred per cent sure he was tailing us. But this is sounding rather odd. I'll try to see what Alice thinks.'

'OK. And thank you for the tip-off. I'll text you. We need to have another chat.'

Matthew feels his forehead furrowing. He hadn't meant for it to be a tip-off exactly and is not at all sure what to make of this. He'd rather imagined this whole case would all be sewn up once they find Alex.

So why would one of Alice's colleagues be following her?

CHAPTER 25

HIM - BEFORE

Fat Brian keeps his face close to the letterbox, pinning the flap open with his fingers.

'I mean it. Open up, young man, or I phone the police.'

'My gran's asleep. You'll wake her up.'

'No, she isn't. I saw her go out. Now look here – I just want to help you. You shouldn't be on your own. You're too little. I can't just leave it now I know you're on your own. I can't have that on my conscience and I can't imagine you like it very much either. All on your own, I mean?'

He doesn't move. For a while he doesn't say anything but fat Brian is right. He doesn't like it on his own at all. He wonders, not for the first time, why his gran thinks it's OK. When Brian doesn't. Adults are very confusing.

'I tell you what – do you have any Lego?' Brian's voice is a bit calmer and he has tilted his head so his eyes are now showing through the letterbox instead of his nose.

'Lego?' He glances into the corner where his gran stores the red plastic box containing all his Lego. They got a huge box from the charity shop last Christmas. He even has animals and letters that spell *zoo*. He wonders if he's allowed to tell Brian this . . .

'It's just I could keep you company, if you like. Play some Lego with you until your gran gets back.'

'I'm not allowed to open the door. It's the rules.'

'It's also the rules that you're not supposed to be on your own, mate. So it's a straight choice. You either let me in to check you're OK, or I phone the police so they can check you're OK.'

He moves his torch to shine it towards the door and walks very slowly towards it. His heart is still really strange, like a super-charged rocket. He stands at the door for a moment. He thinks of his gran's rule about not opening the door but then he thinks of the police turning up with sirens and handcuffs, so he turns the latch.

'That's a good boy. See – that wasn't so very difficult, was it?' Brian is in the room very quickly and closes the door quietly behind him as he speaks. He is holding a small tin with flowers on it and he looks around the sitting room.

'What are you looking for?'

'Nothing. So where's this Lego?'

He fetches the box for Brian and puts it in the middle of the rug between the sofa and the chair. He wants to ask what is in the tin with the flowers but decides to wait.

Brian is surprisingly good at Lego. He builds a small house and they line up the animals outside. It's not really right for it to be a house; it's not big enough to look like a zoo. He finds himself thinking how scary it would be if a real lion and a real zebra turned up outside your house.

Brian says he saw real lions roaming wild in a safari park once and they had a fight over who got the biggest piece of meat when the park staff came round to feed them. He tells some more stories about the safari park. About the giraffes and the cheetahs who can run at zillions of miles per hour.

Then Brian finds some cars in the bottom of the Lego box and they play a game where they build a little wall of Lego and the cars have to try to smash it down. He likes this game a lot and thinks Brian is much nicer than he expected.

'So when does your gran get home?'

'Any minute.' He doesn't know why he says this. He watches Brian frown.

'I don't think that's true, is it? The other Wednesday when I knocked before, I listened out. I didn't hear her key in the door until early in the morning.'

He shrugs. Miss Henderley at school says to use words instead of shrugs, but he rather likes shrugging.

'I don't like to think of you on your own at night. Your gran shouldn't leave you on your own, you know . . .'

'What's in your tin?'

Brian smiles. 'I'm glad you asked me that. Because that's my surprise.'

'What surprise?'

'Well, what I was thinking is that we could do a deal, you and me.'

'What deal?'

'Well, you could do me a favour for keeping you company. And then I could show you my surprise in the tin.'

'What favour?'

CHAPTER 26

ALICE

It's now Thursday evening and I'm once more staring at Leanne across the vast kitchen of the Dorset trophy house.

I've spent most of the day with the police since Alex's disappearance hit the news. Leanne's driven down again as we're both so worried about Mum's reaction.

'It's good that Mum's a bit better this evening. The call from the nurse says her sats levels are almost back to normal.' Leanne is speaking quickly, almost gabbling, as she opens the large stainless-steel fridge. 'Well, not normal – but her normal at least. And the sedatives should mean she'll sleep.'

'Yes.' I take in my sister's expression, which is buttoned up. Tense. So far we've talked mostly about Mum. Leanne's again had to leave my niece and nephew in London. Josh and Annabelle must be missing their mum. Jonathan's taking more time off work but Leanne clearly needs to get back to town as soon as Mum's stable. These emergencies and the geography are taking their toll. She looks tired and drawn.

I'm exhausted too, after such a long session with the police. They're desperate for any crumb from my time with Alex which might suggest where he could have bolted to. The trouble is he lied to me so much, it's impossible to know what to suggest.

Matthew's agreed to stay on the case, thank goodness, but Tom is still quietly furious with him over the fake acid attack so it's all very tense. Tricky. *Exhausting.*

As Leanne makes tea and coffee, a text buzzes into my phone. It's from Jack at the paper. He wants to meet. I'm pleased but also surprised to hear from him. I get this little pull inside – the first pleasant sensation today. His text says he's worried about me and also has news from the Maple Field House campaigners. A date's being set for the demolition. Our editor, Ted, wants to give the coverage to another reporter and Jack wants me in the loop. He thinks it's unfair for me to lose a story I've worked so hard on. I find myself smiling – pleased that Jack's looking out for me.

'Who's that from?' Leanne is now handing me a mug of coffee.

'Guy from work. Wants to meet. There's some stuff we need to talk about.'

'You shouldn't be thinking about work.'

'Well, there you're wrong actually, Leanne. It's driving me completely nuts not being able to work. The editor won't have me back in while the police keep pushing to have my phone extension recorded. There's absolutely no way a paper could ever agree to that, obviously. The nightmare that is HR insists I take all my holiday, and lieu days too, hoping this will blow over. But I have responsibilities. Running stories that I should be working on.' I check my watch. 'He wants to meet me. Quick chat.'

'You're not serious? With all that's been going on? And me driving all the way from London. You're surely not thinking of going out on your own?'

I bite into my lip, reconsidering. 'No, no – you're right. Of course not.' I pause; I *was* thinking about meeting Jack, actually. 'But how about I ask him to come here? It's about an hour's run so he'll probably pass. But – would you mind? If he says yes? I'm dying to know what's going on at work.'

'Why don't you just ring him?'

I don't know how to answer this; I don't like to admit that I'd rather like to see Jack.

'And he's definitely kosher, this guy? Safe, I mean?'

At this, I feel a complete jolt of surprise. 'Jack? Safe? Of *course* he's safe. What are you implying?' I reach up to tighten the band on my ponytail, wondering when it will stop. This appalling circus of everyone in my life becoming a suspect. Of nothing feeling normal anymore. Endless sessions with the police.

'Look – I don't mean to cause offence, Alice. But with everything going on and after what happened with Alex . . .'

'What? So you're saying I'm still a poor judge of character? You really think I haven't learned my lesson about trusting people?'

'No, no.' Leanne is now blushing. 'I'm not saying that.'

There is a long and terrible pause in which we just stand, sipping at our drinks.

'OK. If you really want to invite this Jack over, it's fine. But keep it short. Yes? We're both tired.'

I send a text and finish my coffee. I rather expect Jack to make an excuse, given the distance, but to my surprise he replies quickly to say he'll drive straight to the house. So I text the address and update Leanne.

'Look. Jack was really good to me the day I got that horrid first call in the office. He's a nice guy, Leanne. He's been through a lot himself – he lost his wife a year or so ago. Anyway, he's watching my back in the office. It sounds as if the editor is giving my campaign story away. You know – the demolition of the flats that I've been working on for a long time.'

Leanne narrows her eyes. 'OK. But you need to be careful, Alice. With everyone.'

'You think I don't know that?'

When Jack finally arrives, I take him into the kitchen and Leanne appears immediately from the sitting room, pretending she's looking for sparkling water but clearly keen to give him the once-over.

He has a bottle of red wine and Leanne raises her eyebrows as if she feels this is a bad fit for a quick visit. But I break the ice and pour us each a small glass as Jack asks how I'm doing and says how much everyone in the office misses me and is thinking of me.

'I keep telling her that she should stop worrying about work. Isn't that right, Jack? Don't you agree that she needs a break until this whole wretched business is sorted by the police?' Leanne puts her hand over her glass as I offer her wine.

Jack doesn't reply immediately but does this sort of half-smile at Leanne before turning to me.

'I expect you're finding it quite difficult not being able to work, Alice. Some of us think it's a story we should be covering, actually. This stalking. But Ted has a point that it could make things worse. Give this creep the oxygen of publicity. I can see where he's coming from but it's so frustrating. A story right in our midst that no one's allowed to cover. Christ. I think if it were me, I would want to write about it.'

'Exactly that!' I find myself pointing at him and taking in a long, slow breath before turning back to Leanne. 'You see. Another journalist. *He* understands. We hacks need to write about everything. Yes, Jack. Yes.' I clink our glasses. 'That's exactly how I feel. Furious that I can't write about it.'

'Well, I think you're both crazy. Writing about personal stuff. It's asking for trouble. Obviously.'

Leanne then stands and excuses herself to the sitting room, closing the door behind her. Jack raises his eyebrows at me.

'Sorry, Jack. She's finding it difficult. Our mother isn't well and this whole police inquiry – it's all a bit much.'

'For you too?'

'Yeah.'

'I heard about the fake acid attack. That's mostly why I'm here, actually. It sounded absolutely ghastly.'

'How did you know about that?' For a moment I'm wondering if someone at the café posted something on social media.

'Actually, the police called into the office again.'

'Really?'

'Yeah. That pregnant DI. Routine, I think. Speaking to everyone. And she spoke to me on my own.'

'Why on earth did she do that?'

Jack takes a sip of his wine and holds it in his mouth a moment before swallowing and then replying.

'Mix-up. I was covering a story out near the coast and apparently it wasn't far from where that new attack happened. My car was seen.'

'What – on CCTV?'

'I don't know. But I explained I was on a story. Must have been a coincidence. But I guess it's good they're checking everything. Reassuring, actually.'

'Yeah. I guess so. Though I'm sorry if it felt awkward for you.'

'No. Not at all. Anyway, sounds absolutely terrible – what happened.'

'Yeah. It was pretty terrible actually, but I'm OK now. Tom's got a private investigator helping with security.'

'Right. Good. That sounds good. I mean, a bit surprising . . . but good if it makes you feel more secure.'

'Yeah. I wasn't sure about it to start with, to be honest. But it's just to boost what the police are doing. So – did they say anything else, the police? About me, I mean?' I feel this shift inside, terrified that my double identity will leak.

'No. Just asked me why I was near the coast. Why? Is there something else going on?'

'No, no.' I look into his face and am so very glad he doesn't yet know about my real name. About my link to Alex. There is a little beat when I wonder if I should tell him myself – get it over with. But I let it pass. I'm wondering how long before the tabloids start digging. It may come out very soon anyway.

'OK. So let me update you on the demolition campaign. Like I say, Ted wants someone else to take the story over but I think, if it were me, I'd get in touch with the campaigners. I've brought their latest press release. It's confirming the details on the last residents who moved out ahead of the demolition. They've got a meeting with the demolition company and the housing charity up in London about PR. You could get in touch directly, maybe? And let Ted know you're handling the story from home.'

'Good idea. Thank you, Jack.' I glance at the press release and realise I should have given my key contact a call sooner. I've had so much on my mind. Just a little part of me wonders why Jack didn't simply forward the press release, but then it occurs to me that he probably doesn't have my private email. And I'm not *supposed* to be working.

'Look, I really appreciate this. In fact, can I text you my home email so that if anything else crops up, you can tip me off immediately?'

'Sure. Good idea. If it were my story, I wouldn't want to lose it after all this time.'

I offer Jack a sandwich but he says he doesn't want to intrude for too long, especially as my sister seems a bit touchy.

Within half an hour, I am leading him to the door. I find myself staring at the back of his neck. Jack has this very distinct hairline which I often notice in the office. I find that I would very much like to touch his neck, which causes me immense embarrassment and I pull back, thinking again of that disastrous meal in the Italian restaurant.

Leanne has appeared in the hall to say goodbye, and we watch his car together as it sweeps towards the electronic gates that open and close automatically.

'Bit weird to come out all this way, don't you think?' Leanne says.

'Not really. We're mates, Leanne. He's looking out for me in the office. Making sure I don't get passed over because of this wretched business.'

She just looks at me.

'What?' I lean forward.

'Nothing.'

'No. Spit it out.'

'It's like I said – you need to be careful, Alice.'

'And you really think with this stalker out there and after all I went through over Alex, I don't *know* that?'

CHAPTER 27

ALICE - BEFORE

The day the police came looking for Alex at the home we shared in Scotland, I thought at first that he was dead; that there had been some terrible accident.

I was in the kitchen at the front of the house making toast and saw the marked car pull up outside. I watched the two police officers walk up to our front door and assumed the worst – or what I imagined at that point to be the worst. That Alex had been killed or badly hurt in some accident.

At first, when they explained that they were merely looking for Alex – *Do you know where he is or where he might have gone?* – relief flooded through me. So – Alex was all right. Not hurt. But as their questions began to press me for information, a new panic bubbled up within me.

Why such strange questions? Why were the police looking for Alex? I told them he was getting his car serviced and they said they would check that out but they didn't seem to believe me.

They seemed inexplicably to want to search our home. I was both shocked and at a loss to understand this. I pressed them to explain themselves. What on earth was this really about? The two officers kept exchanging odd glances which slowly morphed from suspicion to pity.

'Will you please just tell me what the hell this is about?' I could feel my heart beating fast in my chest.

Finally they confided that one of Alex's pupils had gone missing from home early that morning. She had taken a suitcase and clothes and her parents had since found 'highly inappropriate references' to Alex in her diary . . .

'What do you mean, *inappropriate?*'

Again they exchanged pitying glances.

'Are you saying this girl has a crush on my fiancé? Because if that's what you're saying, it's hardly his fault, is it? What's her name? What's this girl's name?' As I spoke my heart was beginning to double beat as if I had drunk too much coffee. I was wondering if it was the wretched girl who'd been self-harming and had phoned Alex that weird day we had the row. But the officers gave me a different name and I didn't remember this pupil at all.

I tried to phone Alex but his mobile was unreachable. One of the officers phoned the garage but would not tell me what they said. Then they asked to see Alex's diary, detailing his lesson schedule. We could all see that Alex was due to give a lesson at home within half an hour, and three more later that day.

'So where is he if he's supposed to be teaching today?' The taller of the two officers seemed to be drawing a thick black line under my situation.

'I told you. His car's being serviced.'

I was completely at a loss – shaken and confused by the whole thing. It was my day off and Alex had left very early, saying that the garage had promised to work on his car first. I had offered to drive him but he said he would do some shopping in town until the car was ready. This now made no sense at all, given he had lessons in the diary. I'd assumed he would book the service on a day he was free. It began as a puzzle which all too soon would spiral into a nightmare beyond my worst imagining.

I was told the missing girl was just fifteen. Her diary suggested she'd been in a sexual relationship with Alex for at least six months. Fourteen years old when it started. She had drawn her savings out of the bank and taken all her favourite clothes.

Once the police accepted that I knew absolutely nothing of what was going on, I was assigned a female officer who kept me up to date with each of the next steps.

We believe your fiancé has been in a sexual relationship with at least one underage girl. Maybe more.

It was like being in a film. Yes – like standing against the wall on a set of a film while everyone around me worked on this terrible, terrible story.

As time passed and there was no word from the teenager, an appeal was put out on television with pictures of Alex and the girl. The public was urged to look out for them and contact the incident room.

My phone went bananas. Shocked reactions from my work colleagues. Friends. Family. My own paper ran the story, of course, and wanted an interview with me. *An interview?* Suddenly I was the story, not the journalist. Stepping away from the wall into the film. It was horrific.

I drew the curtains. Stopped answering the phone. Leanne flew up to be with me and we moved out to a small hotel to avoid the press. The irony wasn't lost on me.

I genuinely had no clue where Alex might have gone with the girl. The garage very quickly confirmed there had never been a service booked. Alex had also taken all his favourite clothes. And his passport. So he had clearly been planning this for a while.

There were many more shocks to come. After a week with no progress in the police inquiry, I received a phone call from an estate agent, asking for a meeting 'about the house'. It turned out Alex did not own the property at all. There was no inheritance from a grandparent. He had huge credit card debts, was in rent arrears, and had been fobbing the landlords off that some big new teaching contract was on the horizon. The agency now saw me as the 'sitting tenant' responsible for the mess. I explained that I'd been lied to but I didn't have a leg to stand on. The agency said I could either take over the tenancy by meeting the arrears and monthly rent or I'd have to leave.

Leanne offered to bail me out financially but I was too stubborn at first to accept help. It felt as if I needed to take my punishment for being so naive. The estate agent gave me two weeks' grace. Leanne helped me pack.

The police still had no strong leads. I told them about the row with the other teenager. She was traced and questioned, and eventually broke down and confessed to police that she too had been sleeping with Alex earlier in the year. I was beyond horrified . . .

We all wondered if Alex and the second girl he'd groomed had gone abroad together. I told the police over and over again that I hadn't the foggiest idea of what had been going on, but I started to feel that it was my fault because of my naivety; because I'd accepted his explanation about the telephone call. But there were no sightings of the couple, despite extensive checks of ferry and airport CCTV.

Next, a van came to collect the grand piano, which we discovered was rented too. Leanne promptly put her foot down and insisted on taking me back to London.

Stop being so stubborn, Jennifer. You need help. You need to leave Scotland. And you need to lie low.

Alex and his teenage runaway were eventually discovered on the Isle of Skye in a tiny holiday cottage. Their plan was to hole up secretly until she was sixteen and then marry at Gretna Green. But she fell ill with a bladder infection. The tabloids had a field day speculating where that came from. The infection travelled to her kidney and became so bad that she took an emergency appointment at a local GP surgery. The doctor recognised her from the media coverage and called the police.

The media went nuts. It was all over the papers and local TV too. They were, of course, mostly interested in Alex and the girl, not me, so my picture was rarely used – thankfully – but I was still floored by the whole, terrible experience.

I stopped eating and suffered from what I would realise later was depression.

For all our sibling rivalry and constant niggling, it was Leanne who, in the end, saved me. She took me in. Fed me up. After three months rebuilding my strength, she was the one who suggested I start over. Clean page. So I wrote off the eight months of my journalism training and applied to a new paper in the south of England using my second name and my mother's maiden name. Alice Henderson. I cut my hair and changed the colour. I pretended I was a new trainee, looking for my first break. The paper was impressed with my performance during a trial period and took me on. Within eighteen months, I passed my exams. I felt very guilty deep down in my new clothes as 'Alice', but I worked incredibly hard to earn my second chance. I also got incredibly lucky that no one checked my records or my background.

But my biggest mistake was not that I changed my name; it was thinking I could put Alex Sunningham behind me.

CHAPTER 28

MATTHEW

Matthew is in charge of breakfast while Sal is in the shower.

'It's a Choco Pops day, Daddy.' Amelie is sitting on her little booster seat, beaming at him. Butter wouldn't melt. He tries to remind himself that she is a child and not an opponent.

'No. It's not, darling. It's Friday. Choco Pops day is Saturday. Tomorrow. Treat day *tomorrow*.' Matthew watches his daughter's face darken and there is a creeping dread. How does Sally do this? How does she manage so many hours of this? He starts mentally whizzing through the tip sheet he read just last night on how to head off the impending meltdown. He needs more coffee but remembers that he is not supposed to say 'no' unless absolutely necessary. He is supposed to be smarter than that. *Distract. Distract. Distract.*

'We'll have Choco Pops together tomorrow, sweetie. I'm looking forward to that. How about we do some colouring today while we have breakfast. Or would you like to do a puzzle?' *Give them a choice. Let them feel they have some control over their life.* 'You can choose.'

Amelie looks suspicious. She frowns and narrows her eyes, as if evaluating what is really going on. 'I choose a puzzle.'

'Right. Good.' Matthew turns away quickly before she can clock his smile of surprise, and puts Weetabix and fruit into a bowl with warm milk from the microwave. He tops the breakfast off with more strawberries and grabs two wooden-block puzzles from the basket of toys in the corner of the kitchen.

'Which one?' *More choice.* Matthew is feeling borderline-smug.

A few minutes later Sal appears in her dressing gown with her wet hair wrapped in a towel. She looks at the puzzle alongside Amelie's healthy breakfast bowl and raises her eyebrows with apparent approval.

'Thanks, Matt. You got to run, now?'

'Yeah. Sorry.' He takes a final slurp of coffee and moves swiftly to kiss Amelie and then his wife. 'Be good, both of you. Daddy loves you.' Then he bolts quickly. Such a relief to leave the house after a small triumph instead of a row over shoes or a coat or the car seat . . .

In the driver's seat, still parked on the drive, he checks his watch to confirm that he has just about enough time to try his little experiment for Ian Ellis before he meets Melanie Sanders for another coffee. He double-checks his backpack for his iPad. Yes. Good . . .

He finds himself thinking once more of the day – Friday, a Weetabix day in his household. But for Alice? He wonders what it must be like, waking every day to a countdown. How many days till the next Wednesday . . .

Forty minutes later and Ian Ellis is peeping through the curtains as Matthew pulls in. Poor guy, Matthew thinks. It's wrong to patronise but the truth is Matthew would dearly love to find a small step in the right direction for Ian; at least to stop him calling the emergency services so often. That large, overdue payment from the corporate client has really eased the financial pressure on the agency so he can spare the time.

He has no idea if this is going to work but he's determined to give it a try. He's exchanged several emails with Ian's daughter in Canada and has a hunch.

'So I've been in touch with Jessie by email, and I wanted to run something past you,' he says as Ian leads him into the sitting room.

'Coffee?'

'No, thank you. I've just had breakfast and I don't actually have much time this morning.'

'Why have you been in touch with Jessie?'

'Don't worry. I didn't mention the little people. I was just wondering about whether I can help to put you in touch with Jessie a bit more.'

'I've told you. I'm not getting a mobile phone. They give you brain cancer. And the landline is too expensive. About a pound a minute, I reckon. Maybe more.'

Matthew takes out his iPad from his rucksack, taps in his key code and sets it up in front of them on the coffee table.

'It's an iPad, Ian. Like a little telly – only skinnier. It does lots of things. Look. I found a short tourist film to show you the area your daughter lives in.'

He turns the iPad at an angle and Ian watches the film of the Canadian landscape in utter amazement, as if magic is being performed.

'It's like *Tomorrow's World*.'

Matthew smiles at the mention of the long-forgotten programme highlighting developments in science and technology.

'Is it still on? *Tomorrow's World*? I don't watch telly as much as I used to. Everyone mumbles.' Ian is still staring wide-eyed at the iPad.

'No. I think they axed *Tomorrow's World* a very long time ago, Ian. But never mind that. I have a surprise for you. Now, promise not to pass out on me. Brace yourself for a nice surprise . . .'

Matthew clicks on his Skype icon and connects to Jessie's number. He's already done a test run. She doesn't have a lot of cash, apparently, but she does have a smartphone. Discounted contract. It's five in the morning where she lives in Canada, but Jessie has been on the night shift as a porter at the local hospital and has promised to be standing by.

There's the sound of the call connecting and there she is. A large, smiley woman in a bright blue dressing gown. Matthew adjusts the iPad so that it is pointing directly towards Ian again.

'Hi, Dad. Surprise!'

Ian is at first speechless. For a time he just stares in shock at the screen as if witchcraft is being performed. His daughter then blows him a kiss, her eyes watery. Ian looks at Matthew, his own eyes unblinking, searching for an explanation.

'It's a video call, Ian. It's done through a special service which is free once you have the kit. You can speak. Jessie can see and hear you too. It's not costing me anything so go ahead. You can chat now . . .'

'Jessie?' He says this as if the image is some kind of apparition.

'Yes, Dad. Isn't this great? I can't believe it . . .'

'How about I give you two a few minutes in private and get myself a glass of water. You don't need to touch anything, Ian. Just sit in front of the iPad and talk. Call me if the signal gets funny and the picture freezes. That happens sometimes. I can fix it.'

'So – how are you, Dad?' Jessie says. 'I've just got in from a shift, so I'm sorry I look so shattered. I'll be going back to bed later.'

Matthew stands and moves into the kitchen as Ian begins to speak. Slowly at first and then almost gabbling. Waving too. Like someone who has just spotted a relative in the distance.

Two hours later and Matthew is in a supermarket car park to meet Melanie – no time for their usual café. He's still smiling inside, thinking about Ian, when Mel's car pulls up and she heaves herself out slowly.

'Why's your client going to London? We asked her to stay close, Matt. I thought you said she was up for better cooperation.' Mel has her hand pressed into the base of her back.

'She is, Mel. She's just going to stay with her sister for the weekend. Good security there, apparently. Even better than the Dorset pad. Look – she's tired and she needs a break. She's on her mobile if you need her. And she's got a meeting for a story on Monday morning. Then she's back.'

'Well, I'm not happy about this. Alice out of the patch when we still have no idea where this Alex character is. I don't want to be liaising with the Met on this. You know how I hate that.' She's watching shoppers across the car park collecting trolleys from a bay covered in Perspex like a bus shelter.

Matthew doesn't reply. Melanie is now leaning forward on a railing and she closes her eyes, as if enjoying the breeze on her face. He again takes in the huge bump and remembers that Sal always felt too hot towards the end of her pregnancy. He realises that Mel will get touchy if he again voices his concern but he's worried that she's pushing herself too hard. She's clearly struggling.

'What if he changes the pattern, Matt? What if it stops being Wednesday?'

Matthew is struck by two things immediately. There's a new urgency and a deep-rooted concern in Mel's voice. She's very worried about Alice and very worried about the missing girl too. A good cop and a good person. Also, he finds it uncanny that they still think so alike; it was just the same when he and Mel worked together in the force.

He lets out a long sigh as Melanie opens her eyes and turns to read his expression.

'So it's not just me. You're worried this stalker could change tack too, Matt.'

CHAPTER 29

ALICE

Leanne's car positively purrs. I stretch out my legs in the huge passenger footwell and think of the contrast with my own car – a noisy diesel. I should change it. Yes. Once all of this is over, I will change my car. Come to think of it, I will change a lot of things in my life.

It's Friday and the traffic is bad. Stop, start. Stop, start. The radio is tuned to a commercial station with a lot of quizzes and caller interaction. Leanne likes this. I don't. I prefer music without all the incessant chit-chat and the adverts, but I don't want conflict with Leanne.

Every now and again I glance at my sister as she drives, and try to find the right shape for my gratitude. *Are all siblings like this?* I wonder. The truth is I absolutely hate that I need Leanne to rescue me yet again.

I am remembering the journey back from Scotland after the nightmare that was Alex. The tiny plane from Inverness airport into Gatwick, then Leanne driving me back to her London home. She had been married three, maybe four years, and both children were very small. Leanne and Jonathan had a live-in nanny to step up when they travelled.

I remember quietly disapproving of Leanne having childcare when she didn't work. I feel guilty now for being so judgemental. What do

I know about raising children? And what would I have done without Leanne's support? Then – and now.

'I do appreciate this, Leanne.'

'I know. And I also know it's practically killing you, needing my help. Needing anyone's help.'

I laugh and Leanne bumps the flat of her left hand into my shoulder. 'Hey. Do you remember that time you broke your leg, Alice? How old were you?'

'Twelve.'

'Yeah. And you wouldn't let anyone near to help you with your crutches. You refused to have a bed set up for you downstairs and you used to shuffle up and down the stairs on your bottom.'

'Christ. I'd forgotten that.'

'Me and Mum haven't. Absolute bloody nightmare. One time you slipped and shot down the stairs so fast, we thought you'd have to have the leg reset.'

I laugh and then wait for her to say it, and I promise myself I will not retaliate today – because she's right.

'Our Little Miss Stubborn.'

I take out my phone to pass the time and feel the new sensation that marks every single new day as I gaze at the home screen. *Friday.* Five days and counting; five days until I know what he's going to do next.

I turn to look out of the window and feel suddenly conscious of my breathing. Also my flesh. *I am going to use cheese wire on you.*

Could they be right? Could it be Alex?

I just don't see it myself. Too late, I realised that I never meant anything at all to Alex. I was part of his cover. His cloak of respectability. He drew me into his world for one reason only – so that he could reassure parents and schools and outsiders that he was happily engaged. A lovely man with a lovely fiancée – ipso facto, safe with teenage girls.

I doubt he gave me a second thought after it all blew up. He was furious at the police and the families and media. In court he claimed he was in love with the girl who ran away with him and that age was just a number. He claimed he had been cruelly misjudged. *How can I be condemned for falling in love?*

He never once mentioned me in court, so it just doesn't fit for me to imagine him stalking me now. Why would he bother? Why would he care? And what would he achieve?

'Do you really think it's Alex, Leanne?' I am surprised to hear myself say this out loud.

She fidgets with her seat belt before answering. 'I honestly don't know, but I think you're wrong to so completely discount the possibility. He's had a long time in jail to stew. Who knows what someone like that is capable of. I just want to make sure you're safe until they find him.'

'What's wrong with me, Leanne?' A long sigh leaves my body. I smooth the front of my sweatshirt.

'Whatever do you mean?'

'Well, for all this to happen to me. To one person. It's ridiculous.' I take a hairband from my pocket and pull my hair up into a ponytail.

'I agree that you've had more than your share of bad luck. But you of all people should know from your job that life doesn't play fair when it hands out the drama.' She turns up the radio and I take the hint, returning to my phone.

I've bookmarked several pages on stalking. There's something still nagging at the back of my brain since talking to Jack. He's so right. I really do badly want to *write* about this. It's so frustrating having to keep it all inside.

I flick from page to page – taking in once more all the research I did soon after that very first phone call.

Most stalkers are not killers, apparently. But many killers are stalkers first. Most victims know the stalker. Many don't report the stalking for fear of making the situation worse. Many victims complain that the police don't do enough.

I put a new search into Google and find a link to a charity reaching out to victims. It's not popped up when I've searched before and so I skim through its home page. Its advice page. Its page of statistics. And then I find a page of case histories. There is the story of an actress sent foul messages when she was pregnant. The teacher hounded by a former pupil. The nurse who really was the victim of an acid attack. Page after page of horrible stories.

There are lots of quotes from victims and I devour them, one after another. There's this strange creeping sensation as I recognise the very precise rollercoaster of emotions they all describe. The sense of helplessness. The constant looking over your shoulder. The anger. The disappointment in yourself at being afraid . . .

Then I click through to the website's blog page.

Which is when I suddenly have my idea. And I quietly send the email that I do not realise in this moment is set to make things worse for me.

CHAPTER 30

HIM – BEFORE

He is staring through the classroom window to the trees beyond the playground. There is a huge bird flying in a big circle. Round and round and round.

He wishes he knew more about birds. It looks like some kind of eagle to him, but he once pointed out an eagle to his gran and she said it wasn't an eagle at all. It was a *red kite*. He thought she meant a kite with strings and when he told her this, it made his gran laugh.

She knows loads about birds and all kinds of animals too, from growing up on a farm. She doesn't really like towns and cities. Sometimes they take the bus out of town and go for a walk and a picnic in the school holidays. His gran always looks really happy on those days and he wishes they could run away and live on a farm together. Keep sheep and cows and goats instead of her stinky job.

He turns back to his reading book and traces his finger across the page. He's allowed more difficult books now because he's doing so well. Top of Red Group.

Miss Henderley comes over to his table and sits on the corner.

'Do we have any books on birds, Miss?' He turns back to the window and points to the huge bird which is still circling. 'I'd like to learn the names.'

'I think that's a kestrel but I'm not sure. I'll have a look in the library and see what I can find for you. Everything OK with you?'

'Yes.' A lie. But at least it's Monday and so he's not tired. He won't fall asleep in class; not today. The problem is it's only two more sleeps until his gran leaves him again.

Brian says that if he tells his gran their secret – about the Lego and the favour – then Brian will have to tell the police about his gran leaving him on his own on Wednesday nights and she will be put in prison. Brian says that old people can't cope in prison and she'll probably get sick and possibly die. So he mustn't tell anyone anything at all. Brian says the best and safest thing is for Brian to pop round and keep him company every week when his gran goes out at night. He will bring special biscuits and also chocolate from Belgium, which he says is the best kind in the world.

Thinking about Brian makes him want to punch things and also to cry, so he pushes the backs of his hands into his eyes.

'What are you doing?'

He opens his eyes to see Andrew next to him staring. Andrew repeats the question. 'What are you doing with your hands?'

'I'm trying to see how dark I can make it with my hands in my eyes.'

'That's weird. You're weird.'

'No, I'm not.' He pushes Andrew in the shoulder but Andrew starts to call to the teacher, who is back at her desk now.

'He pushed me, Miss. I didn't do anything but he pushed me.'

'Hey, hey. Both of you calm down and get back to your reading.'

Later, as he walks home from school with his gran, he asks a lot of questions about birds. He's decided that he would like to have a bird of prey and train it to kill Brian. Yes. He will teach it to swoop down and attack him. Then no one would know who was to blame – they would think it was just a bird gone a bit mad – and his gran would not go to prison.

'Can we have a bird? Like a big eagle or something.'

'Don't be silly.' His gran squeezes his hand as they walk. 'You can't keep a big bird in a small place like ours.'

'Some people have parrots. They're quite big.'

'It's not the same. And anyway – I don't like the idea of birds in cages myself. They need to fly.'

'Why did you have to leave the farm? Why can't we live on a farm?'

'It was only a tenancy. It ran out of money.'

Money, money. Always money . . .

He looks back at the sky and wonders if he can train a big bird secretly. In the park or something. He remembers a programme on television that said birds of prey eat mice and things like that. Maybe he could try to catch a mouse and feed a bird in the park. Make it his pet and teach it commands. Then he remembers that he's not allowed to play in the park on his own. He does not understand this. How come he is not allowed to play out on his own but he is allowed to be on his own on Wednesday nights?

He is thinking about this again at bath time.

'I want my bath on my own again. I'm a big boy now.'

His gran looks worried – just like she did the first time he asked. Last Thursday. 'I know you're a big boy but I need to make sure you don't slip in the bath or anything. It's dangerous.'

'We could leave the door a bit ajar again. But I want to do it myself. Every time now.'

The truth is he wants to scrub his body hard. And he's worried that his gran will somehow know. That she will look at his body and guess about the secret with Brian. The favours. And if it all comes out she will have to go to prison. And what if they make him live with Brian?

He looks at his gran once more. He thinks of the biscuits she bakes on Sundays and of the stories she tells about the farm. He thinks of the warm and lovely feeling when she strokes his hair and he has to fight hard not to throw his arms around her waist right now and tell her *everything*. He clenches his hands into fists to stop the wrong words coming out of his mouth. Instead he thinks about the bird he is going to train. Yes. As soon as he is allowed to play out on his own, he is going to secretly train a bird. A huge bird with massive claws that can kill Brian.

'I'm a big boy now, Gran. I'm fine,' he says.

CHAPTER 31

ALICE

I do realise that I'm probably unfair to London. I mean, I can see its appeal – the river, the skyline, the people and the buzz.

My problem with London has nothing to do with logic; I can't deny its very obvious pluses. My problem with London is the assumption by some journalists that it is the centre of the universe – that it has the best buzz. The best restaurants. The best *stories*. My own take as a journalist is that it simply has all the headquarters, which means reporters can speak to the top dogs more easily.

In all honesty, I am probably a bit chippy about this professionally. But I've learned from my time on newspapers in remotest Scotland and then Devon that stories are always first and foremost about people. And people in the countryside have as many issues and problems and challenges as people in London – and they have as much right to be noticed and listened to. And written about.

So, yes. I do see that my problem with London is a question of professional chippiness. The truth is I love the country, and as a journalist I have to fight the assumption from others that I am unambitious (or simply parochial) and I have to work harder to be taken seriously.

But this weekend, I have given London a break. I put Leanne, who adores this city, in charge of our schedule, and I have honestly had a surprisingly good time. On Saturday we took my niece and nephew to the Science Museum, and then to the Tower of London on Sunday. How I reached this age without seeing the Crown Jewels, I don't know. It was all terribly good fun. We then had a very late Sunday lunch at a smart café-cum-restaurant close to Leanne and Jonathan's gated home in Notting Hill.

Turns out that London, like anywhere, is really rather wonderful if you have the time to enjoy it.

And now – Monday – I have my work hat back on. I've belatedly filed my interview with the actress Melinda Belstroy. She messaged me to say that she had thought very carefully and would *not* 'press the button', preferring to accept her bipolar diagnosis and learn to live with it. Ted has emailed to say he'll run the piece within the next couple of days. I'm delighted – so pleased to be *doing* something. And now I'm to meet the three campaigners who've led the charge to get Maple Field House pulled down.

Gill, Naomi and Amy are quite a trio. Mums on a mission, I call them. Mid-thirties and not to be underestimated. I met them a good while back when they sent in their initial press release about the terrible damp. I remember so clearly the first time I visited Maple Field House. About fifteen minutes from Plymouth, the block of flats above shops is shaped around a central courtyard – like a square with one side missing. The mothers explained in their handout that all their children had asthma exacerbated by the terrible damp. But no one on the local council was interested.

Maple Field House was built in a hurry after the war. One of many quick but ugly solutions to the housing need of the times. Owned by the local council, the leasehold shops were once popular and thriving. But as shopping habits changed, so Maple Field House changed too.

Even the charity shops struggled for customers, and most units were just boarded-up shells.

Today Gill, Naomi and Amy are meeting the housing charity which helped fund their campaign to finally push for demolition. I merely reported on their hard work, so am chuffed to be invited. I admire these women, and it was a privilege to put their story in the paper.

At the charity headquarters we're served coffee and delicious cream cakes, in a cosy green room with sunlight streaming in through the window. There's excited chatter, lots of laughter and endless selfies for social media.

'Of course, we couldn't have done it without Alice,' Gill says, leading the charity PR Melody across the small room to meet me. 'No one took much notice until Alice started writing stories about us.'

'Nonsense,' I say. 'Just doing my job. You ladies did all the work. Put together the statistics. Refused to take no for an answer.'

Melody agrees and applauds the trio's work in a little speech, outlining the partnership with the housing association which is to build the replacement homes. She says it's a *win-win* for the council, and a model the charity hopes will roll forward elsewhere too. The local authority is making alternative land available at a peppercorn rent. The housing association is putting up the funds to build.

And then, after applause and more coffee, Gill wanders over to hand me a small, gold foil envelope. I raise my eyebrows, wondering what it is.

'We would like you to be guest of honour at the demolition. They've finally set the date.'

'Don't be silly,' I say. 'I don't need a VIP invitation. I'll just pop along and cover it for the paper.'

'No argument. We want you up front with us when we get to press the button. See the lot go down. It's going to be quite a moment.'

I open the envelope to find a specially printed invitation with my name in gold lettering. The demolition is just two weeks away. And then I skim the details again to find everything around me changing. Suddenly the room feels too crowded and too hot. Suddenly my new appreciation of London is forgotten.

Suddenly his voice is once more back in my ear.

I am going to use cheese wire on you.

Because the date on the invitation is like a cruel and horrible taunt, reminding me that my life – whether in London or in Devon or anywhere else – is no longer my own. No longer normal.

The demolition is set for the 12th.

Which is a Wednesday.

CHAPTER 32

MATTHEW

'Where's your iPad?' Sally is crunching into a thick slice of toast as she watches Matthew across the breakfast table. Amelie is meantime perched on her booster seat, colouring in pictures of fairies. Matthew leans forward to examine his daughter's handiwork.

'Are you sure all fairies are pink, darling?'

'Yes. Of course.' She reaches for an even-brighter pink felt tip, as if to underline her point. 'They're pink so you can see them in the forest.'

'I thought fairies were invisible.'

'Don't be silly, Daddy . . .'

'It's just I've noticed you making notes in a notebook, Matt. Like the old days in the police force in films. So is this nostalgia? Or have you lost your iPad?'

'It's been playing up. I'm thinking of upgrading. Getting a smaller one.' Matthew hopes the truth will not blush on to his face. He's not quite ready to tell his wife that he's loaned his iPad to a man who thinks tiny people want to kidnap him. It's only a temporary solution for Ian, as the SIM has limited data. But Matthew is looking into a cheap Internet package for Ian and is hoping he can be persuaded to sign up.

Then he can give him more lessons so he can Skype his daughter as often as he likes.

'But your iPad's not that old?'

'No. But as I say, it's been playing up. Anyway, I can put the cost of a new one on the business. Legitimate expense.' Thank heavens for that payment from the corporate client. Quite a shock how much companies will pay for consultancy work. Matthew stands and puts his notebook and pen into his backpack and checks his watch.

It's bonkers, of course, to consider gifting his iPad to a virtual stranger – a man who is not even paying him for his time, let alone his technology. He'll visit Ian again shortly to see what difference it's made. But first he needs to speak to Melanie Sanders. Matthew is very pleased to be officially back on the Alice stalker case – even if Sally is less enthusiastic. He spent most of the previous evening reading more articles on the Alex Sunningham case, and something's troubling him. Sort of circling his mind like the annoying buzz of a mosquito. Matthew knows that he cannot fully justify following his instinct when this kind of thing happens. In the police force, he was pressed to base assessment on facts. Evidence and science. But now he's his own man, Matthew likes to listen to his gut. And mosquitoes.

He keeps very still, which for some reason often helps. And there it is – the little something niggling right at the back of his brain.

'Gretna Green,' he suddenly says out loud as all at once the mist clears.

'What about Gretna Green?' Sally tries.

'Sorry. Need to go.'

'Not to Gretna Green, I hope?'

'No. I'll tell you later. A hunch. On the stalker inquiry. Love you both.' He kisses each in turn on the forehead and hurries to the car, where he scans his phone for the feature he was reading last night to recheck the quotes before dialling Mel's mobile from the driver's seat.

'Hi, Mel. Look – this is going to sound a bit nuts but I think you should check the records in Gretna Green.'

'Excuse me?'

'Check for Alex Sunningham's name. I have a feeling the girl may have been playing her parents and playing the media.'

'What on earth do you mean?'

'I don't think he's abducted her. I think she was pretending to have seen the light. That this was all planned.'

There is a beat of silence and Matthew waits.

'You're not seriously suggesting she's still under his spell? Gretna Green. Are you thinking that they're *still* planning to get married? Are you mad? It's been all over the telly. He'd never get away with that . . .'

'But what if he really is that arrogant, Mel? And what if the officials at Gretna Green haven't checked the records? Is there software cross-referencing applications with parole records? I doubt it. And no one would be looking out for his name. I was rereading the interview she gave long after the court case, claiming to have seen the light. It all sounded a bit too pitch perfect, to be honest. What if Alex put her up to it? What if they've somehow stayed in contact? Their original plan was to marry at Gretna Green, remember.'

'But she gave evidence against him, Matt.'

'Yes. Persuaded by her parents and the police. But what if Alex has somehow got under her skin again since. Been in touch. What if he set all this up?'

'Oh Jeez. I have to admit it never occurred to me. But it does actually tie in with the CCTV update this morning.'

'What update?'

'You're not hearing this from me but we've picked him up hiring a car under a false name.'

'Heading north?'

'Yes. Petrol station off the motorway. But no one else in the car. And he must have dumped that car now or changed the plates because we haven't picked it up on any other motorway routes since.'

'He may have switched to the train. And I bet you'll find the girl heading to Scotland by train too. Worth trawling the railway CCTV for her. And him.'

'On it. Long shot, if you ask me – Gretna Green. But we'll check it out all the same and I'll ring you back. No . . . better still. Let's meet at the café. I'll text you a time, and let you know if we find anything meantime.'

A couple of hours later, Matthew is in the café, trying the carrot cake Mel so likes. He is thinking it's actually a bit stodgy as he again googles the Gretna Green rules. It's no longer possible to just turn up and hurry a marriage through. Twenty-nine days seems to be the absolute minimum notice but the process doesn't seem to involve cross-checking prison or parole records so it's possible Alex's plan could be to lie low for a month and then get married. All Gretna Green demands of British citizens are birth certificates and legal confirmation of divorce if they've been married before.

The dates fit Matthew's theory. Alex was released just before Alice's stalking started. He could have filed the paperwork for a Gretna Green wedding soon after he was released. If so – the four weeks would be well up by now and the wedding could be at any time. Which might explain why Alex had suddenly stopped seeing his probation officer. And why the girl had run off.

Matthew again scans the girl's interview, which ran while Alex was serving his second year inside. He notices how often she mentioned her regret and her new life after Alex. The quotes were impressive but, on careful reflection, too impressive. Extremely mature. That was what had rung an alarm bell with him. There was this strange air of 'protesting too much'. Something rehearsed about her comments. It sounded to Matthew as if she were rather too keen to reassure her parents and the world that she had put Alex Sunningham behind her.

Now he's more and more suspicious that the quotes came via her from Alex himself. More grooming. Had Alex found some way to renew contact with the girl and resumed his control over her during his time in jail? It was certainly possible. Prisons were sadly awash with mobile phones.

Matthew sips his drink and thinks of the dreadful Alex and why on earth he might still want this relationship. Alex must know he'll be found out and sent back to prison eventually, to serve his full sentence. Licence terms include telling your probation officer about getting married. Permission would never be given while on parole to marry his victim. So why do something that will get him sent straight back to jail? To stick his finger up to the authorities? To get himself a legal young bride as a cover to chase even younger girls down the line? Maybe he doesn't think he'll be found out. Or maybe he doesn't even care about being found out and serving the balance of his sentence. Maybe he's mad enough to believe he'll reclaim some kind of moral balance by marrying the girl. Creepy. Insidious. Yes – *mad*.

A further half an hour and Matthew looks up to see Melanie Sanders hurrying in, her mac loosely belted around her enormous bump.

'I can't stay long – five minutes. So I won't order anything. But I could kiss you.'

'Feel free.'

She punches his shoulder as she sits down. 'Seriously. I don't know how you do it. I'm almost cross with you for being so clever. You're spot on. Alex Sunningham and the girl, using their real names to make it legitimate, have a wedding booked at Gretna Green. Guess when.'

'No idea.'

'Tomorrow. By coincidence or maybe not a coincidence . . .'

'A Wednesday.' Matthew is almost as stunned as Melanie to have got this right.

'The Gretna Green staff feel terrible for not noticing or remembering the name. But Alex filed the papers weeks ago. Must have been fairly soon after he got out. He looked very different from his media pictures, apparently, and no one remembered this or put two and two together with the recent coverage of his disappearance.'

'Do you think they actually believed they'd get away with it? I mean, surely with the media coverage, the staff would recognise them on the wedding day.' Matthew is turning a sugar sachet over and over between his thumb and fingers. 'Is it just attention he wants, this Alex? A narcissist? To show that he still controls the girl?'

'God knows. But they have so many weddings every day at Gretna – maybe the staff wouldn't have recognised them. Anyway. No matter. The local police are checking all holiday rentals and CCTV in the area to try to find them. If no luck, the last resort is we turn up for the wedding tomorrow and arrest him there before the ceremony.'

'Will you go up there yourself? I thought the whole idea was for this to be a desk job before your mat leave.'

'Technically, yes. But you know me. I like to be hands on, though I'm not entirely sure about Scotland at the moment. The police local to the girl have their own inquiry obviously, so it's a bit of a liaison nightmare. But I'm arguing priority because of the stalker investigation. We'll see. Either way, I'm looking forward to interviewing Mr Alex Sunningham about Alice when it's my turn.'

'You really think he's our stalker, Melanie?'

'Don't you?'

CHAPTER 33

ALICE

It's Tuesday and I'm still in London – more tired today because it's nudging too close to Wednesday for me to sleep. I stare at the cocoa-leaf pattern on my cup of coffee and then across at the violinist. Even for Covent Garden, which always has a good class of busker, he's exceptional. He plays the violin as if it's an extension of his own body. Royal Academy of Music, or something like that? Yes. This is probably how music students pay their way through college. And then there is that inner shudder as I think of music in general. Alex at his grand piano . . .

'He's good, isn't he?' Claire follows my gaze to the musician before turning back to our table. 'So – are you feeling a bit better, Alice?'

'Yes. Sorry about earlier. I have no idea where that came from.' I don't yet know quite what to make of Claire, but I'm mortified to have dissolved into tears earlier.

'Don't apologise. I should have suggested somewhere more private. It's normally quieter here at this time of day, actually. I'm just sorry the office was busy. If there wasn't a meeting going on, we could have found a quiet corner. We'd love a bigger place but we're trying to keep overheads down.'

'My fault. Short notice.' I use my teaspoon to scoop some of the frothy milk into my mouth, then sip at the coffee proper. It's smooth. Nice. Despite my embarrassment earlier, I'm pleased to have arranged this meeting. Talking to Claire about what's going on is such a welcome release.

'I can't tell you how good it is to be with someone who actually understands.'

Claire reaches forward to hold my hand briefly. 'I know. That's precisely why we do this. Everyone says the same when they first contact the charity. It's the most isolating and frightening thing that can happen – stalking. We do what we can. There's no pretending we have a magic solution, but the one thing we can promise is that we understand completely.'

'So, do you not see much of your sister these days, Claire?'

She'd explained on the phone to me previously that she set up the charity after her own sister, Lisa, was the subject of a real acid attack by a fellow student at university. He'd imagined a relationship that never existed and had stalked Lisa throughout their first and second years. Cards and presents and endless text messages. He kept turning up at all her lectures and social events, and her flat too. Lisa reported the pestering to both the police and the pastoral team at the university but no one seemed able to help. The university merely issued the other student with warnings. The police seemed to think the problem would pass.

Then in the third year, in the run-up to exams, the stalker turned up at her flat and threw acid at her as she answered her door. He was jailed. Lisa was left with injuries which required months of surgery.

'She decided to go abroad in the end,' Claire says. 'She said she'd never feel safe in this country again. He's out of prison now, so I don't blame her.'

'So you lost your sister, in effect?'

'We Skype. I visit her when I can. But yeah – I feel I lost her because of him.'

'So this is why you set up the charity? Why you do this?' I am in work gear now. What a story.

Claire nods. 'Someone has to. I managed to secure some funding for four years. We're into our third year and it's a struggle. Not sure what we'll do when the funding runs out.'

I pause. I'd really like to help but I don't want to jump in too soon. I've explained how badly I want to write about my experience. To connect with others. To try to make society realise just how bad it is for victims to go through this hell.

'So what do you think about me writing for your blog anonymously?'

'We'd love it, of course. Someone with your writing talent and personal experience would be such a help to the charity. But I need to be sure it won't make things worse for you, Alice. While the case is live, I mean.'

'To be honest, I don't see how anything can get worse, Claire. I won't include details which could in any way identify me. I won't mention the Wednesday angle; I just want to put my feelings out there. On record.'

'We normally only run personal stories once a case is resolved. Not live. I'm just a bit worried the stalker might see it. Get off on it. We don't want to give the creep what he wants.'

I take in a deep breath. 'Yes – I do see it's a legitimate worry. And it's precisely what my editor says. But I'm climbing the walls not being able to put my feelings out there. I suppose I could start writing and we could hold the material for a bit if you like? I would just feel so much better if I could find an outlet for this. A platform which might actually help other people too.'

'OK.' Claire finishes her drink and hands me her card. 'This has my personal contact details. Email me your first piece and let's talk again. If I'm happy it won't identify you or compromise the police inquiry, we could run it on the website with social media links to our factsheets. Any way of getting our advice out to more victims is a good thing.'

'Great. It's a good website,' I add. 'I certainly found it very helpful.'

'Thank you. I'm glad. And you feel you have enough support? I mean, I realise it's Wednesday tomorrow.' Claire looks graver suddenly.

'I'm travelling back to the south-west later this evening. I have to decide whether to stay at my sister's house, my boyfriend's house or my own tonight.'

'So where do you think you'll feel safest, Alice?'

'The locks have been changed at the house I rent. I've had extra security installed. I should be OK there.'

'And have you got a personal alarm?'

'I've got one that sounds a siren when you press it.'

'No, I don't just mean noise. I mean an alarm that triggers *action*.'

'I'm not following you.'

'An alarm that links directly to the police or a call centre.'

'I had no idea such a thing existed.'

Claire shakes her head as if exasperated.

'What, Claire?'

'I just think the police should issue them as standard. Run this kind of service. They've been known to do it in rare cases. When it's someone high-profile.'

'I've never even heard of this kind of alarm.'

'Well, there are lone worker alarms on the market already that you can wear around your neck. Get straight through to a call centre who can ring the police. We're piloting our own version actually, especially for stalking cases, but I'm not ready to say too much about that yet.'

'Why not? That sounds fantastic. *Exactly* what victims need.'

'It's early days. Expensive to road-test. Not something I'm sure the charity should be investing in.'

'Would you mind sending me details? At least let me look into it.' I keep thinking how fabulous it would feel to wear something like that around my neck at home. One quick button for help instead of fumbling for a phone.

'I'll have a think, Alice. I'll email you some links to the options already on the market if you like, and some details of what we're piloting ourselves.'

'OK.'

And then a text buzzes on my phone. Matthew Hill. I feel a jolt inside.

Some good news. We may be close to finding Alex.

CHAPTER 34

HIM - BEFORE

His gran has made him a birthday cake. Seven candles.

'What's that mark on your arm?' His gran stretches out her hand to try to see better, but he pulls the cuff of his jumper down.

'Nothing. Just scratches from the class guinea pig. He got a bit weird when I was cleaning him out.'

He keeps his thumb on the cuff of his jumper so that it won't ride up as he takes a deep breath for the candles.

'OK then. Don't forget to make a wish, my lovely boy.'

He lets out the huff of air and wishes that Brian were dead. He pictures him in a big pool of blood on the floor. He imagines hitting him with something hard. A hammer. Yeah. *Smash, smash, smash*, right into his brain.

'Now you mustn't tell me the wish or it won't come true.'

'I know that. I'm not stupid.'

'OK, OK. Careful with your tone, my lovely. I know it's your birthday, but we don't want an argument, do we? I just want a nice day for you.'

'My friends have parties.' He feels guilty as he says this but he can't help himself. He is sick of being different from his friends. All their stupid questions all the time. *Why do you have weird jumpers? Does your gran knit them? Ha ha.*

He would love to have a party. Balloons. Games. Normal stuff.

'Yes, well. I'm really sorry about that. I don't think I could manage that on my own. But we're going to the cinema later, remember? And you can have treats. Popcorn and sweets. I've saved some money specially.'

It's Saturday. His gran isn't working today. He looks into her face and sees the sadness in her eyes and he feels even more guilty. He doesn't understand how he can love her so much most of the time and feel cross with her too. It's weird.

'Sorry. I'm really sorry.' He puts his arms around her waist, still holding on to the cuff of his jumper. He uses a compass that he found in school. Mostly he just scratches the skin a little bit, but sometimes when he gets really angry he digs deeper into the flesh until there is blood. He doesn't know why but it feels quite good for a bit. He wants to stop doing it because he's worried the teacher or his gran will find out. It doesn't really look like guinea pig scratches.

Brian knows.

What are those marks on your arm?

Nothing.

You need to stop doing that or I'll need to speak to someone. About your gran. Maybe I should tell the police after all.

Maybe I should tell them about you, Brian.

Now, don't be getting silly. We've talked about this. No one will believe a little boy. And you want to see your gran in jail? You really think she could cope with that?

'Shall we go and say hello to Grandad? Eat the cake outside in a napkin?' He has brightened his tone and he knows that his gran will be pleased with this suggestion. He wants to make up for being grumpy about not having a party.

Sure enough, her eyes look all teary. She glances to the window. The sky is blue. No clouds at all. He tries very hard not to think about

Brian. About how he could get a hammer and what it might be like in jail . . .

'That's a lovely idea. Thank you, my little soldier. He'd like that very much.'

Outside they sit together on Grandad's bench at the edge of the patch of grass. He looks up to the window of their flat. Every morning, from up there, his gran looks down at this bench as she makes their cups of tea for breakfast.

'Morning, my love,' she says every single day to the bench.

It has a plaque on the wood which his grandad's friends made. All his customers from his cobbler's shop. Gran says he used to mend shoes and handbags and belts. He could stitch leather like no one else. He had one of the shops under the flats, and people used to travel from all over town with the things that needed mending.

'Tell me again about Grandad.'

'Your grandad was the best kind of man. Tall and handsome and with a big smile and a big, big heart. He looked after me and he looked after your mum when she was little. He worked all day long in his shop and he used to sit out here on the bench to have his lunch. Sandwiches and a flask of tea.'

'Why didn't he come up to the flat for his lunch?'

'Sometimes he did, but mostly he liked the fresh air. He told me that he liked to breathe in the fresh air and look up at the trees and the birds.'

'I like birds. Was it this bench he had his lunch on?'

'No. That one rotted away. But they put new ones in, and when your grandad died, his customers put the plaque up to remember him. That's why it's so special. Why I like it here so much.' She took a deep breath. 'It's why I never want to live anywhere else. I can see your grandad's bench from the window. And I can picture him sitting here with his sandwich and his flask. It's like he's still nearby.'

'Will I have a heart attack one day?'

'No, lovely. Course not. Your grandad was just very unlucky.'

'So is that why we have no money? Because of grandad's heart attack?'

'Eat your cake, my birthday boy, and don't be worrying about money. Not today. He wouldn't want that. And I told you – I saved a little bit of money for the cinema today. Birthday treat.'

'Can you save enough money to stop working? So you can stay home and not do the night shift?'

She ruffles his hair and he feels his body sort of freeze like a statue. He tries very hard not to think of hammers and pools of blood but he can't help it. It's like there is this big, big volcano in him, waiting to blow its top off. He saw that in a video in school in geography. One minute it was just a mountain and then a huge explosion. *Boom.*

That's me, he thought as he watched the film. *That's me.*

'I thought you were used to me doing Wednesday nights now. I thought now that you're getting a bit bigger, you don't mind so much. It'll get easier and easier as you get bigger . . .'

He stuffs a big piece of chocolate cake into his mouth and looks away at the trees and the birds.

He would like to ask his gran about his mother. He has a picture in a frame by his bed of his first birthday, sitting with his mum in Gran's kitchen. Sometimes he thinks he can remember his mum but mostly he thinks he just remembers the photograph. Some of the other children in school say his mum *did drugs* and that's why she died. They say that their parents told them. He's asked his gran but she doesn't talk about that.

So instead he looks up at the blue, blue sky. He is thinking again of Brian. And of a pool of blood. He is searching the expanse of blue for an eagle. A hunter. A really big bird with sharp claws that can swoop and claw.

Swoop and claw.

CHAPTER 35

ALICE

I'm glad I booked a seat as the train's packed, but I'm regretting the choice of the quiet carriage. I glance around me to take in the faces of the men.

There's a slightly geeky guy watching a film on his laptop. A pensioner doing the crossword with a beautiful fountain pen. For a moment I stare, until he begins to fill in an answer. Careful writing. Capital letters. And then across the aisle there is a tall, balding guy spreading his legs under the seat in front. I narrow my eyes, feeling uneasy. I must have been staring for too long, because suddenly he's looking right back at me. He's also staring. Unblinking. Then he glances down at his crotch and then back at me again, raising his eyebrows. Grinning.

Creep.

I look away. I feel myself blush. Yes, I should have gone for the family carriage. Damn. I normally like to avoid the noisy kids. All those juice cartons and colouring books. But this carriage is full of commuters – men and women travelling on their own. It's Tuesday evening. I should have thought this through; I should have listened to Leanne, who said it wasn't a good idea, leaving my return to Devon so close to

Wednesday. The problem is I still feel ashamed of this fear – this escalating paranoia around men.

Christ. It could be the bald guy. Any of them. None of them. *Calm down, Alice.*

I close my eyes and concentrate on my breathing. I count the breaths in and the breaths out. Just like the cool-down sequence at Pilates. I miss my old routine. Pilates and French classes. I wonder when I will be able to get back to all that.

I try the breathing and counting some more. It helps a bit but not completely.

By the time I reopen my eyes the bald pervert has lost interest and has his headphones in. I glance at the luggage rack to check my small pink case. Good. It's safe. I tell myself again to calm down. I take out a book from my bag, hoping to read, but the words just blur.

Again I look around the carriage, from man to man. I know only the voice of my tormentor through the voice changer from that very first call. I have no idea what he may look like. Or truly sound like without the distortion. I try to picture Alex with a phone and a voice app but I still can't make it fit. It feels somehow too improbable. Too neat. Too obvious.

Matthew says the police now have a strong lead in their search for Alex, but he's not allowed to share details with me yet for fear of scuppering the police operation. DI Sanders has gone out on a limb updating him, apparently. He promises me more information very soon.

The problem is I don't think that finding Alex will stop this. I try to make the leap of faith. I try to imagine that the police are right and I'm wrong. The relief it might bring once he's under arrest and then back in prison. But – no; I just can't make it *fit.*

I can feel my heart starting to quicken. The familiar disappointment in myself. Why can't I be stronger? Braver? Why have I let this faceless man get to me so? Do this to me. Win . . .

You are on a packed train, Alice. He cannot touch you. He cannot do anything to you here. Not with all these people around you.

I take out my phone and put in my earphones. I don't switch on the music but need the prop. The visual cue to step away from all the people in this carriage.

Tom in his last phone call offered to come up to London and accompany me home. He was upset that he hadn't been able to coordinate his work to be in the city to tie in with my visit to Leanne. I said it was over the top and unnecessary for him to make a flying visit to town just to see me home. But that was stubborn Alice talking; right now I'm wishing with every bone in my body that I'd said *yes, please.*

At least he's meeting me in Plymouth and has promised to be on the platform early. He's also booked Matthew again to look out for me from first light tomorrow. *Wednesday.*

I hear the word echo deep inside my head. *Wednesday, Wednesday, Wednesday.* So confusing still. Why Wednesday?

I spool through Tom's recent texts.

You OK? See you soon xx.

He's been trying hard to be calmer about the Alex revelation, but I can tell he's still deeply upset. And who can blame him? I should have told him about Alex. I mean – what must he think of me now? Someone who could be taken in by a man like Alex?

As I reread the texts, I try to picture Tom; to feel the right feelings. But for some reason I find myself thinking of Jack instead. I picture Jack's face, not Tom's. Jack's expression in that Italian restaurant when I behaved so badly.

Why do I do this? *What's the matter with me?*

And then – after ten, maybe fifteen minutes – I begin to fidget. *Damn.* I need the loo. I really shouldn't have drunk that large coffee while waiting for the train. This is how ridiculous my life has become. Nervous about going to the loo on a train. What kind of new madness is this?

I glance yet again around the carriage. Baldy now has his eyes closed. Everyone else seems busy with their laptop or their phone or a book. Outside it's dark, and so all the faces and laptops and phones are reflected in the windows. I lift my handbag over my left shoulder and slip from my seat, deliberately leaning the other way as I pass the bald guy's seat, and walk through to the front of the carriage and into the connecting space.

The automatic doors close behind me. I feel the temperature change; someone must have left the window open to the exit door. I move forward, but before I can decide whether to shut the window, I hear the automatic door fire again behind me. I turn to find that the bald man is there, just a few feet from me. He grins, again widening his eyes.

Blind panic now. My heart is racing and I feel sort of clammy as I turn to stride away from him. What now? What now? What *options*?

I think of hurrying into the toilet and locking myself inside, but – no. *Damn.* I see the flash of red confirming it's engaged. I keep walking – faster, faster – into the next carriage. Yes. Better to walk than be stuck in the quiet of the dividing space between carriages with him.

It's probably not him. The man on the phone. The man with the flowers and the bottle of iced water. Highly unlikely. Just a creep, Alice. You can handle a creep . . .

I keep going through the family carriage. To my left there are two children sitting opposite their mother, playing on their iPads. I push onward, onward, past a woman with grey hair who looks asleep. Two elderly men chatting over a newspaper.

And I turn to find that the bald guy is still behind me. Matching my haste. Following me through the carriage.

Following me?

And now, for the first time, I start to entertain blacker thoughts – that maybe, just maybe, it *could* be him. Blatant. Taunting me? It makes no logical sense – with all these people? Why would he be so stupid? Run the risk of getting caught?

At last I pass the next luggage area. Another interconnecting space and finally into the toilet. I feel a huff of air leave my body as the door closes and the lock clicks into place, but I'm now genuinely desperate for the loo, so I quickly relieve myself and wash my hands before taking out my phone. My hands are still wet. Trembling too. I find it difficult to stand steady as the train takes a corner.

'Matthew?'

'Yes, Alice. What is it?'

'I'm on the train back from London and there's a creep following me. I'm in the toilet and he's right outside. I know it sounds ridiculous but I'm afraid to go out, Matt.' I'm horrified to find that I'm actually crying now. 'I'm sorry.' I move the phone to my chest as I try to compose myself and then put it back up to my ear. 'But I'm really afraid.'

'OK. So I'm here and I'm listening, Alice. You're not alone with this. So what's made you afraid? Are you saying you think it's the stalker? What has this man done? What makes you feel afraid of him?'

'I don't know. I don't know. I mean, he could just be a creep. He's a bit pervy. Staring at his crotch – you know. Just creepy. But now he's followed me through two carriages and I mean – what if it is him, Matthew?'

'Right.' There's a sharp intake of breath before Matthew continues. 'Give me the exact details, Alice. Carriage and train and a description of the man and I'll get on to this. Where are you roughly? I need to work out how strong the mobile signal will be. That's the only way I can get a message to the train staff via transport police.'

'You can do that?'

'Yes. There's a text number for transport police. It's normally pretty slow but I've got a contact. And I can hopefully fast-track it via Mel. I mean DI Sanders. But where are you? Is the signal strong?'

'Not that long out of Paddington. Three strong bars at the moment.'

'Good, that's good. Signal is pretty strong to Reading. OK. Which train and which carriage?'

'I'm now in the toilet between coach C and coach D. The 7.03 p.m. from Paddington.'

'Right. Stay in the toilet, Alice. Ignore anyone who knocks until it's staff. OK? I'll have to ring off to make some calls but I'll ring you back very soon. Do you understand?'

'Yes. I suppose.' I pause. 'But what if someone needs this cubicle?' I can't quite believe this is happening. 'What if I'm just being ridiculous, Matthew . . .'

I think of the bald guy gesturing to his crotch. Leering as he followed me.

'People can use a different toilet, Alice. Creep or stalker, the police need to speak to this guy. And they will. We've got your back. Now, I'm going to ring off to get things in motion. But you stay put. Yes?'

'Yes. OK.' I put my hand out to touch the wall to steady myself. I give Matthew a full description of the man and it feels a tiny bit better sharing this. 'Thank you, Matthew.'

'No need. I'll ring you back very soon.'

Again I try to steady my breathing as I wait.

Someone knocks on the door. I ignore it. I wonder if it's the creep. The stalker?

'I'm unwell,' I call out. 'Sorry. Can you try a different toilet?'

There is more knocking. Then there is a man's voice, low and menacing. 'So what are you doing in there really?' A pause. 'Are you doing something nice for me in there? Did I make you wet? Is that why you won't come out?'

I shift my body to lean properly against the wall, clutching the phone to my chest. I'm ever more conscious of my heart pounding, pounding, pounding. I can feel it against the hand pressing the phone into my chest. I can feel it in my ear too. Also, I feel more and more unsteady. I look to the toilet but can't sit down. It's so unpleasant. Somehow it all feels dirty and wrong in here.

I keep very still, dreading more words through the door. Silence. I look at my phone, willing a text or a call. One minute. Two.

I try hard to steady my breathing. I'm worried I could become faint if I don't get more oxygen into my system. I wait and wait and wait until at last the phone rings. Matthew.

'He's still outside the door, Matthew. He's saying insidious stuff. Sexual. Nasty. What should I do?' I'm whispering.

'OK. So I've set things in motion but I don't know how long this will take. They're trying to get a message through. You need to be brave and just stay put for a bit. Can you do that for me, Alice?'

'Yes. I suppose so.'

Matthew then talks about his day. About his daughter who is apparently going through the terrible twos, which is challenging. He says she loves travelling on trains. He tells me that once they went on a *Thomas the Tank Engine* day and she had never been so happy. I listen, barely able to take in what he's saying but almost tearful at the effort he's making to distract me.

I keep looking at the door, dreading more knocking. More whispering. And then Matthew says a text has just come in. He breaks away to check it and is then more upbeat.

'OK. Alice. Good news. We've called in a favour. Managed to fast-track this. The member of staff coming to help you is called Ben. He's safe, Alice. He's railway staff and he'll be in uniform. He'll introduce himself and then accompany you back to a different seat in first class. He'll also check tickets so we can find out where the bald guy's getting off so we can arrange an arrest. You should pretend you've been feeling unwell . . .'

'I've already said that.'

'Good thinking. Very good. So stay with that story, OK? Wait for Ben. Is this OK, Alice?'

'Yes. I'll wait. You won't ring off?'

'No, no. I'll stay on the phone now until Ben is with you. OK?'

'OK. I don't know how to thank you.' I'm still whispering, clutching the phone so tightly that my knuckles are white.

'Don't be silly. We're going to keep you safe, Alice.'

'Do you think it could be him, Matthew? Do you think I'm being completely ridiculous?'

'No one is being ridiculous, Alice. Just wait . . . OK?'

'OK.'

I wonder if I should keep talking to Matthew but I'm worried about the bald guy hearing even this whispering, so I just wait, the phone pressed hard to my ear.

It seems to be an age. Matthew talks some more about his daughter and then at last there's some kind of new movement outside the door. Then a different voice, speaking up deliberately loudly.

'Excuse me, sir. But could I ask you to step aside, please? This toilet has been occupied for some time. It comes up on the steward's board when this happens. I need to check there isn't a problem. In case someone is unwell inside.'

Next there's knocking. 'Hello? Hello? My name is Ben and I'm railway staff. Are you all right in there?'

'I'm not feeling very well actually, Ben.' I feel my eyes darting from left to right as I raise my voice to be heard through the door.

'OK. Well, can you unlock the door and I'll see if I can help you.'

Slowly I unlock the door.

'I'm sorry. I'm just feeling a little bit faint.'

'Not to worry, madam. I'll help you.'

Ben – a short, stocky man who looks to be in his late thirties – leans forward, widening his eyes as if to reassure me. I let him take my arm and help me into the open space between carriages. I don't have to pretend; I genuinely feel unsteady on my feet. As I move through the wider space, I see the bald man is over by the exit door, pretending to enjoy the fresh air from the partially open window.

As we move towards the carriage, the bald man heads into the toilet and I hear the click of the lock. Ben whispers as we continue forward, 'Another member of staff will keep an eye on him and check his ticket and his destination. I've got you a seat in first class. It's quiet and safe there and we'll bring you a sandwich and a drink. Would you like tea or coffee? Or water?'

'Coffee and some water, please. This is so good of you.'

'Not at all. All part of our service, madam. We're going to keep you safe, OK?'

We continue right through three carriages before Ben settles me into my new seat, returning soon afterwards with drinks and also my pink case, which I pointed out on the way past.

I ring Matthew to update him.

'Good. That's all good. You feeling better, Alice?'

I glance around the carriage. A few of the other passengers have their headphones in. Others are asleep. 'Yes. Still shaken but better. So what happens now? What if I was just overreacting, Matthew? What if he's just a perv, plain and simple?'

'Whether this guy is your stalker or not, he's a first-class creep and he needs to be questioned. You have nothing to feel guilty about, Alice. You did the right thing reporting this, and I'll keep you updated.'

Ten minutes later, and Ben returns to whisper that the man will be getting off at Newton Abbot. It's a long way yet, but police will be on standby to arrest and question him. I'll need to make a full statement when I get off at Plymouth. Is this OK? The police have been in touch and have offered to send a patrol car to meet me.

I nod, feeling close to tears. And then – *damn* – I take out my phone, realising suddenly that I need to update Tom. I wonder if he will be cross that I didn't phone him first.

I think of the police arresting the bald man – and Alex too? I wonder as I press the Call button what precisely to say to Tom. If it's all nearly over.

Or if another nightmare chapter is just beginning . . .

186

CHAPTER 36

ALICE

The next morning, I feel so groggy. I must have fallen asleep at some point but the last time I looked at the clock it was 3 a.m. I don't remember Tom getting up.

I hear clattering. The sound of the milk frother on the coffee machine and at last he appears, holding two mugs.

'Matthew Hill's here. In the kitchen.'

'What? Here *already?*' I check the clock – 7 a.m. – and feel self-conscious in my faded pyjamas and this terrible state of disorientation. I just can't think straight. I remember agreeing to stay here at Tom's rather than returning to my house after giving a statement to the police, but it was very late by the time we got here. We talked for a long time. Drank too many glasses of red wine.

I learned that Matthew and Mel Sanders have a friend in the transport police who, by chance, had been on duty. He pulled some strings for them to get such a fast response on the train. I'd apparently been lucky.

Lucky?

Quite frankly, I feel the unluckiest woman on the planet. If the bald guy isn't my stalker, why the hell did he pick *me* for his perving?

Out of all the women on the train? Am I sending out paranoia signals to attract the world's army of lowlifes? Is there something written on my forehead? *Perfect victim – feel free.* Was that because of Alex? Was all this because . . . of . . . Alex?

I remember so clearly, checking that clock during the early hours and longing for the refuge of sleep. Instead my mind just wouldn't still, rolling the film over and over. Walking me through all the dreadful scenes, one after another. The phone call. The cake box. The spray of ice-cold liquid.

And now? It's once again the day I dread. The day he wants me to dread – and I have no energy left to face it.

Wednesday.

I take in my reflection in one of the mirrored panels of Tom's smart new fitted wardrobe. Panda eyes. Must have left my make-up on. Don't remember brushing my teeth either.

There was a time when I didn't mind looking in the mirror. I got lucky. My mother's genes. I turn to the side to see a copy of her profile. The same neat nose. The problem is I haven't looked at myself for so long; I just look permanently exhausted these days. I take in the dark circles under my eyes and am shocked to find I don't especially care. But then I think of Matthew in the kitchen . . .

'Oh God. Look at me. I need to take a shower.'

Tom leans forward to kiss my shoulder. 'No hurry and no worries, sweets. You've had an awful time. No one cares what you look like. Look – I'm sorry but I can only stay until seven- thirty. I need to leave then – Crown Court. You remember? I can't find anyone to cover. I'm the only one fully briefed and it's an important client.'

'Oh Christ, I'd forgotten actually. But it's fine. Of course. I'll be fine.'

'I've warned Matthew he's to stick to you like glue today. No arguments. Not until we know what's happening with Alex. Or this nut job from the train.'

'Is he still in custody? The guy on the train?'

'Don't know. Matthew's waiting to hear from his police contact. You take a shower – no hurry – and I'll make him some breakfast before I leave.'

'You're not still cross with him, are you, Tom? Over that motorcycle attack? It really wasn't his fault. And he was fantastic on the phone to me yesterday.'

'For you I'm on my best behaviour with him, I promise.' He kisses me a second time and then stands. 'Right. I'll get some toast on.'

Half an hour later and Tom is on the way to court and I'm sitting on the high black-and-chrome stool at the breakfast bar. Matthew's drinking his third coffee after polishing off most of our fresh loaf.

I stare at him. Fair, wavy hair cut quite short. Slim, despite the appetite. I find myself wondering what his wife looks like. And his daughter. He's sitting on the small leather sofa which divides the kitchen and dining space, checking his phone. I wonder if they mind him working like this.

'No word from DI Sanders?' I'm trying for a calm tone but my chin twitches as I speak. Must be the tiredness. I run my right hand through my hair, which I'm allowing to dry naturally. Couldn't face the hair dryer.

'Not yet.' Matthew manages a smile. 'We should have news on Alex by ten a.m. at the very latest.'

'How so?'

'Sorry, but I'm not actually supposed to say, Alice. But they have good intelligence on where he is. So we're confident of an arrest.'

'And the guy on the train?'

'Still in custody but we expect him to get bail today with the help of a duty solicitor.'

'Oh?'

Matthew lets out a long sigh. 'He's got a record, Alice. Exposed himself on a train once before. Accused of stealing underwear from a flatmate. Clearly a first-class weirdo but it's not looking like he has anything to do with your previous stalking. He was in France until the weekend, working in the bar at a campsite. That's been verified already and there's nothing linking him to you that the police can see yet. Obviously Mel Sanders and her team will look into his phone and computer records very carefully before we're sure.'

'Right. So what did he say when he was questioned? About what happened on the train? About why he followed me?'

'Stuff and nonsense. I wouldn't give it any more thought. He's a pest.'

'No. I'd like to know what he *said*, Matthew.'

'He claims you encouraged him to follow you to the toilet.'

'Bastard.'

'Exactly.'

'So why the hell did he target me? And please don't say bad luck.'

'I don't know, Alice. But sometimes creeps cast around for someone they think looks . . .' Matthew pauses.

'Vulnerable?'

Matthew again lets out a sigh. 'I don't want to say the wrong thing here, Alice. But you've been through a lot. Sometimes the strain can just wear someone out. And lowlifes sometimes look out for that. Pick it up.'

'You should be a detective.'

He laughs and finishes his coffee. 'Right. So what's the plan for today? You want to just stay home and try to catch up on some sleep? I can keep out of your way if you want to watch films or whatever. But Tom's right. If you want to go out, then I'm the driver.'

'OK. I'll have a think. I may just stay in and do some writing actually.' I'm remembering now the conversation with Claire from the charity. I'd like to check out that alarm she was talking about. And I've certainly got plenty to write about. I fancy trying the first anonymous blog. Get some of this out of my system and on to paper.

I take out my phone, planning to send a text first to Leanne to update her that Matthew's with me so I'm safe. But as I reach for it, it rings – my sister's name flashing.

'Leanne. Are you psychic? I was literally just about to message you.'

'You haven't seen it, have you?' Leanne's voice is barely recognisable. High-pitched. Desperate.

'Seen what?'

'Go to Twitter, Alice. It's horrible. You're tagged and I'm tagged.'

CHAPTER 37

HIM - BEFORE

The head teacher's office is bigger than he remembers. He's only been in here once before – when his gran was taken ill.

That time, years back, he was collected from his class and led here with no explanation. But he knew something big was up because they brought him lemonade and a chocolate biscuit. The head teacher asked a lot of questions about what relatives he had. She wanted to know if there was anyone she could call because his gran had had *a little upset.*

He told the head teacher that he only had his gran and her face sort of changed and she said he was not to worry but she needed to make some phone calls in the other office. He got more chocolate biscuits.

In the end, a weird woman turned up and told him again *not to worry.* Which made him worry a lot. She took him in her car to a house in town where a lady called Abby said he would be staying with her for a couple of days. He thought it was some kind of trick and was in a terrible panic. He wondered if he should run away but they took him to see his gran in hospital that evening. She said it was all *a fuss about nothing.* She'd collapsed at work and twisted her ankle and they insisted on X-rays. She kept asking the nurses to be allowed home, and when they said it was a bad idea, she began to cry. He remembers it really clearly – watching his gran cry.

There was another lady called Dawn at the hospital who said he could stay with Abby for a couple of nights until his gran was better. He asked to stay in the hospital instead but they wouldn't let him so he lied. He told his gran that he was fine with it all. Abby gave him pyjamas and some spare clothes. She was sort of nice but her house smelled a bit weird and he still didn't know if it was a trick. He had never been so afraid.

Then after two nights his gran turned up in a taxi and took him home, and he clung on to her really, really tight. She promised that they would never, ever have anything to do with *social services* ever again.

What's social services?

Busybodies. We don't need them poking about our lives. They'll take you away. You don't talk to them, you hear me? If anyone asks questions, you say we're fine.

Luckily it was half-term, so he stayed home and helped his gran until she could walk a bit better.

Today in the head teacher's office everything feels quite serious again. This time his gran is sitting right next to him. They had to wait until she finished work.

The head teacher is called Mrs Price and she looks very upset. She's trying to be all calm on the outside but her neck is red, right up to her chin.

He's eight now and he's better at reading people's faces. You learn a lot if you watch people really, really carefully.

'I simply don't believe my grandson would bully anyone,' his gran says. 'I think there's been a misunderstanding. He's a sweet boy. A gentle boy. I think he's the one being picked on.'

'The other child is in hospital with a broken arm.' The head teacher's voice is quiet but the red on her neck gets darker. 'This is serious. There are witnesses to say that this was deliberate. That the other child was punched and pushed to the ground and then kicked. Your grandson had to be pulled off the other child.' Mrs Price looks at him. 'Why did you do this? We can't allow this kind of violence. You are a very clever boy and you could have a great future. But you have to understand that this is very, very serious and I may have to consider a suspension. You need to explain why you did such a terrible thing.'

He remembers exactly. He was upset because of Brian. He was thinking about the disgusting 'favours' and the tin full of sweets and special chocolates which make him want to be sick. He was picturing all the things he would do to Brian when he was bigger. The hammer and the eagle attack. He got the volcano feeling in his tummy. And then Toby was saying some rubbish about his gran being very, very old-looking. Toby's grandfather had just died and they burned him in his coffin until he was just ash, like in the grate after a fire. Toby was saying a lot of stupid stuff about old people dying and how it was just natural; and he just got really, really cross with Toby until the volcano in his tummy exploded.

'It was an accident,' he says.

'There,' his gran says, taking his hand in her own. She squeezes it tight. 'A misunderstanding. Like I said. I'm quite sure there was provocation. My grandson would never hurt anyone on purpose.'

CHAPTER 38

MATTHEW

'It's my mother. Oh no – my mother. My mother!' Alice is now standing and staring at her phone, all the blood gone from her face. Ghost Alice. She sort of buckles, and Matthew's worried she may collapse completely and hit her head as she falls.

He reaches for her elbow to steady her and tries to steer her back to a stool, but she sweeps his arm away and starts shouting.

'No. No. Don't touch me. Oh Jeez. My mother. I think he's got my mother!'

'Show me. Alice. Show me what it is. I'm going to help you. But I need to see. To understand you.'

Alice looks at him as if she hasn't heard. She is gripping the phone, her knuckles white, as if she can't bear to let it go. He widens his eyes to encourage her – trying to coax her out of her shock. Finally, she hands him the phone, her fingers trembling and her eyes huge and wild with fear.

There's a video auto-playing on her Twitter feed. It shows a woman, gasping for breath. Yes. Struggling to breathe, as if suffocating.

For a terrible moment Matthew fears this is the posting of an attack. Some kind of strangulation? That the bastard has attacked

Alice's mother and posted the evidence. He sucks in breath to move into professional gear. He braces to watch the video again as it loops, and this time takes in the detail; he can see that the woman has oxygen tubes feeding into her nose. He frowns. Right. So it looks as if she is in some kind of medical setting. There's an oxygen bottle in the background.

'Has he got her? Is he with her? Has he posted this live? Is this happening this minute?' Alice now has tears streaming down her face.

'I don't know, Alice. But I'm phoning this in to the police and I need you to help me. Look at the video again and tell me if you recognise the place. The room . . .'

She shakes her head. She doesn't want to look.

'I'm sorry, Alice. But you have to help me.'

With his other hand he takes out his own phone. He presses the speed-dial key to Mel Sanders and prays she will answer. It starts ringing . . .

'Please, Alice. I know this is terrible. But you need to look again. Do you recognise the room . . .'

At last, Mel answers.

'Mel. Matt here. New development with the Alice stalker case. A video has been posted online of her mother in respiratory distress.'

'Jeez. So what's it showing? Is her mother hurt? Being hurt? Where do I see this, Matt?'

'It's tagged on Alice's twitter feed. @alicejournohenderson. All lower case, no punctuation. Alice is with me now. She's in shock, but stay on the line and I'll give you what details I can get from her.' He turns. 'Alice. Do you recognise the room?'

She won't look, so he puts the phone right in front of her face. 'I'm sorry, but this is urgent. The room, Alice. Do you know the room?'

At last she looks properly at the phone, a frown appearing instantly on her face. 'Yes. Yes, I do. It's her room at the home. At the nursing home.'

'You sure?'

'Yes. I'm sure. That's her bookcase in the background. With her copy of *Wuthering Heights* on the top. I read *Wuthering Heights* to her when I visit . . .'

Matthew puts his hand up to signal for Alice to wait a moment.

'Right, Mel. The video is apparently showing Alice's mother in her room at her nursing home. What's the name of it, Alice?'

'The Heatherdown Nursing Home. Mitsford. It's on the coast between Brixham and Paignton. Room 14. Second floor.'

He repeats the details to Mel.

'Right, Matt. I've got the video up now. Jeez. This bloody nasty piece of work. What's he up to now? OK – so I'm in Scotland. We're about to arrest Alex. I'll get a DS to phone the home right now. You do the same. See who's quickest to check the status on the mother. I'll get a car sent round immediately; see what we're dealing with.'

'This may not be live or even contemporaneous; this could just be a recording,' Matthew says. 'This could still be Alex.'

'Yes, I know. What a bloody turn of events.'

'Right. You get the call into the home and I'll try this end. Talk soon.'

Matthew ends the call and leans towards Alice. 'Call up the number of your mother's home. Dial it. Now. I'll speak to them.'

'Is he with her? Has he hurt her?'

'Just dial the number for me, Alice. Please. *Now!*'

She picks up her phone and fumbles for a minute through her contacts. Eventually she dials and hands the phone to Matthew.

'What's your mum's full name?'

'Harriet Wallace.'

'Right . . . Hello, I'm a private investigator working with the police. We have an emergency situation – reason to believe someone may intend harm to one of your residents, Harriet Wallace. Room 14. You need to check on her right this minute. I'll stay on the line and you need to report to me what you find. Immediately please. The police will be phoning too. They're on their way. You'll hear police sirens outside very soon.'

The receptionist is at first uncooperative. She asks a lot of questions, wondering if this is some kind of hoax. Matthew barks at her, demanding someone more senior. He's passed to someone else. He repeats himself and at last there appears to be action . . .

'OK. I'm holding on the line. You need to tell me if Harriet Wallace is OK. I have her daughter with me.'

This is now too much for Alice. She's slumped on to the floor – sitting with her back against the wall – tears pouring down her face as she uses the kitchen extension phone to call her sister with this update. She tells Leanne to wait on the line too. Then Alice is sort of mumbling almost incoherently to her sister. Blaming herself. Saying that Leanne was right; that they should have moved their mother to a different home as soon as the stalker used peonies. Mentioned her mother's favourite flower.

'We should have seen this coming. This is my fault,' Alice says finally, looking up at Matthew. But then the senior nurse at the home is back on the line.

'Mrs Wallace is asleep. She's well. She was on her own in her room. Stable. I've ordered a member of staff to stay with her. Do you mind telling me what on earth this is all about? We can hear police sirens. In fact, I can see a police car turning up outside. What the hell is going on?'

CHAPTER 39

ALICE

I watch my mother being wheeled on the trolley bed into the private ambulance. She's wearing a full oxygen mask so I can only see her eyes.

They're strained but I can read them precisely. Mum has raised her eyebrows just a little and is widening her eyes at me. I know from the nurses that she's uncomfortable and has pain in her chest and sides today. She's also very worried about what's going on here but she's trying to hide all this from me. Trying to signal that she's all right. Not to worry. That everything is *going to be all right.*

This breaks me. It's worse than the time with the police. Worse than the row I had with Leanne over the timetable of moving Mum. Worse than the rest of yesterday – *Wednesday, bloody Wednesday* – spent with Matthew Hill and then later with Tom as we all worked out the logistics of how to move my mother somewhere secret. Somewhere safer.

Though Mum's disorientated and tired and has the same severe breathing trouble she's had for the past six months, she knows nothing of what's really gone on. She doesn't know about the camera concealed in the plant delivered to her room, allegedly a 'gift' from me. She's unaware of the video posted of her online. The stalking. She knows only what we've told her, namely that her care needs are changing so we've decided it's best for her to be in a more specialised home near Leanne, who's not working and can visit more easily. And so our mother's priority, true to her nature and her selflessness, is to put us first. To show that she's all right. That people should not worry. Make a fuss.

I climb the two steps into the ambulance to hold my mother's hand and to stroke her hair back from her forehead. I again take in the smile in those pale grey eyes. The same face and the same reassuring expression that kept me safe right through my childhood.

It was always Mum. Only Mum. Dad died very suddenly of a heart attack when I was a baby and I don't remember him at all. But in school I would get upset on Father's Day when everyone else was making cards. Mum would have this same look in her eyes when she comforted me.

And when I sat my first piano exam too. I was nine and I was petrified. I was doing well in my music lessons and my teacher was predicting a distinction. But the pressure was all of a sudden too much. I froze when they called my name in the waiting room. I turned to Mum and asked her to take me home. Legs of lead.

I can't. I can't do it.

Mum stayed completely calm. She wasn't cross. She wasn't disappointed. She simply pressed her palm against my cheek.

Of course you can, my darling girl. I know that you can. There's no hurry. They'll wait a moment. And it doesn't matter how it goes . . . only that it goes. Just do your best and who cares how it turns out. Pass or fail, I certainly don't mind. And then my mother leaned in very close to my face with precisely this expression. Slightly raised eyebrows. A slight widening of her soft grey eyes with a smile of love in them.

Yes. That special smile that reads, *It's all right, Alice. It's going to be all right.*

I turn away to brush a tear forming. I wonder how I will manage without this force of love in my life.

'Now – you know that I'm not allowed to travel in the ambulance with you. Something to do with the insurance.' Another lie. Her mother's daughter. Papering over my worries just as she does. The truth is I'm nervous about being followed. I'm planning to drive in circles again to throw anyone off. I kiss my mother's forehead.

'Will you be OK with the nurse?'

Mum nods and widens her eyes even more.

'OK. Try to rest. And Leanne will be there when you arrive to help settle you in. The place is lovely. I'm sorry you have to move but they have the right nurses for you at the new place. And I'll be back to visit you very, very soon so we can finish *Wuthering Heights*. OK?'

Again Mum nods, moving her right hand to her mask, but I reach out to still her.

'No, Mum. No need to talk. I love you too. Try to rest. Leanne is going to send me pictures of your new room. It looked marvellous from her visit. They're transferring all your things. Your books. You're going to be very comfortable there; you're going to be all right. And I'll visit you very, very soon.'

One final kiss on her forehead and I go back down the steps and blow a kiss as the nurse closes the rear doors of the ambulance.

Why am I not braver? Why am I not braver?

Only now do the tears fall properly, as very slowly the ambulance pulls away.

I watch. A child again, watching Mum leave the playground when I was small, wanting to run after her. I'm back in that piano exam, Mum's voice a whisper in my ear. I'm arriving back in England after the horror of my time with Alex – Mum in the arrival hall at the airport. That same smile in her eyes. *It's going to be all right . . .*

I watch the ambulance get smaller and smaller and feel my nails squeezing into my palms. I wish I could travel with her but Matthew agrees this is best. Safest.

Everyone thinks that any more stalking and tailing is unlikely, which is why Matthew's not booked to watch my back today. Tom – in a complete panic after my mother's video was posted – offered to book

Matthew every single day until the whole investigation is resolved but I don't want that. I've had enough of it all . . .

It's Thursday. Alex is now in custody.

He's the prime suspect for the stalking. And prime suspect for sending the 'gift' of the pot plant with the hidden camera. The footage was eventually taken down after police intervention, but not before it had appeared not just on Twitter but on Facebook and Instagram too.

I take in a deep breath as I remember the messages from Leanne's friends. *Have you seen this? It looks like your mum.*

I try to imagine Alex in the interview room facing DI Sanders.

Will he buckle? Is it him?

Is it finally over?

CHAPTER 40

MATTHEW

Matthew flips three small pancakes with a metal spatula. It's forbidden – metal implement in a non-stick pan – but Sally's not here to police him. The pancakes are a good colour. They're also small and thick; American-style – the kind he and his daughter love best.

Matthew admires Sally's taste on most matters but in two areas, he's baffled. She is obsessed with opera, which he fails to understand. And she is *entirely* wrong about pancakes. She likes traditional pancakes – large and thin, rolled with lemon and sugar. Matthew shudders at the thought of all that flipping and burning and the sharp intake of breath when you taste the lemon. No. *All wrong.* This morning he's in charge, so there is jazz on the radio and the pancakes will be fat and fabulous.

'One order of pancakes with blueberries coming up, madam.'

'It's not a restaurant, Daddy. Why are you talking as if we're in a restaurant?'

'We can pretend it is.'

'Why would we do that? We'll have to pay.'

'No, we won't. My restaurant. My rules. Pancakes are on the house today.'

'Like on the roof?' Amelie frowns. 'You're a very silly daddy. How can I eat the pancakes if you put them on the roof?'

'No, no, no. *On the house* means free. But never mind, sweetie. Here you go.' He puts two of the plump pancakes into a bowl and spoons on some blueberries and a huge dollop of yoghurt. He puts a tea towel over one arm and delivers the breakfast to his daughter on her booster seat with a flourish that makes her giggle.

'Where's Mummy?'

'Mummy is picking up the dry cleaning. Now – be careful because the pancakes are still hot. Try just a little bit. Shall I cut it up so you don't burn your mouth?'

'No. I'm not a baby.' Amelie holds out her arm, rigid and determined, to keep him away. Matthew takes in the familiar warning in her eyes. *Do not let her see that I am a tiny bit afraid*, he thinks. *No tantrums today. Please.*

'OK. Well, try a tiny bit with the yoghurt to see how hot it is? Yes?'

'OK.'

Matthew watches his daughter cut the pancake with her little fork. Her eyes relax. Matthew's shoulders relax. He takes out his phone to see if there's a new message from Mel Sanders. He can still hardly believe how fast the investigation is progressing, and is praying she will say yes to his latest off-piste request.

He knows it's a long shot – asking to watch the Alex interview. More than anything at times like this, Matthew wishes he had an official role. Official status. A long time ago he had toyed with the idea of retraining. He was fascinated with different techniques for interviewing. Also profiling. He did a preliminary negotiation course once and loved that too; for a time he'd wondered if he could get a new qualification which might make him useful again to the force in some new and different guise.

But he looks now at his daughter tucking into her pancakes and reminds himself of the reality here. The need to earn a living. To make a go of his agency. There's no spare time for courses. He won't go back in the force – however much Mel urges him. No. Too late for any of that.

At last, his phone rings.

'Hi, Mel. So what's happening?' He pours some more orange juice into Amelie's bright pink plastic cup and spoons a few more blueberries into her bowl, his phone tucked between his chin and his shoulder.

'Well, he's furious. Claims we've infringed his human rights by stopping the marriage. Is talking about suing us.'

'Good luck with that, Alex. So – delusional?'

'Definitely. No surprise there. We're waiting for the duty solicitor, then they're doing the interviews about breaking his terms of licence first. The team are looking at his phone already. A string of messages to the girl since he got out of prison but we've found nothing yet to link him to Alice.'

'So can I come up? Be useful? I can help out if you go into labour early.'

'Shut up.'

'Seriously, I'd like to see the interview.'

'Oh, come on, Matt. You know I can't authorise that.'

'Unofficially. Sort of adviser. Observer.'

'You gone mad? You seriously want to come all the way up to Scotland?'

'I do. There's a flight from Exeter to Glasgow. I can be with you by mid-afternoon. When do you expect to interview him?'

There's a long pause, as if Mel is seriously considering this. *Good.*

'Oh, come on, Mel. You know we work best as a team. I can be helpful. We can bounce off each other. When are you getting a shot at him?'

'I'm just observing for now. When it's my turn for the stalker inquiry, I'm sending in a very good DS so I can watch and wait. You know how I like to play it.'

'Let me watch too. I want to see him. Please, Mel. I want to figure out if this is our guy.'

'Um. I think that might be my job.'

'Yeah – sorry. But it kind of feels like mine too.'

There's a long sigh at the other end of the line. 'Look. I can't make any promises, Matt. Come up if you want and I'll see what I can do. But it'll all be unofficial. We may have to tell some porkies.'

'You're a star.'

Just as he hangs up, Matthew hears the front door. He checks his watch and winks at Amelie.

'Right, my sweet pea. Mummy is home and Daddy has to go to work. I'm going on an aeroplane and I'm going to bring you back some haggis.'

'What's haggis?'

'It's like sausage only better. Absolutely delicious, I promise you.'

'As nice as pancakes?'

'Definitely.'

In the hire car from Glasgow Airport later, Matthew feels a pang of guilt at the little white lies he's had to tell Sally lately. He's still pretending his iPad is broken, and is planning to call again on Ian as soon as he gets back. Ian's now agreed to the monthly cost of an Internet package and is taking his iPad lessons very seriously. He should be up and running soon. Now Matthew has somehow implied to Sally that Tom is funding this Scottish trip. It's true that Tom is meeting his day rate again since Alice re-engaged him. But there's no sign-off yet for this special trip.

Matthew is well aware that he's more copper than businessman, and is wondering if he dares add these costs to the Alice invoice without prior agreement. In fairness, silver-spoon Tom has said *whatever it takes, I'll pay*, but Matthew can hardly make a legitimate case for this trip. The ball is in Mel's court now. It will take time for the techies to check Alex's phone and go over all the CCTV for his movements over the past few weeks. Matthew thinks it is highly unlikely Alex will admit to anything. He's already playing the victim and won't make it easy for them. In truth, it would make sense to just wait and see what happens. But Matthew is impatient; he badly wants to see Alex's face as he's questioned. He wants to get a feel for where this is going. In the past, he has had a good eye for spotting 'tells'. He trusts his instinct and needs to see this guy in the flesh. The bottom line is he would love for this whole sorry case to be over. For Alice's sake.

As he pulls into a parking space within sight of the police station, he feels the familiar surge of adrenaline that comes when a key suspect is in custody. Mel will be feeling the pressure too.

Inside, he puts in a request for Mel at the front desk and she appears within minutes. The sergeant on reception seems bemused. He queries Matthew's status but Mel suddenly starts fidgeting with her phone, pretending to check messages and then making a quick call, saying simply, 'He's here; five minutes maximum.' There are two other members of the public waiting to be seen by the front desk. Mel raises her eyebrows and stares at her watch. She signs for a visitor badge, giving only cursory explanations that Matthew is 'ex-job'; is deeply involved with the case 'down south' and is needed urgently for the interviews. For a moment Matthew thinks the bluff isn't going to wash, but then the desk sergeant glances between Mel's enormous bump and the people waiting in line.

Matthew gets his visitor's badge.

The station is small and he's led quickly through to a small room adjacent to the interview suite. It's nearly four o'clock in the afternoon and Alex has apparently been making a scene, complaining that he's feeling unwell. That he is being harassed. That *Brexit or no Brexit, I'm going to the European Court of Human Rights over this*. A duty solicitor has turned up and has already taken instructions. Mel explains that

Alex's position is that it is none of anyone's business who he marries. The girl's an adult now.

'So there he is,' Mel says, signalling with her head to the impossibly good-looking man seated on the other side of the one-way glass.

Matthew takes in a long, slow breath and stares at Alex. Suddenly he's thinking again of that terrible moment when the bike swung past them. The squirt of liquid into Alice's face. Those dreadful minutes when he thought it truly was acid and Alice's life would be changed forever.

It would take someone with extraordinary nerve to do that. Chilling arrogance.

He takes in Alex Sunningham's stance. He is leaning back in his chair with his legs stretched out in front of him. Arms folded. Narrowed eyes.

'I'm going to sue you,' Alex says very coolly.

OK. So – definitely arrogant enough, Matthew thinks.

But are you our man? He stares through the glass. *Was all of that really you?*

CHAPTER 41

HIM - BEFORE

Just two weeks and he'll be in double figures. Ten . . . years . . . old.

He has waited a long time for double figures. He thinks of his maths lessons in school. His new teacher has an abacus which she keeps on the shelf. A black frame with shiny red beads. He loves that abacus. In fact, he likes maths a lot now and works even harder in school. Top group. Top dog. He feels sure that things will change; that things will be different once he is no longer a single digit. Double digits on that abacus.

He longs to be taller and stronger too. He thinks of all the things he will be able to do when he is taller and older and can go to the gym and build up his muscles.

'What you thinking about?' his gran says. She is knitting him a new sweater for school. He does not want it. It's the wrong colour; the blue is too dark. The wool will itch and they will tease him. *Maybe your gran could knit you some pants too. Woolly pants . . . Woolly pants.*

'Penny for your thoughts?' She's still staring at him.

'Nothing.'

'Ah – yes. You children spend a lot of time thinking about that.' She is smiling but also glancing at the clock.

Wednesday.

When he's in double digits, everything will be different. When he's in double digits, he will not answer the door to Brian. He will put a chair against the door and pretend he cannot hear him knocking.

He will be going to big school soon and he'll start a gang. He'll tell them about Brian. Not the truth – not the dirty, stinking truth. But he will say that Brian has hurt his gran and needs to be taught a lesson. And they will all teach him a lesson together. They will make him *beg . . . and beg . . . and beg.*

He looks across the room at his gran, who is still smiling at him. He thinks of how tired she always looks. How hard she always works. He thinks of her baking cakes for him every Sunday – butterfly cakes with jam and icing – and making him boiled eggs with soldiers before school. And he thinks of her looking out of the window every day to say good morning to Grandad's bench.

'When I'm big, I'm going to look after you,' he says. 'So that you don't have to go to work at all.'

'Of course you will. And that will be lovely, my sweet boy.' She folds up her knitting and puts it into the bag next to her, glancing again at the clock.

She only works one night shift every two weeks now. She has done some deal with Stan at work. He doesn't know how.

So just once a fortnight there is the tap at the door. Brian with biscuits and banter. His big fat belly. And his little bargain.

One week he thought of just refusing to answer the door, but Brian has said it has been going on so long now that it is too late for second thoughts. No one will believe him and they will put his gran in jail for leaving him.

He closes his eyes and thinks again of maths class in school. He has learned that working hard gets the teachers off your back. He was suspended after hurting the boy that time the head teacher got cross. His gran cried and the suspension wasn't for very long. She said that education was his only chance to make something of himself. And so he decided deep inside never to make her cry again.

Now he has the class merit badge. He is in top groups for everything. And he has just been given a special school award to take music lessons free of charge. He can pick any instrument he likes.

He can't decide. Guitar or piano? He must choose soon.

He pictures himself playing music and he imagines people looking at him and saying, *What a clever boy*. He thinks it will be a good trick. People will listen to his music and will have no idea what is really going on inside his head.

They will never guess the truth. That he is thinking still of hammers and eagles and how long it will be before he grows, with his age in double digits – and is big enough and strong enough to start a gang and pay Brian back.

To make him *beg*.

CHAPTER 42

ALICE

I'm in a café when the email comes in from work. I've used up the 'breathing space' of my spare holiday now, and they agree with me that we need to make some decisions about 'going forward'. There's politically correct rubbish from Helen in HR about my safety being the priority, *blah blah blah*. There's an additional note from the editor saying he's again turned down police requests to tap the phone lines for evidence. I do understand. No paper could function if we agreed to that. But at least they see that a meeting's essential. *Good.*

It's still Thursday. Mum's settling into her new home and I need some routine back. I stir the foaming milk into the rest of the coffee and think. Yes – I so badly need to *get back to work*. I've written a blog for the charity but they haven't published it yet. They're worried about the timing with Alex's arrest, and want to wait to see the outcome. To be honest, Claire's emails have been a bit odd the past couple of days. She keeps going on about me trying her new alarm and writing about that instead. For some reason this is troubling me. I thought she said the alarm project was in its early stages.

No matter. I brush thoughts of Claire and the charity away and reply instead to Helen's email, agreeing to the meeting and stressing that I ideally want to return next week. It's been long enough. I'm not going to get heavy with them just yet, but I will if I need to. I shouldn't be the one paying the price for this creep's behaviour.

I put my phone back in my pocket and then, as I look up, there is the most extraordinary surprise. He's wearing a very smart woollen coat with a bright, striped scarf I have not seen before, so that for a few moments I am not one hundred per cent sure it's him. But then he turns and I'm shocked at the little punch inside. He looks so striking and I feel the familiar guilt because I don't feel this way when I catch sight unexpectedly of Tom.

'*Jack*. What on earth are you doing here?'

He looks utterly shaken too. 'Alice! Goodness.' His expression segues from puzzlement into pleasure, as if he can't quite process this either. But I'm pleased he seems glad to see me. 'I'm after a sandwich before an interview.' He fidgets with his scarf as if suddenly self-conscious. 'Local primary school. Teacher awards. What about you? Bit out of your way here, isn't it?'

'Loose end. Just been driving around. Well, sit down and tell me what's happening. By coincidence, I've just had an email from the office. I'm hoping to be back next week.'

'That would be fabulous. We're all missing you. Everyone thinks it's unfair they're making you take holiday. So, how are things? Have you not got your security guard guy with you?' He glances about, as if checking for Matthew.

'He's not a bodyguard. And no. Not today. Only Wednesdays. The key suspect has just been arrested, though I need you to keep that under your hat.'

'But that's *great news*.' He leans in to read my face. 'Isn't it?'

'Yeah – I guess.'

I am rewinding now to remember when I last saw Jack. Ah yes – at Leanne's, when he warned me that the editor was reallocating my campaign stories. The demolition of Maple Field House. I feel a smile as I remember that Jack has been looking out for me. I'm grateful.

'Sorry, sorry,' I say. 'I suppose I should be more relieved but I guess I won't relax fully until they find some proper evidence. It's a bit of a waiting game.'

'So who is it? The guy in custody. Someone you did a story on?'

'No. Not supposed to say. An ex, actually.'

'Dear Lord, I had no idea.'

And then the waitress appears and Jack orders a double espresso and a toasted sandwich. I wave my hand to signal I'm fine with just my drink.

'By the way – I'm really grateful for you tipping me off about the campaign story. The demolition of the flats . . . I met the organiser up in London so I'm right up to speed. I'm not letting Ted pass the coverage to anyone else. No way. Not after all I've put into that.'

'Oh – you're welcome. Anyway, if you're back next week, it'll be fine. So it's really all over? What a relief.' He's looking into my face as the waitress returns with his coffee, advising him the sandwich will be just a couple of minutes. I notice that he doesn't thank the waitress, doesn't even turn to look at her, and so I do the niceties for him, nodding at her and smiling until she's gone.

'It's just I've been really worried about you, Alice. We all have. I haven't wanted to intrude by email or text. I mean, I know you have Tom looking out for you.' For some reason he flushes – a red patch appearing above the scarf on his neck. I wonder if he is thinking as I am of that awful Italian meal. My faux pas.

'I'm fine, Jack. Well – no, that's not true. But Tom's been great and I'm managing, and I should know very soon if this nightmare is finally over.' I pause then, wondering if I should confide in him more. He seems to sense this, raising his eyebrow by way of question.

'We've just moved my mother to a new nursing home. Better facilities.' I don't know why I don't tell him the truth. He doesn't say anything so I assume he hasn't heard about the video. Some family friends saw it but why would anyone in the office be looking? 'I'm going up there later to make sure she's settled in. I'll feel happier then.'

'Good. That's good.'

The waitress is very soon back with the food, and I look at the melted cheese oozing from the golden bread. It makes me feel hungry and I'm just wondering whether to order one myself after all when my phone rings. I raise my hand by way of apology as I take the call. It's the editor's secretary, Samantha. She babbles an apology but says she's been updated about the meeting by HR and needs to change the time we just agreed. Suggests 3 p.m. instead of noon because Ted has a meeting over lunch.

'That's fine. No problem.' I add that by coincidence I am with Jack and he's packing away a cheese toastie.

Samantha laughs and then adds something which makes no sense at all.

'It's good to know what Jack gets up to on his day off.'

CHAPTER 43

ALICE - BEFORE

The first time my mother saw me with my new hair colour, I watched the change in her eyes. It wasn't long after Alex's trial. She tilted her head, taking in my new look, and there was just this momentary flash of deep sadness.

'Are you shocked, Mum? Do you disapprove horribly? Because if you don't want me to do this. The name change, I mean. If it's going to really upset you—'

'It's fine. The new hair suits you. And if this is what you need to do to put that blessed man behind you, then it's fine by me.'

'And you think you can cope? Me using my second name? That won't freak you out too much?'

And then my mother did that thing with her soft grey eyes. The smile that was set deep within them, to try to reassure me.

'I've watched you lose sleep, Jenny. I've watched you lose weight. I've watched you take those pills for depression to cope with the trial. Don't think I don't know about that. And the truth? It has broken my heart into pieces, and if I could get hold of that man, I wouldn't be responsible for what I might do to him. Leanne is right to have suggested this. I chose Alice for your second name because I love it. I can get used it. I will practise. You make a beautiful Alice.'

'I'm not going to tell them at the new job. I feel so bad about that. A journalist, a supposed seeker of the truth, starting out with a lie myself . . . What does that make me, Mum?'

'It makes you unlucky. Someone who met a snake, my darling. Lots of writers use a different byline. A maiden name or whatever. You have good reason. And it's not a made-up name. It's on your birth certificate. It's a name I chose for you.'

'But do I look different enough from the newspaper picture? I'm very afraid they'll find me out anyway.'

'You look beautiful. My beautiful girl. And the media didn't run much about you.'

I could feel my lip trembling as she hugged me. I still wasn't at all sure about what I was doing – morally or practically – but I didn't want Alex to win. To put an end to my career. To stop me writing. When Leanne first suggested changing my name, I thought she was mad. I said no – absolutely not. I was sure I would slip up, maybe answer the phone as Jenny and be the subject of another story. An exposé? But, over time, I just got angrier and angrier about Alex, and I didn't see what other option I had.

New name. Clean page. Fresh start. What did I have to lose?

I was still staying with Leanne when I decided to consider her idea. She started calling me Alice to see how it went. After a while, it felt OK. And then when – as 'Alice' – I was offered the new job as a trainee reporter in Devon, it suddenly felt doable. Far enough from Scotland for stories and contacts not to overlap, hence less likely for anyone to find me out. I knew that I would see less of Mum and Leanne than in recent times and wondered how I would manage without their support, but it couldn't be more difficult than Scotland in terms of the geography.

'I'll still phone and visit as much as I can, Mum.'

'Course you will.'

And then she asked the same question the police had kept asking me.

'Are you sure there isn't anything you haven't told me, darling? About Alex? About how all this dreadful business started? He didn't *hurt* you ever, did he?'

'No, no.'

'And there wasn't some trigger? Something that might have started—'

'No.'

I answered too quickly. Too loudly. I felt myself blush. I was still tired and weak and overwhelmed. But the truth? At night, something new had been bothering me. One very private thing. One small, embarrassing and intimate thing that I had not yet told the police because I couldn't bring myself to believe that it could have anything to do with what had happened. It was too embarrassing. Too personal.

I had been to counselling and they kept saying over and over that I was not to replay events and blame myself. That Alex was responsible for his perversion. His lies. His behaviour. Not me.

I had been duped. Tricked. *This is not your fault. You must not blame yourself.*

But for all the reassurance, I couldn't help – in the dark and silence of the night – still wondering. Picking over our time together. I felt so guilty for not seeing through Alex when he had the scene with the girl on his phone.

And this other niggling thing. The other private, personal thing that was about Alex but which I had stupidly brought up once and it had made him so very upset.

I didn't want to believe that it could have anything to do with it all. Because if it did? Would that make it my fault after all?

And was it my responsibility to mention it to the police? Even this late in the day . . .

CHAPTER 44

MATTHEW

'Are you sure you don't want a chair, Mel?'

Matthew watches Melanie Sanders press her hand into the small of her back, making her spectacular bump protrude even closer to the one-way glass between them and the interview room.

The police station in Scotland is smaller than any Matthew served in during his time in the force. It is also cleaner and brighter and tidier. He looks at a pinboard on the opposite wall with various posters neatly displayed. Recent appeals. Helpline numbers.

Finally Melanie lets out a long sigh. 'You're right. I'm being stubborn. Trying to put on a show, but the truth is I worry that if I sit down, I'll never get up. Jeez – this baby is in training for the Olympics today. Through there . . .' She points to a small room off the corridor and Matthew darts through to collect a chair, watching several eyes in the room turn to him in puzzlement.

'I've lied,' she confirms as she slumps on to the chair on his return, signalling that he should close the door to the corridor. 'I've told them you're ex-job and that you have crucial inside information on this case.'

'But that's true – not a lie at all.'

'I might have added that you're now a respected profiler.'

'Profiler?'

'Yeah. That shut them up.' She's smiling. 'And we all know what most of them think about profilers. They'll hopefully just gossip behind your back and leave us alone.'

They both stare through the glass. Alex is sitting next to his solicitor but the interviewer handling the parole issue has been replaced by Mel's colleague Mark Fisher, who is to lead the questioning about Alice. Alex is already certain to be returned to jail for breaking the terms of his licence, so has nothing to gain by cooperating.

Matthew does not expect him to be helpful. He strongly suspects his brief will have advised him to say nothing regarding this second inquiry. Sadly there's no evidence to put to Alex yet so this is just a fishing trip in case they get lucky. Matthew's hoping he will at least be able to pick up something from Alex's face and general demeanour while they wait for his phone to be fully checked.

'So, Alex. Back to jail, then. That wasn't very clever, was it?' Mark Fisher is a tad careful with his tone as he pauses, before slapping a picture of Alice – or Jenny, as she was – on the table. A picture of her with her darker, longer hair.

Alex Sunningham looks down at the picture and Matthew leans closer to the glass to watch his face. Not a flicker. Whatever he may be thinking, Alex is careful not to give anything away. *Damn. He's good,* Matthew thinks. *Very good.*

Alongside him, Mel seems to be holding her breath.

'So. Your fiancée. The one who knew absolutely nothing about what was going on.' Mark's tone is still steady. Confident.

Alex glances at his solicitor, who is also looking at the photograph.

'I find myself wondering how you feel about your former fiancée now, Alex? After your time in jail.'

There's silence. No reaction at all.

'Because here's the thing. We think you may have been stewing about what's happened to you these past few years. And that you've developed some kind of grudge. An entirely unfair grudge. Is that true, Alex?'

Still nothing.

Matthew turns to Mel, who still appears to be holding her breath.

Mark won't want to give much away in this early part of the interview. Without any evidence, he's simply goading a bit. He will be looking for Alex to dig a hole – to hopefully give away a small detail that he couldn't know without involvement. A starting point for the interview proper. But Alex doesn't even look puzzled. His face is entirely blank.

'Direct question then. Have you made contact or sent any message to or had communication of any kind with your former fiancée Jennifer Wallace since the court case? And most especially since your release from jail.'

There's a long pause. Again Alex, expressionless, turns to look at his solicitor before turning back to face Mark. And then it starts . . .

At first Matthew simply can't believe it. He exchanges a glance of astonishment with Mel. And then Matthew feels the full irritation and hopelessness of the situation as the noise gets louder and louder . . .

'What the hell is he singing?' Mel says finally.

'Opera,' Matthew replies.

'Yes. I can tell it's bloody opera. I'm not a complete philistine.'

'You need to stop that . . . right . . . now.' Mark keeps his expression calm but raises his voice to be heard over the singing while Matthew closes his eyes to listen.

You get quite a bit of singing in police stations. Drunks mostly, as they're led to the cells to sober up. Mostly it's very poor. Out of tune and the lyrics gibberish.

This is different. This is *good*. Matthew is surprised by something else too. A flicker of recognition. He listens some more, trying desperately to place it. He's frowning as he thinks hard and tries to tune in.

'I'm warning you, Alex, to stop singing right this minute. This is a serious situation you're in.' Mark then turns to the solicitor. 'Can you please advise your client to stop wilfully obstructing our inquiries and to cooperate with this interview.'

The solicitor shrugs as if there's nothing he can do.

'Look. If your client doesn't stop singing, he will be taken straight back to his cell until he quietens down.'

The singing continues . . .

'He's quite good, actually,' Matthew offers, opening his eyes.

'Unhelpful, Matt.' Mel is fidgeting with her wedding ring – twisting it round and round, apparently exasperated.

And then Matthew suddenly recognises it. Yes. The lyrics. *L'amour, l'amour!* . . . *Ah! Lève-toi, soleil* . . .

'This is *Romeo and Juliet.*' He feels a ridiculous sense of pride. 'In French.'

Melanie turns to him, eyes wide. 'And so who are you suddenly – Inspector Morse?'

'Sally likes opera,' Matthew offers sheepishly. 'She's got a recording of this. She doesn't speak Italian, you see. She likes this one because it's in French. Gounod, I think you'll find.'

Melanie shakes her head in astonishment as, inside the interview room, Mark announces for the tape that he's pausing the interview to return Alex to his cell until he stops singing. A sergeant then appears through the door and Alex is accompanied out, still singing at full volume.

'Well, that went well,' Melanie says finally, then stands. 'Shall we get coffee from the machine? They've given me use of an office while we wait to hear if there's anything on Alex's phone. But I rather think we're wasting our time, don't you? Unless we find any evidence, we're snookered. Bet you're sorry you came all this way now.'

In the small office, Melanie has a bulging briefcase with notes from Alex's previous interviews and the court case.

'No videos of the interviews with him last time round?'

'No, just transcripts. I went over them on the flight up.'

Just then, Mark pokes his head around the door of the room. 'Sorry, Melanie. Didn't see that coming. A first for me. An aria mid-interview.'

'Not your fault, Mark. Take a break. Go get a sandwich. I'm going to go over the notes again. Let's give it an hour. See if the Phantom of the Opera gets bored with his cell. If no progress, we'll let them transfer him back to jail and interview him inside once we've hopefully come up with some evidence.'

Mark gives them the thumbs up and closes the door.

'He's a good operator – Mark. Not as good as you of course,' Mel teases. 'But I don't think anyone is going to get anything out of our Mr Sunningham until we have something concrete to put to him. What a bloody waste of everyone's time.'

And then Matthew takes a deep breath.

'Romeo and Juliet. Young lovers.'

'Excuse me?' Mel's expression is once again pure puzzlement.

'I reckon our deluded narcissist is trying to cast himself in the role of romantic hero. That's what Gretna Green was about. Why he wants to marry her.'

'You kidding me? He seduces a fourteen-year-old and thinks casting himself as Romeo will wash?'

'But that's precisely it. He's deluded. Which means he's capable of anything. So can I look at the notes? All the statements from Alice before the trial.'

'No. Of course you can't,' she says – pushing the pile of folders towards him and winking. 'I'll go make us some coffee. See if you can spot anything I've missed. I couldn't find anything in the court notes or Alice's statements – or Jenny, as she was then – which suggests a motive to target her now. Her part in the trial was pretty small actually. It was all about the two girls, especially the one he seduced and dumped.'

Melanie leaves the room, returning after five minutes with drinks in large, chipped mugs. For the next hour they work together through all the statements and the notes on the trial. Matthew is surprised to find reference to a third girl. Also just fourteen.

'There was a *third* victim?'

Melanie takes in a long breath. 'You are absolutely not supposed to have access to that. But yes. Turns out a third girl came forward but she didn't want to give evidence so she was interviewed informally. Same pattern. Alex groomed her, slept with her then dumped her. It was at the very time he was getting engaged to Alice.'

'What a snake.'

'The team decided not to push her. They had enough to nail him without her evidence.'

Matthew continues through the many sheets, appalled at the bitter coffee and wishing they had time to pop out for a decent one. It's only after some forty-five minutes that he puts the trial notes and statements aside and scours through the files for any additional material involving Alice.

And it's then he comes across a single sheet of paper folded within one of the old files of statements. The date is odd. It is some time after Alex was arrested and charged.

Matthew smooths the paper to read half a dozen paragraphs. It's the record of a short conversation with Alice – then Jenny – at a London police station. She'd turned up to give some voluntary additional information to be passed on to the police in Scotland, stressing that she didn't want Alex to be made aware she'd said this. He reads it carefully. There is a stamp to confirm it was referred to the Scottish team but no further action seems to have been taken. Presumably they had more than enough evidence against Alex already, and Alice had said she would not repeat the information in court so didn't want it to be part of her formal statement.

Matthew goes back to the court notes and sees there's no reference to this material being put to Alex or any witness formally during the trial. It was clearly not used and he's not surprised. It wouldn't further the prosecution case and would have been worthless if Alice wasn't happy to back it up in court.

Matthew taps his chin. *Hang on.* What if someone mentioned this little nugget to Alex during the early and extensive interviews before the trial? To wind him up a bit.

What if Alex *knew* Alice had told the police this?

'Don't get excited, Mel. But I might just have found something.'

Matthew turns the piece of paper around to place it in front of Melanie.

'Turns out our Romeo had a sexual dysfunction.'

'What? Impotent?' Melanie is now skimming the sheet of paper, her brow furrowing as she pulls her chin into her neck. 'But he couldn't have been impotent. He was done for sex with the girls.'

'No. Not impotent. Something else. Alice didn't want this to be used in court. She just wanted the police to be aware in case it was relevant. But what if someone slipped up. Off the tapes. To wind Alex up a bit maybe? What if our narcissist guessed it was Alice who said this to police? Well – that would hurt his pride *big time.* He just might have stewed over this in jail. Bit of a long shot, I grant you. But it's just possible this could give us a motive for him to be mad at Alice.'

CHAPTER 45

ALICE – BEFORE

Good Lord – who wants to discuss their sex life with the police? It was bad enough first time round. When Alex was initially arrested, the investigating team wanted to know every blessed detail of our life in the bedroom. Sure – they tried to be sensitive. They apologised for intruding. But the bottom line was they needed to ask me a whole string of mortifying questions. Did Alex have any fetishes? Did he make me do anything strange? Was he ever violent? Was there ever any hint that he was into younger girls? Children?

I answered 'no' honestly to everything. Our sex life was normal. *Ordinary.* I remember using that word quite specifically. But I didn't add the absolute truth – that the question was quite frankly ironic. It was only later, after I returned to London to hole up with Leanne, that I began to stew over everything and wondered if I should have been even franker.

That's why in the end I decided to call into the police station nearest to Leanne's home and add to my statement.

Well, not *officially*. A female police officer took me through to a little interview room and I made her write it down that this was not an official statement.

'I'm not prepared to talk about this in court. No way am I discussing my sex life in detail in court. You need to write that down. It's very important. This is just information that you may find useful. I don't know. It's been on my mind. But I'm not saying any of this in court. The Sunday newspapers would have a field day.' I watched the female officer scratching away on her paper and strained to read upside down to ensure she was keeping up. She had lovely writing and was using a beautiful pen. Expensive.

'So what was it you felt we should know?'

I took a deep breath. It was hard to find the right words.

'No hurry. This can't be easy.'

'Understatement. Look, I was asked when I gave my original statement if Alex was in any way unusual in the bedroom. And I said no, which was the truth. I was asked if we had sex regularly and said yes. Which was also the truth.'

I waited for her writing to catch up before I continued.

'But what I didn't say was that Alex was . . .' I paused to roll my lips together. *Just spit it out.* 'OK. So Alex was actually not very good in the bedroom.' I watched the officer's expression change. She was clearly not sure how to react.

'Oh hell, this is mortifying. He wasn't terrible. Jeez – I wouldn't have got engaged if he wasn't OK. He was an extremely good-looking bloke and I found him very attractive. Before I knew the truth about him, obviously. He was a good kisser. And I suppose you could say that, overall, he was an adequate lover. Like I say – I agreed to marry him and I wouldn't have done that if it was completely terrible in the bedroom. But . . .' I took in another deep breath, aware that I was gabbling. Nervous. 'The truth is there were limitations.'

'Limitations?' The officer poised her pen.

I waited. She waited.

'He had trigger trouble.'

'Excuse me?'

I closed my eyes, wanting to sink into a very deep hole.

'Premature ejaculation. He couldn't last for very long.'

I fancied that I saw her smirk. Was I imagining that? I was certainly blushing.

'Look, I know everyone jokes about this. And it's supposed to be hilarious. But it isn't actually funny in real life. And certainly wasn't to Alex.'

'Right. So why do you think this could be relevant. To the case, I mean?'

'Well, I'm hoping it isn't at all. It's just I was a bit surprised at first with Alex. I mean, he was so sexy and confident when you first met him, that I kind of assumed he would be really good in that department. So the trigger trouble was a bit of a surprise. I didn't like to say anything. He brought it up actually after the first couple of times, and he told me that it was only a problem when he was infatuated. In love. Sort of turned it into a compliment. Said he was a bit overwhelmed by me and it would pass. But then later, when it didn't change, I started to get a bit worried. We got engaged very quickly. It was all very romantic. As I say, he was a good lover all round. He made sure I was – you know – er, *happy*. But this trigger problem didn't change.'

'But you were still happy in the relationship. Happy to get married.'

'Oh yes. I mean – I believed him that he was just a bit overwhelmed. That it would resolve over time. Anyway. After a while I decided to try to have a more open discussion – you know, a few ideas to address it. And he very quickly became really furious.'

'In what way?'

'Oh, just verbally angry. Not physical. I was a bit shocked at first but then I realised I'd hurt his pride. And I felt stupid and a right heel for being so insensitive. I mean, you know what guys are like. I decided to just let it play out over time. I was sure it would sort itself out. And as I say – all round I was very happy. It was before I knew the truth about him. About the girls.'

There was a long pause. 'So why are you mentioning this now?'

'Well, I've been stewing. I've been wondering and worrying if the reason he started chasing after younger girls is they would be less experienced. Might not criticise him. Know any different.'

The officer put her pen down. 'You're not blaming *yourself?* Oh goodness. You really shouldn't do that.'

'No, no. I know that, deep down. But I just felt I should perhaps have mentioned this. In case me upsetting him – you know, me so stupidly commenting on his performance in some way – contributed to his chasing after those young girls.' There. I had said it.

Was it my fault?

The police officer wrote everything down but said I had no reason to feel any guilt at all. She promised to pass the note to the investigating team in person. She checked if I was still seeing a counsellor, as recommended.

Two weeks later I got a phone call from the senior investigating officer, letting me know that they appreciated my additional information. They stressed that my confidentiality would be respected and wanted to reassure me further. They told me in confidence that a third teenager, just fourteen at the time, had come forward to say Alex had groomed and had sex with her *before* I even met him. He was apparently still sleeping with her at the very time he proposed to me. Her case was not to be included in the trial as she couldn't face the trauma, but they hoped it would set my mind at rest. I had played no part in Alex's choices. None at all.

I remember the incredible flood of relief. Then the senior officer was even blunter. He said that Alex's performance in our bed and our row over it was more likely to have been a consequence of his perversion, and certainly not any kind of trigger for it.

I remember taking a long, very hot shower and wishing I could stay under the water forever; wash away the whole sordid business.

What a mug, I thought as I lay on the bed afterwards, in Leanne's spare room. *What a complete and utter mug I was.*

CHAPTER 46

HIM - BEFORE

He had always imagined that once he grew up and got a job, he would move his gran to a nicer place.

Yes. Once he was able to look after her, instead of vice versa, he would rent her a flat somewhere far, far away from those terrible times. Far, far away from disgusting Brian.

So it was a terrible shock to find this wasn't going to happen.

His first job took him to London. His second to Sussex. And when finally he had built up a decent-enough income and savings to offer help, his gran's reaction left him reeling.

'Don't be ridiculous. Move? I can't think of anything worse. I don't need your money and I don't *ever* want to move from this place. Not ever.'

He couldn't quite believe it. He'd had it all worked out. He had saved and saved and he had enough for the deposit to rent a nice, modern flat closer to him.

'But I can get you somewhere so much nicer than this place. Warmer. A nicer area. You're retired now. Wouldn't you like to live somewhere nicer, Gran? I could get you your own place near me. Or I could get a two-bedroom place near to where I work now and we could live together.'

And then her face changed and she looked truly offended. She wandered through to the kitchen area to put on the kettle for tea, and as she waited for it to boil, she moved to stand by the window, staring down at the bench.

There was quite a long silence. A bad atmosphere. She kept glancing at him as if she didn't recognise him.

'You really don't know why I love it here?'

He shrugged, hating every minute of this.

His gran looked again through the window. 'He loved it here too – your grandad. He loved the view from this window. He loved his little shop and he loved sitting out there, having his lunch. It was always good enough for him and for me, this place. I love it here because of him. Why on earth would I want to move?'

'But Grandad would be pleased for you to be somewhere nicer.'

'*Nicer.* Are you saying it's not nice here?' She sounded hurt now. She turned and he fancied he saw tears in her eyes. 'This place you grew up in? I did my best, you know.'

'No, no. I'm not saying it's not nice. And I'm so grateful for all you've done for me.' He moved forward to put his arms around her to hug her. He felt the familiar shock of how small and fragile she felt these days. Like a little bird. It wasn't just that he had grown into a man. She had seemed to sort of shrink over the years.

'I worry about you, Gran. I want to take care of you the way you took care of me.'

'You do take care of me. I'm so proud of you. It makes me so happy to see you making your way. But please – don't *ever* ask me to move. It's what keeps me going. This place.' She stared out at the bench again. 'Saying good morning every day to your grandad's bench. All my memories.'

He watched then as she put teabags into the same red teapot she had used when he was a child.

He closed his eyes and thought of a thousand cups of tea down the years. And now there were other swirling scenes, his mind in overdrive. He had imagined that moving his gran would solve everything. So what now?

The visits from Brian stopped when he was around eleven. He never knew why. He wondered if he had found someone else to torment.

He had thought that when Brian stopped knocking on the door, he would be so happy. So relieved. But strangely, he wasn't. He just felt more and more dirty. And at night, he would get these terrible nightmares. He began to realise that he should have barricaded the door when he was younger. That he should have said no. Told his gran? Called the police? Why didn't he realise that he should have called the police?

He opened his eyes. He looked at his gran as she poured the tea and felt this horrible surge in his stomach like he wanted to be sick. He realised that he badly wanted to stop visiting this place. He had imagined he would move his gran and that would be that. He would never have to visit these horrible flats again.

'You will keep visiting me,' she said suddenly – a frisson of fear moving across her face.

He looked at her hand, trembling slightly as she opened the biscuit barrel to put chocolate digestives on to a plate decorated with roses.

He stared at the plate with its gold rim. He could picture his arm, reaching out for that same plate with his blue school jumper. The one she knitted. The one he was teased about.

And in that moment he realised that once more he would have to be brave. For his gran. To keep her safe. To make her happy.

He had put up with teasing about the jumper. He had put up with so many terrible things . . .

He would do this; he would put up with this place for love.

'Of course I'll keep visiting you. I love you. You know that.'

He was staring at his gran, remembering how on Saturdays she bought a single pork chop because he loved them. Pretended she wasn't hungry herself. How she took him to the library every single week then made him a reading den under the table with sheets and blankets; brought him biscuits and cakes on that same plate with the roses.

'And you won't ever make me move?' she said. 'Let anyone make me move? Put me in a home or anything silly like that. Promise?'

Still he just looked at her.

'Please. I need you to *promise* me.'

'I promise you.'

Her face relaxed and she glanced once more at the bench on the grass below their window. Slowly her smile returned and she signalled they should go across to the sitting room area. And as he followed her, he realised something else.

If his gran wouldn't move, not ever, he would have to do the thing he had dreamed about ever since he was a little boy.

He would have to deal with Brian himself.

CHAPTER 47

ALICE

It's Sunday and I am back in London, staying with Leanne again to check on my mother's new home.

It is very shiny and smart, this place; just as the brochure promised. More like a five-star hotel than a residential home. But it has no view of the sea. As I finish reading to my mother, I notice that her eyes are closing. She seems to sleep more and more these days as her sats levels get poorer.

'Enough for now?'

She nods her reply and I move across to kiss her forehead. She smells of Chanel. Good. They're taking care of the little details here too. Mum has always loved to smell nice.

'Do you miss the view of the sea, Mum?'

'It's fine.' Her eyes are closed so I cannot read the true reply. She seems to be drifting off to sleep and so I whisper that she should rest and I will be back to see her soon. But as I move she suddenly reaches out to grab my hand and squeezes it very tightly.

She holds on for longer than is natural, her eyes still closed, and I feel tears pricking the back of my own eyes.

I know, Mum. I know.

I smooth her hair, kiss her one more time, then put the book back on the top of her bookcase and leave the room.

We had a meeting earlier with the nursing team and I can see that this home is better equipped to deal with the march of my mother's disease. They do full 'end of life' care here. There will be no need to move her again to hospital or a hospice. Leanne has done her research well.

Mum is on maximum oxygen but there's a ceiling on how much this can help her now. The problem, we're told, is not so much getting the oxygen into her lungs but the fact that her badly damaged lungs can no longer process that oxygen. This is measured daily and is getting worse and worse. We're on a graph. The black line is plunging downwards.

We all know where we're going.

The staff are almost impossibly kind. They're efficient and I do trust they're doing everything they can. We are lucky that Leanne can throw money at this. I'm told the NHS is marvellous too, but I like that this home hires the best people. So much for my liberal politics. When it comes to your own, politics go out the window.

I think of my mum puffing away on her cigarettes in the garden when we were kids. She said she took it up after the stress of my father's death. A widow with two small girls. Can I blame her? As we got older Leanne and I both nagged her. But she called it *my one pleasure. My one failing.* In the end we gave up, and I feel guilty for that now.

I sit in reception to check my phone for messages. Nothing from Matthew or Melanie Sanders. What the hell is happening?

Is it Alex? Why would it be Alex? I need to know.

I glance around at the fittings. The beautiful fabrics of the curtains at the window on to the garden. The fresh flowers so carefully arranged on the reception desk. I think back to the time my mother moved into her first home in Devon and I wonder what she really thinks about the transfer here. She must be baffled. A struggle for her to get through each day with her breathing so very strained now. What must she be thinking really? I never ask if she's afraid of what's coming.

I am too afraid myself . . .

When my mother's COPD was first diagnosed, she was living in the family home a few miles from Hastings. It was where Leanne and I grew up and we loved to return there. Thankfully my father had good life insurance and a decent pension so we didn't struggle financially. It was a lovely home and lovely garden.

Her condition progressed slowly at first and we were told there was no set pathway with this disease. Every case is different. She was taught breathing exercises and seemed to manage OK for a while. But then she started to have episodes which put her in hospital, and things deteriorated with each one. Once it was obvious she could no longer live alone, we had a terrible dilemma.

Leanne immediately suggested this home near her in London. But Mum surprised us both by saying she wanted to spend a spell by the sea. Devon. Where we had enjoyed so many holidays when we were little.

Leanne was offended. I was secretly delighted. The truth? I think Mum wanted, for a time at least, to be nearer me. Jenny-turned-Alice, with no husband or family yet. I think my mother with her soft grey eyes – *It's all right, Alice* – wanted to be near me for a time. And so Leanne gave in. She wasn't working but I was. She could leave the children with the nanny to visit Devon more easily than I could travel to London. I had my job to work around and I was working shifts. So we all just got on with it.

And now an email pings into my phone from Claire at the charity. She's pressing again for my thoughts on the personal alarm and whether I would like to write an article for the website about it. I get this strange rumble in my stomach again.

I don't quite understand the switch – from initially implying the personal alarm scheme was perhaps not the right step for the charity to suddenly pressing for my support?

I decide not to reply. Instead I do some googling. I google Claire's background. I find her LinkedIn profile and some interviews about the charity. I find her private Facebook page but then I also discover an older listing not in use. Some of the posts are set to private and I assume she closed the page to protect her sister. But not all the security settings are in place. I find that I'm able to check older photographs and some of the older posts too. It's very strange. Some of it does not tie in at all with the things she told me when we met.

I do some more research, but my phone is too slow and the battery is low. I need to get back to Leanne's.

Something is not right here.

CHAPTER 48

MATTHEW

'So is Romeo still singing?'

'Every time anyone tries to question him.' Mel's tone is pure exasperation. 'Seriously. It should be made a crime, Matt. Opera during police interviews. I blame Morse on the telly.'

'So what's happening?'

'He's being transferred back to jail. Apparently he's very popular there. Runs a choir and smarms everyone to death. Word is he's encouraging his so-called fiancée to launch a media campaign about their "true love story". Her parents are trying hard to dissuade her. We may confide in her about that third teenager Alex seduced. See if that sways her.'

'What an utter creep.' Matthew presses his phone closer to his ear and unclicks his seat belt. He glances across at Ian's front door and checks his watch.

'Precisely. I'm desperate for the techies to come up with something. Alex was using two phones apparently. There were some searches for Alice using her original name Jenny on the second phone but no other evidence. May just have been curiosity. We have nothing concrete yet.'

'And still nothing on the flowers in the cake box? Or the bike used in the fake acid attack?'

There's a long sigh and Matthew regrets asking. Mel's doing her best. It's frustrating all round. They're up against someone clever. No prints. No forensics.

'OK, sorry, sorry. I know it's frustrating for you. Let me know if anything changes. I'm just desperate to know where we are. You know . . . with Wednesday hurtling towards us again.'

'OK, Matt. Speak soon.'

Matthew gets quickly out of the car and hurries across the road. He needs to keep this brief. When Ian answers his door, he's as smartly dressed as ever. Proper shirt. Crease in his trousers. He leads Matthew straight into the dining room to signal the new arrival.

'The module came two days ago. Three months' free trial. Are you absolutely sure it's not sending out dangerous signals? Radiation of some kind? I don't want to be radiated. Also I read somewhere that these devices can listen to you.'

'It's fine, Ian, I promise. There's no microphone in it.' Matthew asks Ian to fetch the iPad still on loan and removes the little square of plastic with password details from the modem. He sets up the iPad and is relieved to see it connect immediately. Ian has thankfully charged it as instructed. He's been practising, using all the notes he made.

'Good. We're up and running, Ian. You now have Wi-Fi, which means you can now use this iPad whenever you like to talk to Jessica. No extra charges – just the monthly Wi-Fi bill. I had a message from her last night to say she's coming off shift around now, so let me show you again how to call her up via Skype.'

Ian now looks a little stressed.

'I promise you'll get the hang of this, Ian, but you will need to concentrate. OK? And make some more notes.'

'OK, Mr Hill. I'm writing it all down.'

Matthew talks Ian through the steps and watches him scribble away in his little exercise book. He decides he will discuss his new hypothesis regarding the little people over tea once father and daughter have caught up.

Half an hour later, he reaches for a chocolate Hobnob and launches in. 'So, your daughter was telling me in our email exchange that it would have been your golden wedding soon. You must miss your wife very much, Ian. I'm so sorry.'

Ian doesn't reply. Matthew presses on. 'Jessie also says that it would have been your wife's seventieth birthday . . . around about the time the little people turned up.'

'I don't talk about the little people with Jessica.'

'I know, I know. I didn't say anything. I just put the dates together.'

Ian now stares at Matthew, his lip trembling. Matthew waits. They each sip their tea.

Finally Ian puts his cup down and lets out a long sigh as if giving in.

'So here's the thing. We were saving up to visit Jessie in Canada. Dream trip to celebrate our golden wedding. We had it all planned out. We scrimped and we saved every spare penny. Barbara wouldn't buy herself anything new. Put all the money in the travel fund. That green dress. It was her favourite. She wore it every birthday. I said she should have a new dress for her seventieth but she wouldn't have it. Wanted to save to see our daughter instead.

'And then she got sick. Pancreatic cancer. It was all terribly quick. And in the end I had to spend the holiday fund on her funeral.'

Matthew feels a change in the air temperature around him. The room is suddenly too still. Too quiet. He stares at Ian's perfectly ironed shirt and the crease in his trousers.

'I hung the green dress on the door because it made me feel she was still around. That she might get up and put it on. But then suddenly it upset me too much. I wished I'd made her buy herself some new things. Nice things. Why didn't I insist, Mr Hill?' He turns to look at Matthew. 'Anyway. I got in a pickle, staring at that green dress, but I didn't want to move it from the wardrobe door so I moved myself instead. Into the spare room.'

'Is that when the little people turned up? Guarding the room. Guarding the green dress?'

'I know what you're thinking, Mr Hill. You're thinking I'm completely barmy. A silly old fool.'

'I don't think that, Ian. Not at all. But I think the little people don't like solutions. Modems . . . and happier times. So let's see how things go now with you chatting more regularly to Jessie.'

'Good plan, Mr Hill.' Ian clears his throat and Matthew can hardly bear to see the strain on his face.

'You can borrow the iPad long-term, by the way.' Matthew tries to make this sound casual. 'I meant to say. I'm getting a new one. I don't need it at the moment.'

Ian stares at him and then takes in a long, slow breath.

'But we haven't even talked about your fee yet? I expect to pay. I've been putting a little aside from my pension. Every week—'

'Oh. Don't be worrying about that. We can talk about that another time.'

There is another pause.

'You are a very decent man, Mr Hill.' Again Ian clears his throat. Smooths his trousers. 'Very decent indeed.'

CHAPTER 49

ALICE

It's now Monday and I am booked on to a train this evening to return to Devon for tomorrow's work meeting. First-class ticket this time.

The police are going ahead with a harassment charge against the perv on my last train journey. Technically I'm pleased, though I'm not looking forward to giving evidence. I'm nervous of my link to Alex coming out – but what choice do I have? The guy who hassled me needs to be punished; I don't want him doing that to others.

This morning, I'm in work mode, using Leanne's study. It overlooks their garden with impressive views across Notting Hill. More and more I can see that living in London has its appeal. Last night Leanne and Jonathan took me for a meal on the South Bank. Seventh-floor restaurant with a vista to die for. I looked out over the city, street lights twinkling and car headlamps sweeping across the canvas which is so very different from my own landscape. Yes. Little by little I'm coming to understand my sister better.

I turn back to my laptop. The more research I do, the more it baffles and troubles me. I've traced the company records for the personal alarm that Claire has been trialling and there is no mention of the charity as a shareholder or interested party. Instead the company is in Claire's maiden name (which I found easily via her social media channels) and a mystery guy – Paul Crosswell. Googling him, he seems to have a chequered history in various areas of security. He's run several companies – two went bankrupt and a third, specialising in general home alarms, is currently in receivership.

All very odd. No option now but to make the phone call I've been putting off. It's a risk and it feels sneaky. If my suspicions are wrong, Claire will find out I've been digging behind her back and will rightly be furious with me.

But what if I'm right? It's taken more than an hour to get this number and I can't let this go.

I dial. Three rings. Four.

'Hello?' The woman's voice is hesitant. She answers the phone as if baffled at the technology. I wonder if she uses her mobile mostly and it's rare for the landline to ring.

'I'm very sorry to trouble you. But is that Claire's mother? Claire Hardy?'

'Who is this?'

'I really am sorry to intrude, but I'm a journalist doing a feature on stalking. And someone suggested I get in touch with your daughter Claire.'

'How did you get this number? Who are you?'

'My name is Alice. And, as I say – I'm a journalist. I'm hoping to speak to Claire about her sister and about her charity.'

'Claire doesn't have a sister. Whatever kind of journalist you are, you've got your facts wrong.'

'But I was told that Claire's sister had been involved in a stalking incident. Which led to Claire's involvement with the charity.'

'What charity? I have absolutely no idea what you're talking about. Look, Claire and I have been estranged for many years. She's an only child and quite frankly that's a relief. One daughter has been quite enough trouble, thank you very much.'

And then she hangs up.

I turn once again to the garden to watch a robin sitting on the chimney of my niece's playhouse. My mind is racing – in contrast to the robin, which is resting, tilting its head as if asking what I'm thinking.

I narrow my eyes, trying to work out what the hell is going on with Claire but my mind is wandering. The playhouse is making me think instead of my niece. It's a beautiful timber house, designed with a deliberately crooked door and crooked chimney. Yesterday I played tea parties with little Annabelle in there and remembered the games Leanne and I used to play when we were small. Dolls' hospital. Our favourite. We had a doctor's kit and would diagnose all our dolls' illnesses and prescribe treatments.

The memory of the doctor's kit makes me think again of my mother. That camera put in her room. I feel hatred suddenly. Anger and a knot of violent thoughts towards the man who posted that gross video of my mother's breathing. Her new home has been fully briefed. She's to receive no mail or gifts or anything at all to her room. No visitors unless cleared by Leanne or myself. She should be safe now.

Should be . . .

I think once more of that cold water squirted in my face. I put my hand up to my cheek, remembering the fear of pain and disfigurement. And then I think of what my poor mother faces so stoically every single day and my fear makes me feel ashamed.

Finally, I trek to the kitchen to make coffee, a headache starting. I'm still trying to process the puzzle of Claire and her charity. Is she a fraud? A trickster? What the hell is going on?

I return to the office with my drink and bury myself in more research. It's good to be working but it's liking diving down a rabbit hole. The deeper you go, the weirder it all gets. I find more evidence on social media linking Claire and Paul Crosswell. I find an old newspaper cutting of a civil court case against him over a security contract for a shopping centre. The court case failed and there was little press coverage. But with more digging I discover that Paul Crosswell was accused of providing false promises and disreputable business practices. So – Claire and Paul. *What exactly are you up to?*

I tap my fingers against my lips. This personal alarm. What if it's a scam? Linked to Paul's businesses? What if this is purely about making money; what if they're just using the women targeted by stalkers.

I realise I need more evidence. But why would Claire make up such a dreadful story about a sister? I realise that I am quite possibly on to a very good story here. It feels shocking that Claire would dare to try to use me, a journalist. But then I think of how vulnerable I must have seemed to her when I first made contact. My anger at her audacity now morphs to something else. Excitement? Yes. The adrenaline is pumping. I'm glad to have happened across a proper story after too long out of the office. If Claire really is duping genuine victims of stalking, she deserves everything I can throw at this.

I pick up my mobile and dial Matthew Hill's number. He may be able to help me investigate Claire and Paul. Also, I need to know what the hell is happening regarding Alex.

Is it Alex?

Is it over?

CHAPTER 50

HIM - BEFORE

He takes two weeks off work and watches Brian every day. He takes great care not to be spotted by his gran. A hat. Sunglasses. A large scarf wrapped round and round, covering his mouth. Shabby clothes.

Brian is a slob – even heavier now. He must be in his late fifties but looks much older. In the past he claimed to work for a bus company but there's no evidence of working now. These days Brian doesn't take his filthy, fat self far – mostly to the pub, the off-licence and the bookies. But there *is* a pattern. Good.

He makes notes on his phone checking Brian's precise movements each day.

His stomach crawls as he sees that some mornings Brian sits on a bench near a children's play park. Just watching.

And then he gets lucky. At the same time and on the same day each week, Brian makes a trip to the bookies, using the long and narrow alley behind the disused garages near the old shoe factory. Most people don't like to use that alley. Children are warned to keep away. Only a creep like Brian would take that route.

He checks the alley very carefully. No CCTV cameras anywhere near. Good.

He goes back to work and thinks every single day about how to do this. He has horrible dreams about the past. And then delicious dreams showing Brian's face as he turns and sees him.

Sees the hammer.

Just occasionally he wonders if he can really do this. But most days he's surprised to find that he is looking forward to it. The full stop. If his gran is determined to stay in her flat – if the place really means so very much to her – then this has to be done.

He waits a month and takes another week's holiday. He checks very carefully what to wear to limit the risk. Gloves, obviously. But there is so much more to think about. Forensics will look for fibres and hairs too.

He realises that however careful he is, he may be caught. Still, he finds that it is decided.

So he packs his change of clothes inside a sealed bag in his rucksack. He puts on his gloves, his hat and scarf and his sunglasses.

He checks himself in the mirror. And he feels alive.

For the first time in as long as he can remember, he feels *alive*.

CHAPTER 51

ALICE

I jiggle my right foot up and down and glance around me. It feels so weird to be back in the editor's office. It's Tuesday and I am thinking of that first phone call, when Jack brought me in here to report it to Ted. It feels a lifetime ago. A different Alice.

'So – are you happy with what Helen has suggested?' Ted raises his voice a little as if to draw me back into the room. Helen from HR is smiling, gathering her things.

I uncross my legs and put both feet flat on the floor. 'Yeah. Yeah. Sure. I'll start back on Thursday. I've got a good story to work on actually, Ted.' I see the glint of interest in his eyes. The paper may be dying but Ted's hunger for a story is not. He's old-school and will never stop chasing the headlines. I wonder what he will do when redundancy comes.

I wonder what I will do.

We both wait for Helen to make her excuses and leave the room. The compromise is that I've had to agree not to work Wednesdays until the police feel more sure that any threat to me has diminished. I will work Saturday or Sunday instead, taking each Wednesday as a day in lieu unless and until Alex is charged. The company claims to be thinking of my safety but is clearly still worried about what might happen on their premises. I suspect insurance might be an issue, quite apart from the moral debate.

'So, here's hoping it really is all over for you, Alice.' Ted is leaning back in his chair. 'Right. Let's hear what this story's about.'

I look at him and wonder if I should tell him that other truth. Who I really am. How I tricked him into giving me this job in the first place. No. Not yet . . .

'Got some more digging to do, Ted. But it's someone trying to rip off victims of stalking.'

His expression changes completely.

'Don't worry,' I say. 'I know what you're thinking but I can make this work without making it a totally personal piece. I'll find other victims. Hopefully someone local to comment other than me.'

He tilts his head.

'It's a good story, Ted. I have more work to do but it's about someone making up nasty stories to win people over and make a fast buck.'

'I thought we agreed no personal crusades, Alice.' He looks anxious. 'We can't be drawing attention to you on this topic. Not until the guy targeting you is caught, so if you work on this story, you keep me fully in the picture. No risk-taking.'

'Promise.'

Ted pauses then, frowning. He shuffles some pieces of paper before continuing.

'Look. I've not found this easy, Alice. Stuck in the middle with HR breathing down my neck. I want you to know that we'll do your own case justice, when the time is right; when they nail the guy. Trust me, we'll put the bastard on the front page, but I need a charge and a case. I've just got my hands tied for now.' He looks sheepish. Maybe even guilty? I don't know what to say in reply. I do feel upset that HR made me take holiday. But I haven't been straight with Ted myself, so who am

I to judge? 'We've missed you in the office, Alice. The place hasn't been the same without you. And we've all been worried.'

I feel touched. Ted never talks like this. I just nod my thanks as my phone buzzes. A message from Gill, one of the campaigners over the demolition of Maple Field House. I've already sneakily told her I'm back on the story full-time. She wants to meet up to go over coverage of the demolition. I daren't tell her yet that I'm not supposed to be working Wednesdays. I'll need to find a way round it.

I stand and move across to open the door, noticing again who's in the office and who is missing.

'Is Jack out on a story?' I glance across at my empty desk and Jack's space alongside it, then back at Ted.

'Late shifts this week. He's *definitely* been missing you. Like a bear with a sore head.'

'He just misses me fetching his coffee.' I try to sound light as I leave Ted's cubicle. I chat briefly to the three others bashing away on deadlines and then head out to my car.

I phone Gill to confirm I'm properly back from my break. She suggests doing a feature on one of the families already moved from the flats to a new house with a garden. She wants the story on the demolition to focus on the positives going forward. I agree and promise to talk it over further. Families are moving into new homes in phases. A lot are still in temporary accommodation while the new housing is completed by the local housing association. But I need to be careful that I don't put a gloss on the situation too soon. I need to check that things are moving forward smoothly and that everyone is keeping the promises made when the demolition was agreed.

Next I realise I must decide whether to stay on at Tom's or move back to my own house. I try ringing my landlord to double-check that the light fitting has been sorted and that the change of locks has been signed off. We've agreed a new, stricter procedure for who's allowed to handle spare keys for the property, and I need reassurance all is well before I return. There's no reply, only an answerphone, so I head back to Exeter to Tom's.

He'll be pleased, but I find as I drive that I am thinking of Jack – out of sorts while I've been off. I feel the frown. Why did the office think Jack was on a day off when I bumped into him at the café? He said something about a teacher-award story but I wonder if he's working on a different story on the quiet that he doesn't want anyone to know about. Maybe something for the nationals?

Jack's ambitious. I don't want to drop him in it with Ted if he's freelancing on the side. I'll ask him discreetly when I see him.

CHAPTER 52

HIM - BEFORE

It was not at all as he expected.

There was more adrenaline. More blood. More buzz . . .

Changing his clothes in one of the disused garages afterwards, he can feel his heart still pounding in his chest. He always knew this would be the most vulnerable time. If someone finds Brian too soon – before he has time to change and get away – he will almost certainly be discovered.

It will break his gran's heart.

But he has planned well and he finds that he is more exhilarated than scared. He moves quickly. He strips the bloody clothes and puts them in the bin bag inside his rucksack. The blood spurted further than he expected and he notices some flecks on the backpack straps. *Damn.* He should have thought to bring a second bag. No matter. They are only small specks and he will burn the bag along with all the kit later.

He changes his gloves, hat and scarf – careful to have brought spares of each. And then he sets off across the derelict car park past the old shoe factory, over the fence and across the patch of rough grass, weaving his way the mile back to his car.

He has checked all the camera positions and is meticulous with his route. He throws the rucksack in the boot of the car, on top of a plastic liner, and retrieves his wallet from the glove compartment, taking off the hat and scarf so he will appear different – calm and ordinary – if picked up on any road cameras.

He drives home carefully – no speeding – and avoids the motorway, then he quickly lights the log burner in his small sitting room. He watches the hot flames as he cuts up the bloodied evidence, feeding pieces one by one into the fire. Then he scrubs his hands and his nails and sets out on foot to buy fish and chips, making sure he strikes up a jokey conversation with the server. An alibi. Just in case. *No. I was home. Just watching telly, then fish and chips. Why?*

Later he sits with his chips and his tomato sauce and he finds that he is still exhilarated. There is no call from his gran. Or the police.

Nothing on the news yet.

He looks at the ketchup. And he closes his eyes to replay the scene over and over. Brian's shocked face. The thud of the hammer against flesh. And skull.

The shock at *so . . . much . . . blood.*

In his head, remembering all those years in school, dreaming of power; dreaming of an eagle with sharp claws. Swooping. Slashing.

Dreaming of being a grown-up.

On such a high now that his grown-up self feels so alive; that it was all much more satisfying than he could ever have imagined. So that in the end he couldn't help himself in that alleyway earlier; he kept the hammer blows coming long after Brian was still.

CHAPTER 53

ALICE

I place my hand just above the frying pan to test if it's hot enough for the fish. *Wow.* Searing.

'Not long to supper.' I raise my voice so Tom can hear me in the sitting room but there's no reply. I stand in the doorway to see that he has headphones on. I repeat myself even louder. He lifts one cup away from his ear – hears me say *supper* – and gives me a thumbs up. I smile. He smiles. I feel quite up this evening. It's Tuesday still, nudging ever closer to the next D-Day, but with Alex safely behind bars again, I'm starting to feel a little less afraid. And the thought of returning to work has really buoyed me. Also – I am moving back into my house on Friday. The keys are all carefully logged.

It's going to be all right, Alice.

I twist a little more salt and pepper on to each tuna steak before lowering them into the pan, stepping back to avoid the first sizzle. I want it to be a nice meal tonight, to thank Tom for his patience. For making me so welcome. I haven't found it easy spending so much time together. He knows this, and he knows too that I wouldn't have chosen for us to, in effect, live together like this so soon. But it's been a good bridge and I'm grateful. I can finally see a path back to calmer times.

I just need to be wrong; I need the police to say it was Alex after all. That it's over.

I check the clock on the kitchen wall and flip the fish. Great colour. I feel hungry and reach across the counter to pour two glasses of wine as my phone rings in my pocket.

Jack's name. I feel an involuntary frown – not understanding why he would ring at this hour. We're eating late. 'Hi, Jack. Sorry. Listen, I'm right in the middle of cooking. Late supper. Can I call you straight back?'

'I'm sorry, Alice, but I'm at work and I don't know how to tell you this.' His tone is terrible. Too quiet. Sort of sucked-in.

I move the pan off the flame.

'What is it?' Yes, I remember now that Ted said Jack was on lates. He'll be in the office for another hour or so.

'There's a big fire, Alice. I've just picked it up on the final round of calls.'

'What?' I don't quite understand. Then I feel a change in my stomach. I picture Jack making the routine check calls to the police and the fire service. But why is he calling me? Is he not able to cover it? Needs my help?

'Right. So why the call, Jack? Anyone hurt?'

'No. Not as far as we know.' A long exhalation of breath. 'Look, the thing is . . .' There is a strange pause.

'What, Jack?'

'It's *your house*, Alice.' Another pause, as if to let me take this in. 'The fire's at the house you rent. Two pumps are there. Neighbours have got out safely. I don't know how much damage yet. I'm going there right now.'

It takes about forty minutes by car. Tom insists on driving. I just sit in the passenger seat. Mute. Dazed. Both my hands trembling in my lap.

A million thoughts are swirling around my brain. I realise that I really was banking on being wrong; that it was Alex after all. *So does this mean it isn't? And why Tuesday night? Not Wednesday? Did the stalker think I was at the house?*

As we approach the final corner, I can see the flashing lights of the emergency services reflected in the windows of neighbouring homes and off the shiny finish of cars parked along the street. And then we are on the road itself and the shock is electric. No flames now but thick, black smoke soaring into the night sky. Maybe a dozen people still on the street, huddled together with alarmed faces. Some on their phones. Others trying to manage their children.

I stay in the car for a moment, just staring up at my bedroom window. The frame is entirely blackened and a large part of the roof is caved in. I cannot help it; I imagine myself in there. The heat. The flames. I cannot think of anything worse than being trapped in a fire. I find myself wondering if I would jump. I think of the many terrible stories where people have had to make that choice.

'Would you jump?'

'What?' Tom is clearly thrown by the question. He screws up his face, looking up at the building.

'If you were trapped in a fire, would you jump?'

He unclips his seat belt and shakes his head. 'You need to stop thinking like this, Alice. Look at me. You're OK. You're safe. We should probably get you a cup of tea or something – for the shock. I don't think you're ready to talk to the police yet.'

'Sorry?' Still I am imagining myself at the window. Would the smoke overcome you before you could decide?

And next there is a new and terrible thought. *My things.* I don't care about my clothes but I am suddenly remembering there are other precious things . . .

'Oh no – my things, Tom. All my mother's letters. My mother's letters were in there.'

'Oh, goodness. I'm so, so sorry. Look, are you really sure you're up to this? To speaking to the police? Or is it too much, Alice? Do you want to leave – get a hot drink or something first?' Tom puts his hand gently on my arm.

'No, no. I'm fine. I need to find out everything I can. And I need to know if anything can be salvaged.'

I get out of the car. Automatic pilot. Reporter mode. I speak first to the fire officer in charge, explaining it's my house and pressing for what we know so far. He confirms no one was hurt.

'And how bad's the damage? Is everything lost?' I am picturing the bundle of my mother's letters. They were in a drawer beside my bed.

'I'm so sorry. We did what we could but it's very bad inside.' He pauses. 'Especially upstairs.'

I see the neighbours watching me, their faces turning away to whisper as he leads me a few steps away from the throng to bring me right up to date. Apparently the fire took hold really rapidly. It will take time to confirm the cause but it looks like some kind of crude petrol bomb was posted through the letterbox. No witnesses. Neighbours heard a bang but by the time they realised what was happening and got everyone out of the attached homes, there was no sign of who may have done this. No car. No bike. No shadowy figure. Nothing.

'And *definitely* no one hurt?' I stare into the fire officer's eyes, needing to hear the answer again.

'Thankfully not. The neighbours were quick. Could have been very much worse. We're just checking everything over. Police are involved, obviously. They'll want to speak to you. And we'll be liaising with them when the cause is confirmed.'

'Of course.' I glance across the road and for the first time notice two uniformed officers talking to some of the witnesses. I wonder if the news will have reached Melanie Sanders yet.

And then I see Jack. He's just finishing talking to some of the neighbours, scribbling furiously in his notebook and signalling to the photographer to get a picture of the family.

I watch him doing his job calmly and assuredly – careful to reassure the witnesses as they stand, solemn-faced, for the picture. A couple in their early thirties. At first they have their backs to me but as they turn, I recognise them. James and Louise from three doors down. Their two children – a boy of around ten and a girl much younger – are in pyjamas with blankets thrown around their shoulders. I watch them, trying to remember the children's names. Jack thanks them all before turning to suddenly spot me, immediately heading across the road towards me.

'Alice, I'm so sorry. How are you doing?' He puts his hand on my arm.

'How do you think she's doing?' Tom's tone is clipped. His expression guarded. I notice him glance at Jack's hand on my coat and feel awkward; I am pleased that Jack is here – as awful as this scene is – but I don't want Tom to know this.

'Thanks for ringing me, Jack.' I reach up to move a strand of hair from my forehead so that Jack has to move his hand away.

And then I look into Jack's face and try very hard to read it. He looks concerned but there's something else; some other strange frisson. I can't help thinking back to bumping into him at the café when he said that he was working but the editor's secretary said he was off. I badly want to ask him about that. But not in front of Tom.

'Sorry. I need to make some calls, Jack. My landlord.' I turn to Tom then. 'Melanie Sanders. And Matthew Hill too. We need to phone Matthew.' I try to sound calm and in control but my mind is now racing and there is a tremor to my voice. I can feel my hands beginning to tremble; I realise that I cannot keep this up and I turn suddenly back to Jack.

'I've lost everything, Jack.' My tone is incredulous, as if I am only now truly taking in that this is real – not just a story for the paper but *my* story. I put my hands into my pockets to hide them as I look back up at the blackened window of my bedroom. '*Everything.*'

CHAPTER 54

MATTHEW

Matthew cannot stop pacing. The phone call from Alice has confirmed his worst fears.

Escalation. The word is bouncing around his head, his brain spooling through all the research he's read. But why the fire on Tuesday and not Wednesday? Is there even more – maybe even worse – to come tomorrow?

Mel is not answering her phone, which is not surprising. She's probably en route to the scene of the fire.

He's in the kitchen and can hear, via the baby monitor on the dresser, Sally trying to soothe Amelie, who has woken after a bad dream. Something to do with a dog. He pauses for a moment to listen to his daughter, his heart lurching as she describes teeth. *The dog had really big teeth, Mummy.* Sally is trying to coax Amelie back into the real world. *You're awake now, sweetie. You're perfectly safe.* Matthew finds himself holding his breath. Amelie at last seems to be calming down. Next, Sally begins to sing. Matthew can imagine his wife smoothing their daughter's hair. He moves to the dresser to turn down the monitor and begins pacing again.

Arson. He saw it often enough in his time in the force and feels a shiver right through him as he realises what this means. This is not like the fake acid attack. The nasty video. The cake box. This is a big step up. Yes. *Escalation.* It's the key word used in all the stalking research papers. The issue researchers are so keen to analyse and try to understand. The tipping point – the signal that stalking might lead to physical violence, even murder.

Escalation.

Up until now, Alice's stalker has been about terror. Fear. Control. But – *arson?*

Matthew is trying to work out if the timing of this points to Alex or away from him now.

On the phone, Alice had assumed this now ruled Alex out, but Matthew's not so sure and has warned against early assumptions. Alex could well have made some dark contacts in jail and might be using them – quietly furious that he's back inside. It's way too early to draw conclusions.

The most critical challenge now is how to keep Alice safe. Matthew finds he's pacing again. He badly needs to speak to Mel to see what resources she can muster off the back of this attack. It raises the bar on the threat to Alice but he still doubts police protection will be an option. The police can't even provide surveillance for domestic abuse victims.

The huge dread and associated responsibility is fully dawning. He will remain the first line of defence for Alice. Tomorrow . . . Wednesday . . . and going forward.

Matthew thinks back to that awful case in training. The pictures of Rachel Allen's body on her bathroom floor. So young. Such a waste. He thinks too of that first meeting with Tom and Alice in his office and remembers precisely why he was nervous to take this case. Short of providing bodyguard protection 24/7, stalking is almost impossible to counter.

He glances again at the baby monitor to see the flickering light calming; Amelie must be settling down properly. Just a few minutes later, there are footsteps on the stairs and Sally appears in the doorway.

'She OK?'

'Yes. She'll be fine I think. I don't know where that came from. I don't want her to be frightened of dogs. But what's up with you, Matt? You look terrible.'

'Arson attack on Alice's home. She wasn't there but it takes everything up a gear.'

'Dear Lord. Anyone hurt?'

'No. Thankfully not.'

'But it's a Tuesday. I thought this nutter struck on Wednesdays.'

'Yeah. So did we.'

Sally sits down on the chair by the dresser. 'Oh heavens, I really don't like the sound of this, Matthew. I mean, I feel for this woman – of course I do. But aren't you booked to mind her tomorrow? No, no . . . no, Matt. I don't want you putting yourself in harm's way like this. I thought there would be way less danger out of the police force. Having your own business. Picking your cases. We've just had that big payment in. You don't need to *do* this—'

'Come here.' He beckons to Sally and takes her into his arms. He knows she's right really. He can't make this OK for Alice, not on his own. Sally had been relieved when Tom fired him temporarily and was upset when Matthew agreed to go forward with the case after all.

'You have to think of me and Amelie now, Matt. You can't be putting yourself in danger. I mean . . . *arson*.'

He smooths Sal's hair and pulls back so that he can kiss her on the forehead, the moment interrupted by his phone. He takes it from his pocket. Mel's name at last.

'So what's happening?' He pulls a face by way of apology to Sal, who shakes her head in resignation and moves through to the sitting room.

'Definitely arson, Matt. We're going to speak to Alex again. He could be using a contact.'

'That's what I wondered.'

'But he may just sing in our faces again so I'm feeling pretty stressed, between you and me.'

'There could be something on CCTV this time. Every new incident means a new risk of him making a mistake.'

'I guess.' There is a long pause.

'You OK, Mel?'

'Not really. This will get me more resources for the investigation, and I need to know where Alice plans to be tomorrow – and going forward. I can get uniformed patrol cars to do drive-pasts but you know I can't protect her properly.'

'I know, Mel.' He pauses. 'But that's not your fault.'

'But it *feels* like it, Matt. So what do you think? Is this Alex paying someone . . . or is it someone else entirely? Do you think whoever it is really wants to *kill* her, Matt? Just between us. I'll be honest and say that, after that fake acid attack, I thought it was all about terrorising her. Inciting fear rather than actual violence. But now I'm afraid he could go the whole way. That this could be Rachel Allen *all over again*. Is that what you think now? That he may try to kill her?'

Matthew takes in a long, slow breath. The word *escalation* echoes once again in his head. He is remembering not just Rachel Allen but another case cited in the research, of a woman who was stalked for ten months. She kept telling her mother that she was sure she would one day end up on the news. She did. Her stalker drowned her.

'I won't be saying this to Alice, but I think it's possible, Mel.'

'Yeah. Me too.'

CHAPTER 55

ALICE

I am back in Leanne's huge, shiny Dorset kitchen in a strange agitated daze, exacerbated by too much caffeine. *Wednesday now.* Tom has taken the day off and Matthew Hill is here too, monitoring the TV security system and forever marching around – checking the doors and the windows and occasionally outside too, pacing the grounds.

Leanne has been on the phone, talking about hiring bodyguards. Putting the cost on the company, but I can't be going down that route. No way to live. I mean – when would it ever end?

The arson attack has been on the local TV news all day and something new is suddenly occurring to me.

'Hang on. Do you think *that's* why he seemed to change the day – why he did it late last night? Tuesday night, I mean.' I address the question to Matthew, who has just come back in from the garden and is closing the bolts on the French doors from the kitchen on to the patio.

'Sorry – I'm not following you, Alice.'

'So it would be on the news all day today. *Wednesday.* That this is my torture this week. My burned home on the telly . . . all day Wednesday.' I tilt my head towards the large TV screen on the wall near the large stainless-steel fridge. The sound is off but the picture is zooming in on the upper floor of my house. The ticker tape beneath the picture confirms arson and that a full investigation is under way. I notice the police have been careful not to mention the stalking threat or the link.

Matthew shrugs but then narrows his eyes as if reconsidering the point. 'Possibly. But why not just do it early Wednesday?'

'Because he needed it to be dark not to be caught. If he'd done it late Wednesday, most of the coverage would have been Thursday. An attack very late Tuesday guaranteed coverage all day Wednesday.' I realise as I listen to my voice that a part of me wants to believe this narrative because I don't want to imagine yet more trauma. *Today.*

'It's possible, I suppose. Who knows how this kind of mind works? But we can't assume nothing else will happen today. We need to be vigilant. And the important thing now is to talk through how we go forward from this, Alice. After today, I mean. And what's happening about the plan to return to work. I take it you're reconsidering that?'

'No choice, actually. My editor's been in touch. Asked me to take another week off, minimum. Until we hear more from the fire investigation team. I think he's worried they'll burn the office down. Or that the stalker will pose as an interviewee. Something like that.'

Matthew exchanges a glance with Tom and I feel some new tension in the room – something I can't quite read.

'What? What's going on between you two?'

'Nothing. It's just we were talking, when you had a nap.' Tom is trying to soften his voice. He glances again at Matthew. 'And we were just wondering if you should maybe get away for a bit, Alice. Complete change of scene.'

'What – *run away*, you mean?'

'No. But – look, my parents are still on this cruise, as you know. They're just about to spend some time in Italy. How about we join them for a bit? Meet up for a few days in Italy.'

'On the cruise?'

'No, not the cruise. We could get a hotel on the coast somewhere and just meet up with them. Relax. De-stress a bit while the police look into this.'

I don't know why I feel so cross at this suggestion. Tom has wanted me to meet his parents before – in Paris. I said no to that too. It's too soon. One day I walked in on him Skyping them and he asked if I wanted to say hi, and I made an excuse. I felt he was cornering me. It's too full on. Meeting the parents. It makes me think of my time with Alex. The engagement ring. The whole blessed nonsense.

'I don't want to go to Italy. I don't want to run away. I mean – how long would I have to keep running? *Hiding?* This is ridiculous. I've done nothing wrong and yet it's my life that's been completely turned upside down.' I can feel tears coming and that's not what I want either. 'Anyway, my mother's not good. The nursing staff are worried. Leanne just brought me up to date. I can't be going on trips. I need to visit her this weekend as normal. There's no way I'm missing the visit to my mother.'

Again they exchange a strange look. More resigned. More worried.

'Of course. Sorry. It was just an idea.' Tom's tone is apologetic. 'Shall I make some more coffee?'

'If I drink any more coffee, I suspect I'll start bouncing off these walls.'

'OK. Peppermint tea it is.' He heads over to the kettle and I stare at his back as he tries two drawers, looking for cutlery.

I hate peppermint tea but Tom is doing his best. I am being a cow. I can't help it because I'm not sure how much more of this I can take. This feeling of utter helplessness. Playing the sitting duck.

'Actually, can we forget the tea? I think I'm going to take a bath. Try to calm myself down. Any more from Melanie Sanders?' I look again at Matthew, who checks his phone and shakes his head.

I don't know why I keep clinging to the hope the police inquiry will come good. Alex has been questioned again but is still refusing to cooperate. To make matters worse, I mentioned to Matthew about Claire Hardy at the charity and that has now backfired on me. He's informed Melanie Sanders as if Claire might be a suspect in my own stalking. Ridiculous. She's trying to con people as far as I can see, not stalk them. I made it clear that I made contact with the charity, not the other way around, but Matthew says they could have used Facebook ads to target my stream – to put the name of the charity in my mind. They can't afford to miss any possible line of inquiry. And Claire has a dicey boyfriend. So they're now checking her out. Complete waste of police time, if you ask me.

I watch Matthew put his phone away in his pocket and head upstairs.

Leanne's Dorset home has four bedrooms with their own bathrooms, plus a huge separate guest bathroom with a beautiful roll-top bath. I decide against the small shower adjoining my bedroom, as I feel a bit more nervous in there. The guest bathroom is off the main landing and somehow feels better. This is what my life has become. Worrying which bathroom feels safer . . .

I lock the door and glance to make sure the window is closed. I find some bath oil on the shelf and fill the tub to three-quarters so I can sink right in. The scent is lovely. Vanilla with some other note I can't quite make out. The warmth of the water does indeed feel soothing and for a moment I feel better. But then as I sweep the bubbles over my arms there is suddenly a strange tapping noise at the window. I freeze. I listen – hoping I imagined it. But no. There it is again.

Now I sit bolt upright, the water surging as I do so – creating a wave which sends water splashing over the top on to the marble floor tiles. I want to leap out of the bath but am worried I'll slip on the wet floor. I have to twist my neck awkwardly to get a view of the window. And now – a myriad of emotions. Because the moment I look at the window, I see the ridiculous truth. The clear shadow of a branch from a tree, simply tapping against the glass in the wind.

It is then that the tears come. The shame of the depths of my fear. My overreaction. Frightened by a mere branch. The horror burning a stamp on my flesh that my life has been reduced to this. I can't work. I can't function. My home has been burned down. My mother is sick. I honestly can't imagine that my life will ever be normal again.

CHAPTER 56

HIM - BEFORE

When the police turn up at his home, he imagines it's about Brian. After all these years, he wonders what has finally led them here. Some new forensic discovery? Some witness who never came forward before?

He's settled in a new job now and his mind is all at once buzzing. What mistake did he make? What have they found? Most of all he's worried about his gran. Who will look out for his gran if he's arrested? His mind is in overdrive and his heart is pumping but he keeps his face calm. Maybe there is still some way out of this. He will admit nothing.

He will *say* nothing.

He allows them into his home. They stand in his sitting room, glancing around. And then the female officer says that she is very sorry but there is 'some bad news about your gran'.

The two officers exchange a strange look. He thinks it might be pity. He doesn't understand. And then he can feel his head twitching and there is this strange dizziness deep within him. They are still speaking but he's now in this bubble so their words cannot quite reach him.

He is looking at their mouths, watching their lips move and willing them out of his home. He does not want them here. Does not need to hear any more of this rubbish.

'You must have made a mistake. I'm sorry but I'm going to have to ask you to leave now.'

'I'm so very sorry but there's no mistake. Can I perhaps make you a cup of tea?'

'No.'

Much later he is in this terrible place which smells of chemicals and some other floral scent that is perhaps supposed to cover up the chemical smell. It fails. They have tried to make the room look respectful and calm. They have wasted their time.

It looks as terrible a place as he can ever imagine.

There is a sheet over the face of the woman who is dead. Still he is certain there has been some mistake. His gran would not do this. He's warned again that the circumstances of death have led to a distortion of her appearance. He must brace himself. They need him to identify her. They are *very, very sorry.*

The sheet is lifted back and there is that terrible twitching of his head again. He cannot believe it and so he closes his eyes. It is as if time is this long, slim tunnel and he is being sucked away from this room – back, back, back. He is a small boy blowing out the candles of his birthday cake – his gran smiling at him. He is in the park on the slide – his gran waiting at the bottom, beaming. He is in his bedroom, knees curled up to his chin, dreading the knock-knocking on the door on a Wednesday night.

There is a voice now. He opens his eyes to find they are asking him if he is able to confirm this is his grandmother. He's back in the bubble and they repeat themselves and so he nods. They move to replace the sheet but he shakes his head and holds up his hand to stop them.

He looks some more.

He cannot believe what has happened to her. He looks at the dark distortion that was once his grandmother's beautiful, soft and ever-smiling face, and he swears deep inside himself that he will find who made her do this.

He will make them pay.

He will go to the ends of the earth until he has understood who drove her to this terrible thing. And he will *make . . . them . . . pay.*

CHAPTER 57

ALICE

Leanne has sent their company driver to take me to London this time. No more trains. It's Friday and the traffic is dreadful. I feel a bit ridiculous sitting in the back, to be honest. Like royalty or something. But the chauffeur is a nice bloke; he drives well and, though he's friendly, he's taken the hint that I don't want to chat.

We are only about ten minutes away from Mum's new nursing home, and so I message Jack again. He tipped me off early this morning that he's now been pencilled in on the news desk diary to cover the demolition of the Maple Field flats in my place. He feels bad about this; he's worried I'll be upset with him for taking on *my story*. My position? Quite frankly I'm furious with Ted, but there's also this small relief that he chose Jack – as I would still like to find a way to quietly play a part. *Somehow.*

I've bounced this past Jack and asked him to keep it under his hat. Tom and Matthew will go nuts if I share this plan too soon. But Jack is more nervous than I anticipated. He's like an echo of Ted now – worrying about my safety. The demolition is Wednesday, after all. My thinking is I will go along – low-key and entirely in the background – if Matthew can be persuaded to come too. That story means a lot to me. I'd just like to see it through. See the wretched place come down. The look on the campaigners' faces.

I won't step forward. I won't make any kind of fuss. I just want to be there.

'Right. Here we are. My instructions are to walk you inside. That OK?' The chauffeur is unclicking his seat belt.

'Fine by me. Thank you.'

He gets out and opens my door. Again, it feels a bit formal, but I don't want to cause offence. Good of Leanne to arrange this. She means well.

Inside I am pleased to see they follow strict procedure at reception, checking my ID before issuing a visitor pass. They also confirm that rules about deliveries are in place regarding my mother. *Good.*

I am escorted to the lift and up to the second floor by a second member of staff. Not sure if this is the norm or they are trying to impress, given the police have been in touch too.

My mother's room is as lovely as I remember it from the last visit. I glance at the little table in the corner where there are fresh white roses in a glass vase. I feel worried for a moment, remembering the pot plant and the concealed camera at the last home, but the nurse follows my gaze and confirms that Leanne brought them with her yesterday.

And then I turn to my mother. Who is still in bed in a pale blue nightie, propped up with pillows.

'She's feeling a little weak today so we're going to leave it a bit longer before she's dressed. Is that a problem? Were you planning to go out into the garden?'

I shake my head. *No.* I don't have the courage to take my mother outside. Not with all this unresolved.

There is a pale pink velvet chair alongside the bed, and I find it is unbelievably comfortable.

'Hello, Mum.'

Her eyes open instantly at my voice.

'My *lovely girl.*'

Three words. Still her maximum.

I smile, fighting the surge of tears inside at seeing her deterioration. For the first time, her skin looks the wrong colour. Her lips have a bluish tinge. Leanne warned me about all of this on the phone, but every change with every visit still shocks me.

My mother nods towards the bedside table where *Wuthering Heights* is ready. We always keep to this deal. Leanne will sometimes play cards with my mother. Or Scrabble. Other times they will sketch together – a skill I do not have. But the reading job is *mine*.

'So. Where were we?' I open the book. There is a new bookmark at Chapter Twenty. It's a child's effort and it takes me a moment to recognise it. Pressed flowers – pink and purple – under some kind of plastic covering. Not properly laminated; this is like the cruder covering we used to use for schoolbooks. Yes. I remember now these sheets, with paper which you had to peel off the back. There is a hole punched in the bottom of the marker and a faded pink ribbon tied through it in a bow. I tied that ribbon myself. Primary school? I was probably no more than eight.

'Where did this come from?'

'The box.' My mother tilts her head again. By the fireplace on the opposite wall there is a silver storage box which Leanne must have brought on her visit. I picture it in a different place – stored at my mother's home under the stairs. We haven't rooted through that box for years. It's full of all sorts of family memorabilia, mostly things that Leanne and I made in school.

'You getting sentimental?' I try to make my tone teasing, but in truth I am thinking of all those precious letters that I lost in the fire. I don't want my mother to know any of my nightmare so I fight the tears and find a smile instead. My mother shrugs before smiling back and signalling with her hand that I should start reading. She closes her eyes. Wheezes. Her chest barely rising at all with each breath. Lips still too blue.

I read for no more than fifteen minutes before she falls asleep again. I ring the button and the nurse arrives to confirm that this is the normal pattern now. My mother finds it difficult to stay awake for very long. The lack of oxygen.

'We talked about this?' The nurse is searching my face as if to check if I'm facing up to what is really going on here. I just nod. Can't speak.

I ask her to say goodbye for me and to tell my mother that I'll visit again very soon, then I carefully place the book with my bookmark back on the table. I press my hand on the cover for quite some time before I feel ready to peel myself away.

Outside, I tell the driver that we need to take a small detour on the way back to Leanne's home, and give him the postcode for Claire's mother's address. She may not be home and she may refuse to see me, but I am still a journalist, even if they won't allow me back into the office just yet, so working on this story feels like the right thing to do. If Claire and her partner are trying to rip off the victims of stalkers, I have to do something.

The address is a terraced house divided into three flats and I realise the odds are stacked against me. I would have better luck with a bell and a front door. An intercom gives me less of a chance to plead my case. She won't be able to see my face. *Damn.*

I press the small buzzer.

'Yes. Who is it?'

'It's Alice – the journalist. I phoned about your daughter Claire. I have some new information that I need to share with you. It's very important.'

'I told you, we're estranged. You need to go.'

'I think you're going to want to hear this.' A punt. A fib. There is a long pause, and then to my astonishment there is the buzz of her releasing the door lock.

'Come up.'

Claire's mother looks curious as she lets me into her small flat. It is neat and bright with a red velvet sofa and cream cushions. Not what I was expecting at all. For some reason I had imagined something sadder and more disorganised.

'So, what's this new information you think I'll want to hear?'

'I don't want to cause offence, and there's no easy way to say this, but I'm worried that Claire may be involved in something shady – possibly illegal.' I watch her face. She does not look shocked at all. 'OK, so my research suggests Claire and her partner may be using a charity to try to trick people out of money.'

She makes an odd noise, letting out a puff of air. 'Well, that wouldn't surprise me.'

'Really?'

'I take it she's still hanging around with Paul Crosswell?'

'I don't know for sure, but she's set up a company – an alarm company for victims of stalking – with him. She told me she had a sister who'd been stalked. A nasty attack. She said she'd had to move abroad and that's why Claire is running the charity.'

'Utter rubbish. She's an only child, like I told you. He'll have put her up to this.'

'Can I sit down?' I take out my notebook and pen from my bag.

'If you must. But I can only give you five minutes.'

There's no offer of a drink, and despite my best efforts Mrs Bruce is clearly keen for me to leave. She doesn't want to go on the record but she shares enough for me to know that I'm on the right track with this story.

Paul Crosswell is the reason Claire and her mother are estranged. And Hardy isn't Claire's married name, as I'd assumed. Just a new cover, apparently.

Claire and Paul apparently have serious financial difficulties. He first tried to set up a different kind of security alarm system – for business users. It went to the wall and there was a police inquiry which came to nothing. Turns out he told customers there was a call centre which put queries straight through to the police where necessary. Just like the pitch Claire gave me. But there was no call centre. No grand system. The calls just went through to Paul's personal phone. He was charging customers a hefty monthly fee for a service which was a scam. Users would have been better off phoning the police themselves.

I tell Mrs Bruce that I think they're trying a new version of the same scam with the stalking charity.

'How would they pull that off? Are there not checks and balances with charities? Regulations?'

'Technically, yes. But criminals can work round them.'

'That sounds like Paul. He's certainly set up and dissolved a whole string of businesses.' There is a pause, and she stands as if deciding this is enough.

'Look, it's why we're estranged,' she says finally. 'I told Claire I want nothing to do with her until she steps away from that dreadful man. I made her choose.' She looks sad for a moment. 'Naive of me. Stupidly, I thought she would choose me. I'm sorry, but I really do need to ask you to go now.'

I leave my card, and in the car to Leanne's London home, I ring Matthew to update him. I feel sad for Mrs Bruce but am quietly excited about the story.

He's not.

'I thought we agreed that you need to leave this to the police, Alice.'

'I'm sorry?' I'm a little shocked at his tone. We agreed no such thing. He just said it would be wise to let Mel look into Claire and her boyfriend. It's the first time since my real name came out that Matthew has sounded truly cross with me.

'Mel's still looking into Paul Crosswell and he's a nasty character. Not just fraud. There's stuff you don't know; he's had a couple of charges for actual bodily harm too. He could be a suspect, Alice.'

'Oh, come on, Matthew. I told you – I approached the charity, not the other way around. There's no way this pair are involved with my stalking. They're just trying to rip people off and they're hoping to use my writing.'

'Please, Alice. We're still checking this out on our end. You need to keep a low profile. Keep yourself safe. And you need to leave this alone.'

CHAPTER 58

ALICE

Somehow the days pass. The weekend. Monday. Tuesday. And now here we are again . . . *Wednesday.* Every week now I ricochet between fear, anger and boredom. I've endured well over a month of this and I'm exhausted.

I'm fed up especially with feeling so isolated. Too many people telling me I can't be a journalist just now is extra salt in my wounds. I fire an email to the head of HR at my paper, telling them that I have now used up all my spare holiday as requested and I demand to return to work. I reiterate that I'm prepared to take every Wednesday off, as we agreed, but warn that I'll take my case to an employment lawyer if they continue to keep me from my desk.

As soon as I've sent the email, I slightly regret it. A part of me can see their point of view. In our last meeting, I cited cases of much higher-profile journalists facing trouble with stalkers. They weren't stopped from working. 'We're not the BBC,' was the response. 'We're a local paper in financial difficulties, fighting to survive. We don't have the resources the BBC has. We don't even have someone full-time on reception, Alice. We can't just get all the mail X-rayed. It's difficult.'

Difficult? They think I don't know this is *difficult?*

I stare at the screen of my phone. *Wed* – white lettering on a blue background . . . again. So soon. I am at Tom's flat and the agreement for today is that he will keep an eye on me until Matthew turns up at 10 a.m. It's very early still but I have been awake since the early hours and so he brings me coffee. He is as patient as ever but I'm like a cat on a hot tin roof. Pacing. Sounding off. Wound up.

I am just updating Tom about the email to work when the intercom buzzer sounds. It's an early courier with a parcel. Tom is visibly relieved. He's expecting important papers for a tricky contract he's negotiating. He tells the courier to bring the parcel of papers 'up to the second floor, please'. But the guy says he's wearing a motorcycle helmet and the company rule is they're not allowed to visit upstairs flats with their helmets on. People complain. Tom tells him to take his helmet off. But the courier says he's pushed for time – *Do you have any idea how little time they allow for each delivery?* – and either Tom has to come down or he'll mark it as a non-delivery.

Tom tries arguing but the guy says he's not paid to argue.

'Oh, just go down, Tom,' I say.

'No way. I don't like to leave you.'

'The flat's secure. You need the paperwork. Are we saying we can't receive any deliveries any Wednesday ever now? Even for your work? I mean, this is no life, is it? It's getting ridiculous. Just go down. Get your papers. Stop fretting.'

I move through into the kitchen and flick the switch on the coffee machine. It's still dark outside and I check the time on my phone as I wait for the green light for an espresso. There are a few emails. I flick through them one by one. Nothing very important.

It is as I am still turned towards the worktop that it happens.

It is all so fast that I have no time to think. Or to hit back. To grab anything to stop this.

There is suddenly this gloved hand cupped round my face with a large cloth over my mouth. I can smell chemicals. And leather.

I struggle hard, flailing my arms and trying to reach the worktop. But it's no good. I can smell something sweet now. I expect to collapse but this does not happen immediately. I feel my brain numbing and am suddenly being sucked into this dark tunnel. I keep flailing my arms. I struggle hard and I try to scream through the cloth. I know that I must not go into the tunnel but the lights are fading into the distance until I am so far, far away that they are gone completely. Consumed by the darkness.

When I wake up, my head is thump-thumping and I cannot see properly. Still there is this strange smell. Slightly sweet. My mouth is covered but my eyes are not. But I cannot see anything at all. Somehow I cannot make my vision work properly and so I close my eyes, trying to sense how long I was out, where I am and what is happening.

Am I still in Tom's flat? I can't tell. *Oh dear Lord. What has he done to Tom?*

I am sitting. I can feel a hard surface beneath my bottom. My hands are tightly bound at the wrists. I'm on a chair? Yes. It's a wooden chair of some kind. I can't think of a chair like this in Tom's flat. So I've been moved?

I try opening my eyes again and this time they slowly begin to adjust.

I am in a room that I do not recognise. At least not at first. I look around. Some kind of kitchen-cum-sitting room with the curtains drawn and a main door to the right. I try to take in other details. To place where I might be.

There is a strange mix of pictures on the wall. The Queen. A rather kitsch print of some rural setting with ducks and geese, and alongside it a large framed school picture of a boy with a big smile and a big gap between his front teeth. I glance around, my head still pounding, but there is nothing else to help me. A wooden magazine rack. Empty. Some kind of bag on the floor by a tall-backed chair. Shelving in the corner of the kitchen area.

Only now do I take in just how tightly my mouth is covered. Taped. I move my hands instinctively to try to reach up to take the tape from my mouth but they are tied firmly to the arms of the chair.

True panic is rising now. Sometimes, at night, I struggle to breathe through my nose – especially during the hay fever season. I start to feel this deep, deep dread. What if my nose gets blocked now? If I can't breathe through my nose, I will simply suffocate. I will die. I look around this bleak and terrible space and imagine that this is where everything could end for me. I can feel my breathing quicken with my panicked thoughts and I tell myself that I have to find a way to calm myself. Have to keep my nose clear. *You have to breathe, Alice.*

And that is when he appears from an adjoining room. He's dressed all in black. Black trousers. Black jumper. Black gloves and some kind of black balaclava.

And this is when I realise that what I thought was fear before was nothing of the sort. All those weeks – afraid of my stalker? That wasn't real fear.

I let out this strange animal noise, stifled through the gag as the dark figure sits on the high-backed chair across the room from me.

This is what real fear is.

CHAPTER 59

HIM - BEFORE

He is shown his gran's suicide note at the police station. It is in a plastic evidence bag. A single line on a sheet of white paper. Her familiar neat writing in blue biro. They let him take a photograph, using his phone, but he's told that he cannot have the note and file back until after the inquest.

'What file?'

They produce an A4 folder in another, larger evidence bag, and tell him that his gran was collecting cuttings from the local newspaper about the future of the flats. She had also just received a final notice to quit from the company responsible for the housing block, along with a letter from the local council urging her to agree to a meeting with the housing association which would offer alternative accommodation.

The police officer tells him that his gran did not respond to any of the letters about sorting out her new home. All this will be set before the inquest.

He struggles to compose himself in front of the police officer. He had talked with his gran in the past about the stupid local campaign to get the building demolished.

It'll come to nothing, she had said. *They're always sounding off. Been moaning for years. But I'll be fine.*

He'd been busy at work. He'd not visited his gran as often as he should. A little part of him was worried because of the inquiry into Brian's death. But he consoled himself that his gran was happy. She was in the place she loved and he had promised that she could stay there. He had helped make it safer. He had got rid of the putrid infection who lived next door. He had done his bit.

Two months later, at the inquest, he is the only person to attend. No press. No other friends. There are just a few people waiting for the next hearing.

Only now does he alone fully *understand* what really happened.

He received a package from his gran two days after her death. A long letter and her diary. She must have posted them to him before she . . .

He closes his eyes during the hearing, picturing her writing the letter at the table. The police said he must hand over anything relevant – but no. He will not give the letter or the diary to the police; he will give them nothing more of his grandmother. What do they care? Justice is *his* job now, not theirs.

The A4 file found at the flat contained cuttings from six months back, when a local journalist suddenly took up the campaigners' case. Alice Henderson.

The coroner is shown the many cuttings from the A4 folder and seems puzzled. Questions are asked. Was this elderly woman tired of waiting for a new home? Was that it? Was she struggling with the poor conditions in the flat?

The police say neighbours were questioned but had no helpful insights. The elderly woman was a very private person. Kept herself to herself. She was not involved in the campaign and was not known to have discussed it with anyone. There was no record of correspondence with the local authority.

The post-mortem confirms severe arthritis and there is speculation that the pain from this might have been magnified by the damp conditions.

There are no neat conclusions. All the court has is the short suicide note left on the kitchen table.

I can't go on. I'm sorry.

He watches the coroner looking through the pages of newspaper cuttings once again. And then the man rereads his gran's note – not out loud but quietly. His face is grave and sad.

The coroner leaves the room for a bit, then returns to say that he is satisfied that his gran took her own life, though the precise reason remains unclear. The verdict is suicide. The horrible truth is his poor gran took many pills and then put her head into the gas oven. The gas eventually cut out apparently, but not before she had suffered. Vomited. The reason her face was so red and distorted when he was asked to identify her body.

He wonders – this terrible burning inside him – how long it took for her to die. What she felt. What his beloved gran *felt*. All alone.

After the hearing, he is called to the police station and is allowed to take the final single-line note and the folder stuffed with all the newspaper cuttings. All written by Alice Henderson. Her picture is at the top of some of the longer features. He stares at the face. Alice with her neat hair and her neat smile. Do-gooder Alice. Know-it-all Alice. Some middle-class, privileged bitch who knows nothing of real people's lives, and just took it upon herself to back the stupid campaign and to push and push and push until the politicians began to listen.

At home, he rereads his gran's diary. The true story. The *whole* story – how she became more and more desperate week by week when the campaign suddenly and unexpectedly found wings through Alice wretched Henderson. The tone of his gran's daily jottings changed further as the campaign gained even greater momentum. From the final entries, it was clear she was beside herself. She wrote that she simply could not face a future living somewhere else. Away from her memories. Away from the beloved bench. She had always thought the campaign would come to nothing and was shocked to be proven wrong. She cursed Alice Henderson and her stupid local paper. *Why couldn't she leave it alone?* She scribbled that she told no one how she felt because what was the point? Local authorities never listened to people like her. So when the notice to quit arrived, she made her decision. She would not move. No way . . .

She asked him in her letter to keep the diary safe, as she did not want strangers poking about in her business.

He holds that final letter in his hand again. He has read it so many times that he can recite it in his head. Once more he imagines her sitting that last time at the table to write it . . . all alone.

He has not cried since he was a child. Since those terrible Wednesdays with Brian. He thinks of what he did later to try to keep his gran safe. He thinks of Brian in that alley. The blood spraying. The hammer blows. *Bash, bash, bash.*

He hated that place – the housing block. But she *loved* it. His gran. And he loved her. So he came to accept its future in his life for the sake of the only person who had ever cared for him. He did the right thing for her. He was strong. And he *promised* his gran she could stay.

He watches a tear drop on to the letter as he scans the words, his gran's voice in his head.

> *My dearest boy.*
> *I am writing to explain a bit. You must try not to be too cross with me or too sad. This is best for me. I am so proud of what you have become. Please, please forgive me and go forward in your wonderful new life.*
>
> *I am just not strong enough to move. I cannot bear it. Too old and much too tired, my beloved little soldier.*

*I honestly never believed it would come to anything –
this demolition campaign. They've been moaning for years.
But this Alice woman has suddenly whipped it all up. It's
in the paper every week. And it's all gone wrong. They've
given me a date to get out.*

*And I can't face it, my sweet boy. I'm so sorry. I just
can't.*

Your loving gran. Xxx

*PS I'm sending you my diary because I don't want
people poking about in my business. We never liked
that – me and your grandfather. People knowing our
business.*

He wipes his face and tells himself that he will never cry again. He needs
to find something better than tears. He looks again at the final newspaper
feature – tucked into his gran's diary – trumpeting the decision to
demolish the flats. The headline: WE DID IT!

He spits on the picture of the journalist and recites her name out
loud.

Alice Henderson.

CHAPTER 60

MATTHEW

Amelie is perched on her booster seat, ready for her second breakfast. She woke early again this morning and Sally was a heroine, leaving him to lie in while she negotiated early cereal, early warm milk and cartoons on the telly. Matthew smiles, remembering the days when they were sure they would *never* allow telly early in the morning.

'Still hungry, princess?'

'I'm not a princess. I don't have a crown.' Amelie pauses and tilts her head as if reconsidering. 'Could we get me a crown?'

'I'll look into it,' Matthew says, avoiding eye contact. Negotiations over royal apparel could most definitely go downhill.

'Why does Mummy make skinny pancakes?' Amelie is frowning as Sally puts a plate of large, traditional pancakes in the centre of the kitchen table. She rolls one on to a smaller plate for Amelie, sprinkling sugar and drizzling lemon juice and slicing the long tube into bite-size pieces.

'I like fat pancakes. Daddy makes fat pancakes. Why are some pancakes skinny and some pancakes fat?'

Matthew is about to intervene when his phone rings. Caller not recognised. It's a call forwarded from his office.

'Hi. Matthew Hill. Can I help you?' He's not on duty with Alice until 10 a.m. and was hoping for a quiet breakfast first. He expects a long and difficult day.

'You don't know me but I'm very worried about Alice Henderson. Someone's taken her car. And she's not answering at her boyfriend's flat.'

'Sorry? And you are?'

'It doesn't matter who I am. What matters is we need your help. Urgently.'

'I'm sorry but I need to know who's calling. Why are you at the flat?'

'Look – I'm not there now. I followed the car and I don't know what to do. It's been abandoned. There's no sign of her.'

'Right. Give me the location. I'll get there and I'll ring . . .' He almost adds 'the police' but realises he has no idea what he's dealing with. He will phone Melanie Sanders quietly. Secretly. As soon as he can.

Matthew stands. 'Listen. Can you stay on the line? I'm just going to my car. Don't hang up. I just need a minute, then you can give me the details.'

'You're not going already?' Sally's face is all alarm. 'I thought you were starting later today.'

'Change of plan. No choice. I'll be fine. You're not to worry.' He kisses his wife and daughter on their foreheads, his phone still clamped to his ear, and heads for the door, grabbing his car keys on the way.

He has no idea if this is a trick – the stalker himself calling as some kind of sick wind-up – or someone genuine. He will need to be very, very careful. He doesn't want Sally to worry but his mind is racing with options.

He needs to keep this guy on the line. Try to get a name. More information. But he also needs to find a way to phone Mel Sanders for backup. Jeez.

What the hell is going on?

CHAPTER 61

ALICE

I try so hard to calm my breathing. *Slowly, Alice. Slowly.* I breathe in for three beats and out for three beats, praying that my nose will stay clear. I don't want him to see my fear. I have this strong feeling that's what he wants. My fear. The truth is he has it completely. I am utterly terrified. I am so afraid that it feels as if I may wet myself. I clench my muscles and try to keep my head above the water but it feels like drowning. Yes. As if I am actually drowning in my own fear.

In . . . two . . . three . . . Out . . . two . . . three . . . My laboured breathing makes me close my eyes and I picture my mother with her little plastic tubes into her nose for her oxygen. I realise how truly awful it must be for her all of the time. Not being able to breathe properly.

I can't help it; the image of my mother makes me buckle.

He seems to take in this movement but says nothing. He has not said a single word yet. He just sits there, all dressed in black. In the shadows of the room so that I cannot see his eyes.

I am trying to remember his height as he first walked into the room and sat down. Is this Alex? Is he the right height? Could he have escaped? Alex has been in an open prison for some time and I'm wondering if this is possible. An escape. If this was his plan all along. Did he set this up while he was on parole?

I try to imagine what Alex is capable of. Would he really hurt me – face to face? Could he have hurt Tom? Worse? Oh dear Lord. What has he done to Tom? I think of Alex in a motorcycle helmet and Tom totally unsuspecting.

I cannot bear this. Him just staring at me in this silence. Me not knowing what is coming *next*. I have glanced around and can see no evidence of the things I fear the most – cheese wire. Acid. I am trying not to let myself think of these things. The objects I fear. No. I need to focus on breathing. I need to stop imagining what he is going to do.

I keep my head still but move my eyes from left to right to take in the room again. And now something strange is happening. There is this odd wave of familiarity. Yes. The shape of this place feels somehow familiar. Not this room per se, but the *layout*. I can feel myself frowning as my eyes dart from left to right and my brain tries to process this.

What is it? Why does it look familiar?

I take in the shape again. The left-hand side of the room is the kitchen with old-fashioned cupboards fitted around a window with its curtains drawn. There is a sort of breakfast bar which divides this space from the rest of the sitting room and this is what feels familiar. The front door is directly across from the breakfast bar.

There is an internal door ahead of me which is ajar and seems to lead to a small corridor and to a bathroom and possibly a bedroom.

And now it is dawning on me. The layout is the mirror image of a flat I know quite well. It is much smarter than this one, the cupboards replaced with painted wood. The furnishings much more stylish in that other place. But – yes. The same layout as here but a mirror image. This is the same as the flat lived in by Gill, one of the demolition campaigners. I have interviewed her there many times. I glance around again. I can imagine myself walking in the front door of Gill's place. She is on the top floor. The third floor.

I don't understand. It makes no sense. Why is this room so like Gill's place?

And now he is fidgeting in his seat and taking a phone out from his pocket. I can't see it properly but he puts it right up close to his mouth. He takes off one glove to press the screen several times and then he talks through it. It's on loudspeaker. And it is the voice from that very first phone call to the office. Distorted through software of some kind. Low. Robotic. Menacing.

'Are you figuring it out yet, Alice?'

CHAPTER 62

MATTHEW

Matthew checks the postcode which was texted to him, and sees two cars on a patch of wasteland ahead. He recognises Alice's car, and in front of it a second, darker model. Very odd. It looks like the black Golf that he thought was following them once before. The one owned by her work colleague.

Matthew pulls his phone from his pocket and rings Melanie again. 'I've just arrived, Mel.'

'Uniformed should be there very soon, Matt. I'll be ten, maybe fifteen minutes. What's happening?'

'It looks like it's her colleague, Jack.'

'Jeez. But he's a suspect. We've interviewed him. Any sign of Alice?'

'No.'

'You wait for us, yes?'

'I'll keep you posted. I've got to go.'

Matthew hangs up and gets out of the car slowly. Jack then does the same, hurrying over. 'OK, Jack. So what's happening here? Where's Alice?'

'That's the whole point. I don't know. I just followed the car but I kept losing it. It was too far ahead. I lost quite a lot of time. Took a wrong turn. By the time I finally found it, there was no one inside.'

'So why didn't you give me your name on the phone, Jack?'

'I was afraid you wouldn't come. That you would think it was a wind-up or that you would just tell the police. They've been hassling me. They seem to think I'm a suspect. I was afraid that I would just be arrested.'

Matthew is walking towards Jack very slowly. He keeps his hands out from his sides slightly with his palms open – a gesture to try to keep things calm. The guy is incredibly agitated, scraping his hands through his hair and jerking his head left to right. Matthew is trying to work out if this could be their man. If he's hurt Alice and this is some kind of trap.

Once closer, he takes in Jack's eyes. They are wide and alarmed, the pupils huge.

'Why have you been following Alice, Jack? Why would you do that?'

'Because I *care* about her, man. And I've been worried sick. The police don't seem to be able to do much at all. I've been following her to try to help her.'

'Right. So what's really going on here, Jack?'

'I don't know. I don't know. That's why I need you. We have to find her, Matthew. We have to find Alice.'

Matthew glances around. It's quite possible Jack is telling the truth. It's also possible he's obsessed with Alice. Matthew moves over to Alice's car and glances inside. No clues. He tries all the doors. All locked. But then, alongside the car, he spots wide drag marks in the dirt. They lead right across the patch of rough ground to fencing surrounding a large old housing block which is boarded up. Some of the fencing has been cut and the drag marks continue beyond the fence towards the back of the block itself.

'Right. So this is not good.' Matthew takes his phone out again. He's aware Jack could have done this. Taken Alice inside already and then staged this concern.

'Mel. A hunch at this stage but it looks as if it's possible someone has taken Alice into a derelict block of flats near the postcode I gave you. Fencing's been cut. Drag marks. I'm here with Jack right now.' Matthew glances back at Jack.

'Do you know this place, Jack?'

'Yes, I do. It's the place Alice was doing stories on. It's Maple Field House – the block that's going to be demolished later this afternoon. I don't understand. Why here? Why is her car here now?'

'OK, Mel. So it seems to be a place Alice has been doing stories on. We don't understand. But there is a connection. And it's set for demolition today.'

'OK. Stay put. We're on it. Is there a sign with the name of the demolition company?'

'Not that I can see from here.'

Matthew hangs up just as a uniformed security guard suddenly approaches from a small white van.

'Hey. What you two up to? This is private property. There's a demolition here later today. It's not safe. Did you not see the signs around the other side?'

'Oh hell. Why didn't I put it together?' Jack's expression is all alarm. He glances around. 'Why *here*? What the hell is going on, Matthew?'

'OK. So the police are on their way.' Matthew is now looking directly at the security guard. 'But you need to contact the demolition crew and get someone senior here immediately. Get the whole thing halted. I need the name of the company.'

'And on what authority? Who the hell are you anyway? The place is all set. Fully wired. There's another security guard watching the front. We're in charge until the demo team return.'

Matthew then turns to Jack. 'Right, Jack. You stay right here and you tell the police everything when they arrive.'

'No. I want to come with you. I need to find Alice.'

'You can be more help here, Jack. I need you to meet the police. Get the details of the demolition company and get them on site immediately. Yes? It's very important.'

Finally Jack nods, and then Matthew heads towards the gap in the wire fence.

'Oh no, no, no. You can't go in there. No way.' The security guard tone's is firm but he doesn't challenge Matthew physically. Instead he's dialling his phone. 'I'm warning you. This is a dangerous site. I'm serious. You absolutely cannot go in there . . .'

In one two. Ou[...]
'Open your ey[...]
I do as he says,[...]
'She took tabl[...]
because of you. You[...]

I let out this st[...]
my lungs even mor[...]
And I can't make an[...]
to the campaign; w[...]

I glance across[...]
kitchen area. There[...]
and on the left at th[...]
and feel a pang of n[...]
board with a metal[...]
A little board with [...]

He sees me look[...]
board and then he's[...]

'That scare you[...]
into me and clearly[...]
make sandwiches fo[...]
Every day. Cheese a[...]
thinly. Wire's so mu[...]

He is speaking[...]
coming. Feel faint.[...]

I am going to us[...]
'Oh, Alice. Awf[...]
Here's the beauty of[...]
don't need to hurt y[...]

I have no idea w[...]
ing that he's going t[...]
just about claiming [...]

CHAPTER 63

ALICE

'You really have no idea, Alice?' The voice through the software sounds so very menacing. Like something from a film. Still he is in the shadows so I cannot see his eyes.

In, one, two . . . out, one, two.

I close my own eyes to tune out his voice and concentrate on my breathing. Again, the struggle to fill my lungs properly makes me think of my mother.

I picture her in her new home with its lovely staff. The vase of roses on her table. I picture the copy of *Wuthering Heights* on the shelf, waiting for me. I try to think of other family scenes. Better pictures. Lying on the grass, making daisy chains. My mother calling us – Leanne and me – over to the picnic rug. *Lunch, girls.* Egg sandwiches – smelly but delicious. Ice-cold drinks poured from a thermos into red plastic beakers.

I summon more scenes. Grey school socks and scuffed shoes. My mother standing behind me, plaiting my hair. My mother singing to me. Stroking my hair after a nightmare. *It's going to be all right, my darling. Just a dream. It's going to be all right . . .*

'I used to live here, Alice. In this flat. With my grandmother.'

I don't know what
look at him again. I do

'She killed herself i

I feel utter shock. I
have done nothing. I d
He's mad. He must be

And then very slov
he takes off the balacla

My left eye starts t
ture, even in this gloon

It's *Tom*.

I can see that it's h
But my brain is saying

Tom is at the flat.
I don't understand.

He is laughing. An
My eye is still twitchin

'You really had no
to side. Tom's voice. A
not Tom.

'You bought it all.
smart family. The smar
it from a magazine, Ali
the Skyping? I just mac
to them.'

He is actually laug

'Oh, and hiring Ma
plain sight. I've enjoyed
kitchen area now. 'I pai
I'm recovering family m
now he looks back at r
inquest. She died. My g

'You are going to *kill yourself*, Alice.' He laughs. 'In the same place.' He looks across at the oven again.

What now? I picture him forcing me over there. Towards the oven. I try not to think but I imagine that he is going to give me pills. Fake my suicide. Is that it? This mad person. This mad version of Tom.

He leans forward and seems to examine my face. 'You still not getting it?' Again there is a low laugh. 'I am simply going to leave you here, Alice. I'm going to text the guard to confirm I'm out. And they are going to blow this place up. *Boom*. With you in it.'

Suddenly my heart is thumping even harder. The demolition. Oh dear Lord.

'After all, it's what you wanted, Alice, isn't it? This place *gone*.'

And now, all of a sudden, I start to see it. I have no idea why he's doing this. I have no idea how this version of Tom even exists. This narrative about his grandmother. This background so far from the story he told me. But I do understand where I am now. Maple Field House. I also know what is going to happen.

There is a pause in which he just stares at me as if trying to read my reaction. But the bigger shock for me is that my fear does not grow. I picture what is going to happen and with that picture comes the shock of relief that it is going to be quick. Somehow, blackly and bizarrely, this helps. Yes. Knowing at last – after all these weeks – what I am dealing with.

There is a long silence, and in the hole of stillness, my next thoughts are another complete surprise to me. There is this jolt. A chemical surge. Almost like euphoria. Like a cloud lifting.

If he is here, seeing this through, he cannot be with my mother; he cannot hurt my mother. That is not what this is about. It's about me, not her.

The realisation that it is just about *me* is both terrifying and strangely reassuring. So that the next emotion is the final and the biggest shock. *Relief.*

Yes. Relief that he is not going to hurt my mother.

I feel tears welling in my eyes because I realise suddenly that I love her so much more than I care about myself.

I am afraid – yes. But my fear is suddenly less significant. Because it matters so much more to me that she is OK. That he is not going to *hurt her.*

I feel something I never thought I would feel. Especially not here. Like this.

I feel brave.

Yes. I am actually trembling with the shock of discovering that I am not a coward after all.

This man, this twisted version of Tom, cannot do any more to me. Because he does not understand the relief I feel. He doesn't understand *love.*

I picture my mother with her nurse and her cosy room. White roses on the table and *Wuthering Heights* on the shelf.

I feel strangely jubilant now. Resigned. Relieved. Nothing matters now. My mother is safe. And so I start kicking with my foot against the table in front of me to make a noise. Maybe someone will hear. I don't know. I don't care. It doesn't actually matter anymore.

'You need to stop that, Alice.'

I kick some more, harder and louder. He moves to pull the table away from me but I twist to reach to the left to kick the sideboard instead.

'Stop that, Alice. I'm warning you.'

I kick louder and louder until he roars like a wounded animal. He leaps forward and puts his hands around my throat but still I kick.

His grasp around my neck is tighter but I don't care. *My mother is safe. My mother is safe.* I don't care about him.

Kick, kick, kick.

And then suddenly there is this huge crashing noise. For a moment I fear it is one of the explosions being triggered too early. I feel faint from the struggle to breathe. My neck is so very sore and I want it to be over.

I manage to move my head to the right. Is it the explosion? Is it all happening early? But there is no dust. No. It is not the demolition. It's the door. Something is smashing – *bang, bang, bang* – against the door. Three huge blows until the wood is finally splintered.

I am fading now. It feels like falling. Blackness on the periphery of my vision. I can't see. I can't breathe. I am falling, falling, and when I manage to open my eyes again, I still can't take it in.

Somehow, Matthew is in the room now. Yes – it's *Matthew* with a fire extinguisher in his hand. He swings it to hit Tom in the back.

The hands around my neck are released but I feel giddy. Trying to get enough oxygen. Falling still.

Through a haze I watch them fighting. I see Tom strike Matthew hard and then pull away. Tom is trying to open the window in the kitchen. I see him stepping up on the sink. I think he is going to jump and I think: *Good. Jump.*

But Matthew pulls him back down. There is more struggling. They are on the floor. The sound of blows. Flesh hitting flesh. Groaning. And finally, through the haze and the dimness, I hear Matthew talking to me. He has Tom pinned to the floor, over by the kitchen units now.

'Alice. You need to try to breathe slowly for me. Can you do that, Alice?'

I can hear sirens. Still I am falling. Fading. Through the gag across my mouth, I call out for her. For my mother . . .

'The police are here. It's going to be all right, Alice. You need to breathe slowly and hang in there, Alice.'

Not his voice now. My mother's hand stroking my hair. Her voice in my ear.

It's going to be all right, darling.

EPILOGUE

ALICE

It is one of those classic October days – a mostly clear sky but surprisingly cold, with a strong breeze that sends the few clouds scurrying across the blue as if late for an appointment. I watch them in their billowy haste as laughter ripples through the small crowd.

The mayor is still speaking; he must have told a joke but I am no longer listening. I am mesmerised by the sunlight catching his chain and also the steel of the scissors in his hand, sending starbursts of gold patterning across the coats of the children, huddled near the front and clearly eager to be allowed to play.

There is a yellow ribbon waiting for those scissors. It is tied in an ostentatious bow across the entrance to the new park – the final phase of the redevelopment project for the former residents of Maple Field House.

There is applause, and at last the ribbon is cut and the children are ushered through the entrance by smiling parents. I watch the photographer from the paper that was once mine calling for smiles and posing little groups at each piece of new equipment. A double slide set on a tasteful bed of bark clippings. Little wooden animals on huge springs with handles shaped as ears. All carved in muted shades. Yes. All so beautifully designed, and a million miles from the rising damp and the boarded-up shops of Maple Field House.

And now, as the crowd begins to scatter, I see Matthew approaching and he gives me a small wave. Ah. He said he might come along but I did wonder. He has his daughter with him. She is quite lovely – golden ringlets to her shoulders. She is pointing, eager to try the slide, but Matthew is telling the photographer: 'No pictures. Not my daughter. Sorry.'

I move towards them. 'You came.'

'I wanted to see how it turned out. And to see you too, Alice. How are you doing?'

I shrug. 'Better.'

'Good.'

We watch his daughter negotiate the steps to the smaller of the slides. Matthew moves closer, saying, 'Sorry, Alice. Excuse me.' He is all at once distracted and stands protectively behind the wooden ladder, then rushes around to the front to greet her at the bottom of the shiny steel. His daughter repeats the cycle three times and then agrees to try the swing where it is a little easier for us to talk.

'So are you still staying locally, Alice?'

'Some of the time. I've been travelling a bit. With my sister and her children.'

'Good. Yes. I remember you saying.'

'How's Melanie, by the way? Did you give her my best?'

'I did. In fact – here.' He takes his phone from his pocket and skims through several pages before holding the screen out to me. The picture is a close-up – Melanie laughing with a smiling, chubby-faced baby on her knee.

'Oh wow. He looks gorgeous. *Big*.' I laugh. 'So how is Melanie coping?'

'She's exhausted, permanently covered in sick. And very, very happy.'

'I'm so pleased.'

We pause as he puts the phone away and pushes the swing higher still.

'You know, I've never really thanked you, Matthew. I mean – not properly. I was a bit of state through the court case.' It's been a long haul – the legal process moving so slowly. Matthew turns away from me, his gaze fixed on the swing.

I watch him, guessing what he's thinking. At first, he wouldn't even let Leanne settle his bill. He blamed himself for not seeing through Tom. But it was no one's fault. Even the judge said that.

An unlucky cycle of trust. Matthew trusted in DI Sanders' checks on Tom. But she'd delegated the background checks on Tom to a DS. He said he'd done a thorough job but in truth cut corners; he made the mistake of allowing Tom's lawyer colleagues to vouch for him. A single phone call to the private school Tom never attended would have rumbled him.

'It wasn't your fault and it wasn't Melanie Sanders' fault either. He was very clever,' I say. 'He fooled everyone, Matthew. Even the judge commented on that in his summing up.' I remember the words. *You went to extraordinary lengths to reinvent yourself and to weave a particularly wicked web of lies.*

Tom had been in the drama society at university, we learned, and had taken voice coaching to achieve a middle England tone. None of his legal pals rumbled him.

'Not everyone would have come in to that building after me. I *am* grateful, Matthew.'

He keeps pushing the swing and then at last reaches between beats to gently touch my arm. 'No need for thanks, Alice.'

The gesture – touching my arm – makes tears prick the back of my eyes and so I say nothing more. Just nod.

I see a counsellor still – once a fortnight, struggling to trust my judgement. Taken in by Alex then Tom. Leanne and my counsellor say it's because I'm a good person and see the best in people. They say the self-doubt will pass.

I also have this terrible phobia now about colds. Anything blocking my nose. I have become a bit obsessive about it – every night using sprays to try to keep my nose as clear as possible.

Breathe, two, three. Breathe, two, three.

Tom is serving life now but the trial was terrible. He pleaded not guilty to everything and simply refused to answer any questions at all. As if his silence could somehow defeat us.

At first we could only surmise Tom's motive. He refused in all police interviews to fully explain himself. His grandmother did indeed kill herself, just as he told me in the flat, but initially no one understood *why*. The grandmother had some of my cuttings in a file but that's all anyone knew. The only link to me. Her inquest wasn't covered by the paper as we were short of staff that day. But the inquest records were checked and the motive for the grandmother's suicide was never clear.

Then a search of Tom's home found a letter and the gran's diary, which finally explained it all. Tom's grandmother apparently loved her flat and desperately wanted to *stay* there. It sent a shiver right through me when I found that out. We honestly had no idea that anyone opposed the demolition campaign. I knocked on so many doors to get the full picture but don't remember ever speaking to her. The campaigners were certainly never aware of any opposition.

The diary suggests only Tom knew his gran's true feelings. And the timing confirms Tom targeted me quite deliberately. We started dating just a few weeks after his gran's inquest. I go cold when I think of it. Those early dates. Me in his flat. Me in his bed. Unaware of the mask. All that hatred . . .

He used accomplices, the police discovered. Mostly young criminals he met through his early years as a duty lawyer. Turns out he paid someone to spray that water in my face. To buy the plant for my mother. To call that morning at his flat, pretending to be a courier. And he paid off the security guards so he could drag me into the building. CCTV shows a large diving bag – a huge zip-up affair on wheels. I feel faint just thinking about it. I could have died in that bag.

And then came the even bigger shock that stalking was not the only charge. When Tom's DNA was taken, it matched evidence at the scene of an unsolved murder. Some loner who lived next door to his gran – bludgeoned in an alley a few years back.

We have no idea why.

Just as we still don't know why *Wednesdays*. Why did he have a thing about Wednesday? The police asked over and over. But he refused to say.

◆ ◆ ◆

The breeze is suddenly stronger, blowing my hair across my face. I move a strand and then find myself staring at my right hand.

Now there's this shudder right through me as I picture it exactly. Her hand in mine . . .

I was called to London just three days after Tom attacked me. We stayed by Mum's bed – Leanne on a little camp bed on the left and me on the right. I held one hand and she held the other.

They had to give Mum a lot of drugs to keep her comfortable and so she slipped into a coma. I lay on my little bed on the floor, reaching up to hold her hand. All night I watched her chest rise and fall and I was counting and chanting in my head. *Breathe, one, two. Breathe, one, two.*

When the chest was finally still, I was utterly bereft. I thought I would be relieved for her but I wasn't. I made so much noise that people came running.

'You have to calm down, darling.' Leanne was distraught to see me like that. 'Please, Alice. You have to calm down.'

◆ ◆ ◆

I put my hand in my pocket now and look up to see Matthew signalling with his head that I should look behind me.

Goodness. *Jack.*

Matthew lifts his daughter from the swing and says his goodbyes. They are meeting Sally, his wife, for lunch. Have to hurry.

I watch them leave, Amelie on her father's hip, as Jack moves over, putting his notebook and pen in his pocket.

'So you're covering this?'

'Yeah. Got everything I need. Nice pictures.' He glances at the park, a dozen children still enjoying the new equipment, some of the parents sitting on the smart new benches.

'It's nice that there's plenty of seating,' I say.

'Yes. They transferred some plaques from those rickety benches in the centre of the grass at the old place. Nice touch. Dedicated to some of the first residents, apparently.'

I just nod. I didn't know that. I am taking in how well Jack looks. It's an odd sensation. He looks so familiar and yet it feels strange to be in the same space as him again. I get this a lot – a sense of not quite fitting in the world as I should. Some days it feels as if I drift through scenes, watching them rather than taking part. The counsellor says it is a phase of adjustment and will pass.

'Thank you for all your texts, Jack. I'm sorry I don't always reply. I've been travelling a bit.'

'That's OK. I saw your piece, by the way, in the *Sunday Herald*. The exposé on that stalker charity. The alarm scam. Really good work, Alice.'

'Thank you. It was nice to have something to do. Take my mind off the trial.'

'Right. Good. Yes, of course. So – have you been offered a contract off the back of that? In London, I mean?'

'No, no. Not sure journalism is right for me anymore, actually.' I am very aware that Jack must know, as everyone knows now, about my name change. About Alex and what happened in my past. It all came out in the media coverage of Tom's case. Not quite sure how, but it doesn't matter now.

'Really? So what are your plans then? Are you still local?' He sounds wary. Maybe disappointed. I can't tell.

'I'm using Leanne's place in Dorset at the moment.'

'Ah. Slumming it, then?'

I laugh. He smiles.

'I'm doing some comms work with a charity now. A proper charity, supporting research into lung disease.'

'Oh, right.'

'Want to put something back for a bit. While I work out what to do long-term.'

He just nods.

Once again the wind whips up suddenly and I have to take my hands out of my pockets again to tuck my hair into the back of my coat collar.

'Look, Alice, you must absolutely say if this is too soon. Or inappropriate. Or a bad idea.'

I clench my right hand so that the nails are just digging into the palm; I am thinking once again of how terribly I behaved with Jack at that Italian restaurant all that time ago. I think of him losing his wife. Letting go of her hand as I had to let go of my mother's. *You need to calm down, Alice. Please.*

What was I thinking? How crass of me. I want to interrupt him to say sorry again; that I understand a little better now.

But he's blushing. 'Look, if it's too soon you must say, but I was wondering if we could meet up. Try dinner again?'

I am a little shaken now and stare into his face. '*Dinner?*'

Surprised – yes. So that I don't know quite what to say. I look down at my left hand. It looks pale in the cold. Jack's right hand is alongside mine. Pinker.

'As friends, you mean?' I desperately want him to know that I'm sorry I upset him that last time. That I truly understand a little better now.

'Well, no. Actually.' The flush on his neck deepens so that you can see the red emerge just above his tartan scarf, creeping upwards towards his chin. 'I meant like a date, actually. Like I say – if it's too soon, you must absolutely say, Alice.' He is talking much too quickly. Gabbling almost. 'I bolted the last time because I wasn't ready. I mean – I still miss my wife, Alice. I'm not going to lie. But the thing is, I really care about you very much. And I'd really like to see if—'

I move my hand just a fraction and he clasps it suddenly. Tight. His flesh so much warmer than mine.

'Sorry. Cold hands . . .' I say.

'Warm heart. Is that a yes, Alice?'

I just nod and look down at our two hands, joined.

Grief, I learn, is the strangest thing. Sometimes I am convinced that I see her. My mother. I conjure up her ghost and I fancy that she turns to wave at me from across the street. And sometimes in the quiet and the stillness of the night, I am certain that I hear her voice.

Jack is staring at me and I am listening hard because deep inside me I fancy that I hear her voice right this minute. A whisper like a shell held up tight, tight to my ear.

It is going to be all right, my darling girl.

Jack is smiling at me now.

I am smiling too.

It is going to be all right.

AUTHOR'S NOTE

When I was a young reporter just starting out, I really did take a threatening call – just like Alice in this story. My caller rang me three times . . . the same day each week. First he threatened me. Then he taunted me over where I had been that day. And then finally (and bizarrely) he apologised for upsetting me. He said he had been going through a rough time and was very sorry to have taken it out on me. He promised he meant me no harm . . . and I never heard from him again.

I remember feeling so relieved that this horrid spell was over. But the experience never left me. I was very afraid during those few weeks when I did not know what the calls were about. Or how serious they were.

When I realised all these decades later that I wanted to examine this theme in an entirely fictional story, I promised myself that I would only do so if I could counter the negative with a celebration of courage and love. And that's why I put Alice and her mother's love at the heart of this story . . .

Because fear is a terrible thing. But, as I know from my many years in journalism, courage and love are thankfully always more powerful in the end.

Thank you again for reading *I Will Make You Pay*. If you have enjoyed the novel, I would enormously appreciate a review on Amazon. They really do help other people to discover my books.

I also love to hear from readers, so feel free to get in touch. You can find my website at www.teresadriscoll.com and also say hello on Twitter @teresadriscoll or via my Facebook author page: www.facebook/TeresaDriscollAuthor.

Warm wishes to you all,

Teresa

ACKNOWLEDGMENTS

There should be a special award for the families of writers who never know which version of the author they will meet each day. The confident one. The panicked one. The one declaring that a deadline simply *cannot* be met.

So above all I send my thanks and love to my gorgeous folk – Pete and James and Ed – with my eternal gratitude for your patience and support. I would like to tell you that I will be so much calmer over the next book. But we all know better!

A special thank you next to the amazing folk at Thomas & Mercer, who champion my novels with extraordinary energy and expertise – with a special shout-out to my truly wonderful editors, Jane Snelgrove and Ian Pindar.

My eternal gratitude as always to my lovely agent Madeleine Milburn and her team, whose support, expertise and cheerleading skills are just *incredible*.

A group hug also to the warm and wonderful writing community – by which I mean those fellow authors who so generously share wisdom (along with virtual, late-night clinking of glasses when things are going awry).

And finally – a thank you from the bottom of my heart to all my lovely readers. Your reviews and your messages really do mean the world.

ABOUT THE AUTHOR

Photo © 2015 Claire Tregaskis

For more than twenty-five years as a journalist – including fifteen years as a BBC TV news presenter – Teresa Driscoll followed stories into the shadows of life. Covering crime for so long, she watched and was deeply moved by all the ripples each case caused, and the haunting impact on the families, friends and witnesses involved. It's those ripples that she explores in her darker fiction.

Teresa lives in beautiful Devon with her family. She writes women's fiction as well as thrillers and her novels have been sold for translation in twenty languages. You can find out more about her books on her website, www.teresadriscoll.com, or by following her on Twitter @TeresaDriscoll or on Facebook at www.facebook.com/TeresaDriscollAuthor.